W9-AAS-009

first & then

then

emma mills

SQUARE
FISH

Henry Holt and Company

New York

SQUARE
FISH

An Imprint of Macmillan
175 Fifth Avenue
New York, NY 10010
fiercereads.com

FIRST & THEN. Copyright © 2015 by Emma Mills.
All rights reserved. Printed in the United States of America by
LSC Communications, Harrisonburg, Virginia.

Square Fish and the Square Fish logo are trademarks of Macmillan and are used by
Henry Holt and Company, LLC under license from Macmillan.

Our books may be purchased in bulk for promotional, educational, or business use.
Please contact your local bookseller or the Macmillan Corporate and Premium
Sales Department at (800) 221-7945 ext. 5442 or by e-mail at
MacmillanSpecialMarkets@macmillan.com.

Library of Congress Cataloging-in-Publication Data
Mills, Emma, 1989– author.
First & then / Emma Mills.
pages   cm
Summary: Devon is a high school senior, wondering if she really wants to go to college,
what to do with her cousin Foster (a freshman) who has moved in with her
family in Florida, and whether she likes Ezra, the stuck-up football star
at her school, or cannot stand him.
ISBN 978-1-250-09068-3 (paperback)   ISBN 978-1-62779-521-0 (ebook)
1. High schools—Florida—Juvenile fiction.   2. Football players—Juvenile fiction.
3. Dating (Social customs)—Juvenile fiction.   4. Cousins—Juvenile fiction.
5. Families—Florida—Juvenile fiction.   6. Florida—Juvenile fiction.   [1. High
schools—Fiction.   2. Schools—Fiction.   3. Dating (Social customs)—Fiction.
4. Cousins—Fiction.   5. Family life—Florida—Fiction.   6. Florida—Fiction.]
I. Title.   II. Title: First and then.
PZ7.1.M6Fi 2015   [Fic]—dc23   2014043456

Originally published in the United States by Henry Holt and Company, LLC
First Square Fish Edition: 2016
Square Fish logo designed by Filomena Tuosto

3   5   7   9   10   8   6   4   2

AR: 4.8 / LEXILE: HL720L

For Mama, Poppy,
Hannah, and David

1

My college essay was titled "School Lunches, TS High, and Me," and it was every bit as terrible as you'd expect.

I stared at a poster on the wall behind Mrs. Wentworth's desk while she read. It was this *National Geographic*–looking photo of a pride of lions on a veldt. One was out front, looking particularly majestic. Golden sun dappled its mane, and whereas the background lions were looking here and there, this one's dark eyes gazed right at me. Underneath the picture, the word ACHIEVEMENT was printed in big serif letters.

Clearly, this was supposed to inspire something in me. I wasn't quite sure what. Run faster. Kill more gazelles. Be better than those riffraff lions hanging at the periphery.

Mrs. Wentworth cleared her throat eventually, and all she said was, "School lunches." It posed the question "why?" without formally asking it.

"The prompt said to write a page from the story of my life. You eat an awful lot of school lunches in your lifetime, don't you?"

"And this cafeteria food was somehow . . . meaningful to you?"

"There were some deeply moving mashed potatoes—I'm not going to lie."

There was something strange happening around her lips, a weird sort of twitching motion. I think a frown and a smile were locked in mortal combat. "Devon, I really need you to take this seriously."

She meant take it seriously like go home and write an essay about a dead relative, or a sick bird I had nursed back to health when I was little, or a mission trip to build houses in Guadalajara. I just couldn't find it in my heart to do that. I'd never been to Mexico.

But then she surprised me. "Don't get me wrong," she said. "It's not the topic. It's the execution. You could've run with this. It could've been witty and inventive and really captivating. But it reads like you wrote it during a commercial break."

I took offense to that. I wrote it during at least four commercial breaks.

"How much thought did you really give this?"

It wasn't like I hadn't given *any* thought to it. I had even gone as far as composing an essay in my head, written in the style of Jane Austen. Jane was my favorite author, hands down, and I knew that my true life's story would be told in her style.

Jane didn't shy away from the truth about people. I felt like I knew her from reading her books, like I knew the kind of person she had been, and it was someone I liked a great deal. Someone who saw people for who they really were, someone who was capable of calling bullshit in the most elegant way imaginable. Jane would tell it like it was.

Unfortunately, how it was for me wouldn't make the best sort of college essay. *Miss Devon Tennyson requests admission to your university, despite the fact that she is stunningly average.*

I couldn't say any of this to Mrs. Wentworth. I didn't expect her to understand it, how I took comfort in seeing things through Jane's lens sometimes. She couldn't possibly comprehend the satisfaction I drew from imagining myself as *Miss Devon Tennyson* and unextraordinary, as opposed to regular Devon Tennyson and just plain boring.

When I didn't speak, Mrs. Wentworth set my essay aside. "Devon, this is crunch time. You've got a lot of work to do this semester if you want to get your applications competitive. Your GPA isn't bad, but your extracurriculars are definitely lacking. Are you at least aware of this?"

One brief tryst as girls' cross-country team manager. One failed run for Homecoming Court. One nonspeaking role in the drama department's annual desecration of *Beauty and the Beast*. I was definitely aware of it.

I would've pointed out that I had joined Mrs. Wentworth's own club—the Road-to-College Club—but it was hardly optional, and as of now, I was the only member. So I just nodded and tried to look solemn.

"You've still got time. It's only August, but before you know it, deadlines are going to start creeping up. You've expressed some interest in Reeding. Let's pursue it. But we need to explore all our options. If there are any other schools you've got in mind, let's visit them."

"Visit?" For a brief second, I imagined myself on the road with Mrs. Wentworth, arguing over complimentary shower caps in some cheesy motel room.

"You can't make informed decisions without knowing what you're getting into," said Mrs. Wentworth. "You wouldn't buy a dress without trying it on first, would you?"

3

I choked back *Maybe if I bought it online* and just shook my head. It wasn't the idea of college visits I was apprehensive about. It was the concept of Road-to-College Club in general. *I think this will be good for you*, my mom had said, holding up a flyer sent home in the mail and officially making Road-to-College Club akin to broccoli and sunscreen. Maybe it would be good for me. But that didn't mean I had to like it.

"Are there any particular majors you're interested in?"

"Not really." Saying *advanced breakfast with a minor in cable television* would surely bring about some epic battle that Mrs. Wentworth's smile was doomed to lose.

"Well, you've got some things to think about. This week I want you to look for extracurricular activities. Join a club. Start your own. It's not too late to get yourself out there and get involved."

Ugh. She sounded like a brochure. I suppressed an eye roll and opted for a noncommittal head bob.

It was quiet for a moment. I thought she was going to dismiss me, but when I looked up, Mrs. Wentworth was examining me through narrowed eyes.

Her first name was Isobel. She wasn't very old in the grand scheme of things, but by high school standards, she seemed it. She wore patterned sweaters and long, shapeless floral skirts. Still, Mrs. Wentworth's eyes were very beautiful. Her lashes were thick and dark, and the color of her eyes was just as vibrant, just as green as it must've been when she was my age. I liked to think that she was incredibly popular in those days. All the guys would follow her around and offer to drive her home and tell her that she looked like the girls in the magazines. And she would laugh and flip her dark curls and have no idea that there would be a time in her life when she would be Mrs. Wentworth, and care what some obnoxious girl wrote to get into Reeding University.

"Devon," she said, and somehow it felt like the voice speaking was a little more Isobel and a little less Mrs. Wentworth. "Do you *want* to go to college?"

No one had ever asked me that. College was the natural order of things. According to my parents, between birth and death, there had to be college.

"I don't know what else I would do," I said.

"Join the army," was her simple reply.

I made a face. "I hate being yelled at."

"The Peace Corps, then."

A choking noise erupted from my throat, something like a cat being strangled. "I hate being selfless."

"All right." The twitching around Mrs. Wentworth's lips started up again. "Get a job."

"Just start working? Just like that?"

"Lots of people do it. Some very successful people never went to college."

"Yeah. Look at Hollywood."

"There's one. Go to Hollywood. Become a star."

"But I can't act. I've never even *talked* in a play."

"So join drama club."

"Oh yeah, chorus member number twelve will be my ticket to stardom."

"Why not?"

"First, you have to like doing that kind of stuff, which I don't, and second, you have to be good at it, which I'm not."

"So what are you good at?"

"I don't know. Nothing, really."

"Now, how can you say that?"

I couldn't express it right, not without Jane's help. Those turns of phrases she used that gave elegance to even the unpleasant things. She would say I was *wanting in singularity*. Staunchly average. Spectacularly . . . insufficient, in situations like this. In the face of all-caps ACHIEVEMENT. Because what if you didn't have it in you? What if, deep down, you were just one of those background lions?

"Everyone's good at something," Mrs. Wentworth said after observing me for a moment. "You'll find your niche. And you know a good place to find it?"

"College?"

"See, you're a good guesser. There's something already."

I smiled a little.

"I think you're a perfect candidate for college. Don't think I'm trying to dissuade you here. I just want to know why you want to continue your education."

"My parents," I said. She could've just asked that straight out of the blocks.

"To get away from them?"

"To keep them from murdering me."

A particularly fierce twitch seized her lips. "I want you to get involved," she said, sticking the essay back into my file. It was the only thing in there, save the crumpled postcard from Reeding University I showed her at our first meeting. "And give the personal statement another try. Heck, write the whole life's story while you're at it."

I made another face.

"All right, all right, I won't get ahead of myself. Have a good day, Devon."

"You, too," I said, and left the office.

I walked down to the football field after our session and thought about what Mrs. Wentworth had said. Mostly I thought about the essay—a page from the story of my life. I imagined writing about myself in the Peace Corps: a philanthropic Devon, traversing jungles and deserts, filled to the brim with the opportunity to self-sacrifice for the good of others. That's the kind of shit those college people wanted—some spectacular tale of unflinching originality, sandwiched between your grade point average and your ACT scores. How many volunteer hours have you performed, and tell us exactly when your stunning triumph over adversity occurred.

I felt like I had never done anything. I had never suffered. I had never triumphed. I was a middle-class kid from the burbs who had managed to be rather unspectacular for the last seventeen years. A triumph over mediocrity—that was what I needed.

"Did college club get out early?"

Wherever I was, Foster had a way of finding me.

Until this past summer, he had been the kind of cousin you see only every fourth Christmas or so. His family lived in California, we were in Florida, and that had been perfectly fine, a perfectly acceptable dose of Foster. But things had changed, and the new dosage of Foster in my life was pretty hard to tolerate at times.

He threw his bag to the ground and plunked down next to me on the bleachers.

"Did moron club get out early?" I said.

He looked at me for a moment. Then he said, "I see what you did there. I said 'college' for your club, and you said 'moron' for my club. Clever."

I looked out at the field, partially to avoid having to reply to that, and partially because practice was just starting and this was my favorite part. All the players would circle up on the field to do cal-isthenics. I liked the jumping jacks best, the way they'd chant each count aloud together. It was hard to see faces when everyone had their equipment on, but I could spot Cas Kincaid from anywhere. His jumping jacks were always half-assed.

Foster didn't like Cas, but I didn't like Foster. I probably should've felt bad for him, but Foster had this inability to do or say anything remotely human. Sometimes I thought the earth could rip open and swallow our house up whole and he would just stand there on the sidewalk changing tracks on his iPod.

"What'd you learn in college club?"

"Stop calling it college club."

Like "Road-to-College Club" was so much cooler.

"Stop calling it moron club," Foster countered.

Ironically enough, if any club was "college club," it was his. At freshman orientation, Foster signed up for the Future Science Revolutionaries of America Club. It was a biweekly meeting of those genius kids who like to build robots and memorize the digits of pi. Most of them could probably get into more colleges as freshmen than I could as a senior.

The chanting stopped as the guys moved on to a new exercise. Foster followed my gaze to the field and, more particularly, to Cas.

"Don't you feel dumb always following him around?"

I didn't answer, but I wasn't really listening.

"Don't you feel dumb hanging around and waiting for him?" he repeated as he bounced up and down a little in his seat, a rub-ber band perpetually wound too tight.

"Why would I feel dumb?"

"Because he doesn't hang around and wait for you. Don't you want a boyfriend who waits for you?"

"He's not my boyfriend. We're friends."

"So how come you close the door to your room whenever he comes over?"

"So you won't come in."

"You don't have sex in there?"

"No!" I looked over at Foster. I was fairly confident he was the scrawniest, most immature fourteen-year-old in all of Florida, quite possibly in the entire world. "No. No one's having sex anywhere."

"I'm sure there are people having sex right now. All the way around the world. I'm sure there are millions of people having sex right now. It's nighttime in Europe. People have more sex at night, don't they?"

"Stop talking about sex, Foster."

"Why? Does it make you uncomfortable? Does Cas make you uncomfortable? I could punch him, you know. I know how to punch."

"No punching. No talking. Let's just be quiet, okay? Let's play Zip Lip."

"Okay." Foster liked to think he was best at this game. I was old enough to know that my mom only invented it to keep me quiet when I was little. He should've been old enough to realize that, too.

"But wait. Is your dad picking us up? Because I'm not driving with Cas. He smells."

"You smell."

A pause. "I see what you did there."

I sighed. "Zip your lips, Foster."

"Do yours first."

I drew my fingers across my lips. Foster did his, and there was temporary peace.

The peace lasted through the drive home, even after I greeted my dad, effectively losing Zip Lip.

9

"How was school?" My mom asked that evening, with one hand resting on her hip and the other stirring a wooden spoon in a pot of pasta sauce. Foster was tucked away in front of the television, and my dad was in his office. The house was quiet, aside from the gentle bursting of bubbles in the sauce and the dull hum of Foster's TV.

"It was fine." I took to setting the table, because I knew she was going to ask me to do it anyway.

"How was Foster?"

I hated questions like that. What can you possibly say? It made him sound like a weather system. Foster was cloudy with an 80 percent chance of precipitation.

"He seemed fine," I said as I grabbed some napkins out of the cupboard. I still wasn't quite used to getting four instead of three.

"Do you . . ." She was trying so hard to sound casual. "Do you think he's fitting in well?"

"It's only the third day."

"But do you think he's making friends?"

"I don't know." That was a lie. "I haven't seen much of him." That was a lie, too. I knew he couldn't have been making friends, or else he wouldn't be trying to hang around me so much.

"What about gym class?"

Physical education wasn't a freshman requirement until my sophomore year, so after having put it off for so long, I was dutifully bound to two semesters as the only senior in a class of hormone-ridden freshmen. A class that happened to include my cousin Foster. I hated sports and I wasn't too fond of freshmen, so gym class was a blight on my otherwise seamless senior schedule.

"We've only had one class," I said.

"And?"

"And Mr. Sellers told us about dressing out and lectured about the sports schedule and that was it." Mom opened her mouth to speak, but I went on. "As far as I know, nobody's shoving him into lockers or calling him names or treating him any different than any other freshman."

This seemed to satisfy her, but I knew it could only be temporary, so I threw some silverware on the table and hurried up to my room before she could ask any more questions.

I got Cas on the phone that night before bed. It was one of my favorite things—curling up under the covers with the phone pressed to my ear, knowing I could drift off to sleep as soon as I hit End.

"A number four," I heard Cas's muffled voice say on the other end of the line, "with a Pepsi and no—hey, Dev, remind me to tell you about practice—and no pickles on the burger and extra ketchup."

Cas was nearly unable to devote his entire attention to a single conversation at any given time. But it was difficult to ever reproach him for it; he just thrived on constant engagement—interested in everything and everybody. When you really needed him as a friend, he'd rein it in.

"What happened at practice?"

"Coach reamed Marburry because"—to the drive-through window, "Thanks, man, could I get a couple napkins?" and back to me—"because he nearly killed himself trying to take Ezra down."

"Why would he do something like that?"

"Because he's a fucking idiot," Cas said thickly, because now he was eating and talking and driving all at one time. "No, but seriously, he's pissed he got moved to safety and Ezra's still starting running back." There was just the slightest hint of darkness to his voice, something that I heard only because I had known him so long. "And, you know, because of the Bowl."

Everyone knew. In addition to being named a *Parade* All-American, Ezra Lynley had been chosen for the army's All-American Bowl East team. The entire town made such a big deal out of it that you couldn't use a public restroom without a CELEBRATE TEMPLE STERLING'S OWN ALL-AMERICAN poster staring down at you from the back of the stall door.

"Yeah," I said. "What an exciting and unexpected opportunity for him."

Cas laughed. That was the tagline under CELEBRATE TEMPLE STERLING'S OWN ALL-AMERICAN: AN EXCITING AND UNEXPECTED OPPORTUNITY FOR TS HIGH'S EZRA LYNLEY.

There was a pause during which I'm sure Cas shoved a few more french fries into his mouth, and then, "How's your new brother?"

"Don't call him that."

"Well, that's what he is."

"Is it bad that I don't want to be around him at school? I mean, I see him all the time at home, but does that, like, make me a bad person?"

"Why would that make you a bad person?"

"I don't know." Except I did know. "His mom just abandoned him like that."

"So? Joe Perry's mom abandoned him, and last time I checked, you said he was the most obnoxious person in the world ever ever."

"I did *not*—"

"You did so, two *ever*s. Twice the *ever* is, like, the obnoxiousness squared."

"That's probably the nerdiest thing you've ever said."

"Don't change the subject. You hate abandoned children."

"I don't hate anybody!" I knew he was goading me, but I always played along. "And Joe's mom left in, like, the second grade. It's different."

"No matter how long it's been, an abandoned child is still an abandoned child."

"Stop saying *abandoned child*!"

"You said it, too." I could hear the grin in Cas's voice. "Hey, you know somewhere a kid is, like, being abandoned because of this conversation."

"Don't say stuff like that."

"Don't censor me! *I've got freedom of expression that will never be broken!*"

"Shut up," I said, but I was laughing all the same. "You're going to drive off the road."

"I'm almost home."

"And it would be tragic to die a block from your house, wouldn't it?"

"This from the girl who didn't want to say *abandoned child*."

"Foster wasn't really abandoned," I said, the smile slipping off my face. "He was just kind of . . . sent away."

"Doesn't make it any better, does it?"

"Maybe it does. She's coming back for him."

"Yeah," Cas said evenly, and I wasn't sure how much either of us believed it.

2

As far as I was concerned, physical education was evil.

You take a bunch of teenagers, make them strip down in front of each other in a locker room, have them don hideous matching uniforms, and then measure their worth based on their ability to chuck balls at a net, into a hoop, or at each other. It was just. Evil.

I dragged myself into the locker room at third period, dropped my gym bag on the floor, and ignored the gaze of anyone who might be looking at me. To be honest, some of the other girls really scared me.

When I was a freshman, I had braces and more pimples than I could count. I didn't wear makeup. I didn't own short-shorts. I had never tasted alcohol, and I certainly didn't know how or why you would ever want to blow anything.

Being in this class kind of made me feel like the stereotypical old man who sits with his cane outside the grocery store in cheesy movies, ranting *"In my day . . ."* Sodas cost a nickel. Kids respected their elders. Freshmen didn't show major cleavage. Or wear thongs. Or—my eyes widened but my mouth stayed clamped shut—tan BITE ME onto their backsides.

With no one to share in my disbelief, I kept it inside, mentally noting that maybe I should do like the Reeding application says and write it in the story of my life. Chapter One: How the TS freshman locker room has more push-up bras than a sale at Victoria's Secret.

Most of the boys weren't any better. They acted like the guys on teen soaps, preening and showing off, but the fact that they were as close to middle school as the senior guys were to college made calling them fresh*men* almost laughable. *Freshboys* was more like it.

If I had to be with these kids for two semesters, I wanted to surround myself with the quieter ones, the ones who looked and acted their age. The regular ones. But there were so few of them that I think the prostitots and freshboys were what was considered normal.

As for Foster, he didn't resemble anything closely related to normal. Unfortunately, the only thing he was closely related to in this class was me.

"Hey, Devon! Dev!"

He jumped up and down, waving his arms in my direction as I left the locker room. I took a deep breath and went over to him.

He was wearing the same TS gym uniform as the rest of us, but even that couldn't look right. All the boys ordered their shorts big so that they hung down to their knees or lower. Foster's were well above his knees, and his shirt was crammed in unevenly around the waistline. His socks were pulled up as far as they could go, and the laces on the cross trainers my mother had insisted on buying him were tied in big fat bows.

I could tell—in my very high school roots, my senior class inner core—I could tell that no one was going to push Foster around. They wouldn't slam his books to the ground when they saw him after class. They wouldn't pull his chair out from under him in the cafeteria.

"Hey, Foster!" A couple of PTs nearby waved at Foster. Foster, looking mildly confused, wiggled a few fingers in their direction. They all giggled, but it sure wasn't because they thought Foster was cute.

What these kids would do was laugh at him, and somehow that seemed just as bad to me. How do you stop people from laughing at you? How do you make them take you seriously?

By being cool. By fitting in. By . . . becoming friends with Fonzie. Fuck if I know.

I gave Foster a weary "Hello" and then wandered over under a basketball hoop, trying to inconspicuously distance myself from him. I wanted to maintain my senior mystique, but it's pretty hard to seem grown-up and sophisticated when you're wearing cotton briefs in a locker room full of girls with BITE ME butts.

Foster bounced along after me. "Hey, Dev, have you met everyone? Do you know everyone yet?"

I realized he was referring to the other freshmen.

"Uh . . . no."

"You don't talk to the girls in the locker room?"

"No."

"Not even Gracie Holtzer? You haven't met Gracie Holtzer?"

He gestured to what must've been the queen prostitot, a girl whose hair was so painstakingly flat-ironed that not one single twist of frizz dared leap off her chestnut mane. She tossed that silken hair back over her shoulder and smiled coyly at a band of freshboys standing nearby.

"Not even Gracie Holtzer," I said, glancing now at Foster. He wasn't looking at Gracie Holtzer the way the other boys were. They were all just shy of lighting themselves on fire to get her attention. Foster, however, was eyeing her like he eyed the wasp nest in the eaves of our back shed. It was a look of mingled curiosity and fear.

"Let's circle up!" Mr. Sellers emerged from his office, clapping his hands and heading to the center of the floor. The other students made their way over and formed a large, lopsided circle around him, which I dutifully joined, Foster in tow.

The girls whispered loudly to each other while Mr. Sellers started talking to us about fall sports. I tried to pay attention for the sake of not having to rehash the latest *Cosmo* tips, but my attention was broken, ironically enough, when the whispers all at once ceased. I looked around the circle and realized that all eyes were on the door.

A very familiar frame stood there. Any student at Temple Sterling probably could've picked it out of a lineup, even without a bright red 25 emblazoned across the chest.

I thought back to the bathroom stalls—there under CELEBRATE TEMPLE STERLING'S OWN ALL-AMERICAN, under AN EXCITING AND UNEXPECTED OPPORTUNITY, was the black-and-white image of this face.

I had never really seen Ezra Lynley close up. We had never had any classes together. No postgame-party run-ins. It was always me in the bleachers and him on the field.

He wasn't thick-necked and huge like some of the football guys, but he wasn't scrawny, either. Strong enough to take a tackle, but light enough to run in that way he was famous for. And he had good bones, as my mom would say. His jaw curved nicely, and his nose had this great line to it, but all in all, as the gym class and I stood shamelessly appraising him, I felt like his face left something to be desired. The right features had been assembled, but there was no shine to his eyes, and the spot on Cas's mouth where a smile always seemed to lurk lay particularly slack on him.

After an awkward moment's pause, Mr. Sellers sprang to life. "Ezra! Coach said you'd be joining us! Hurry up and get changed. We're just getting started."

Ezra gave Mr. Sellers a look that said he wasn't about to hurry up for anyone. Twenty-five pairs of eyes watched him saunter off to the locker rooms. When I looked back at Mr. Sellers, he didn't look aggravated by Ezra's attitude in the least. In fact, as he caught my gaze, he gave me a sheepish "Boys will be boys!" sort of smile.

I rolled my eyes.

Today's activities, Mr. Sellers informed us, would begin with some warm-up exercises. Our first unit was football. So after learning the proper way to grip a football (a few of the guys exchanged knowing looks), we were supposed to get a partner and practice passing.

There was a mad dash for partners. Most of the girls grabbed their nearest friend, but a few of the PTs broke the boy-girl divide and giggled on over to chat up some freshboys.

I glanced around. People were pairing off fast. I locked my eyes on Ezra Lynley as he left the locker room and strode over to him.

"Hi," I said when I reached him. "I'm Devon."

I extended a hand toward him. He stared at it for a second before taking it briefly.

He didn't introduce himself. Of course I already knew him, but there was something instantly off-putting about that. Still, it was better than partnering with Foster, which was my only other option—an option that I could clearly see ending with Foster beaning me in the face with the football and breaking my nose, Marcia Brady–style.

"Do you want to be partners?" I asked, forcing some brightness into my voice. "Seniors, uh, sticking together?"

Ezra stared. "You're a senior?"

I would've liked to think I looked a little more mature than the rest of the girls in the class. Then again, with the majority of them being PTs, I probably looked the most like a fourteen-year-old.

"Yeah. I'm a senior."

He evaluated me for a moment and then said, "Get a ball."

"Get it yourself," I replied, because who did he think he was? Who did he think *I* was, for that matter—some football groupie eager to bask in his glory?

Ezra just looked at me, expressionless, and it was like being tested without knowing the criteria.

Apparently I passed, because he turned and crossed the gym to the bin of footballs by Mr. Sellers's office. Turning back with a ball in hand, he chucked it from right where he stood, one smooth sweep of his arm that sent the ball sailing across the gym. Of course I didn't catch it. It soared over the fingertips of my outstretched hands and bounced lopsidedly off toward the basketball hoop.

Ezra just stood there.

I turned and retrieved the ball, jaw clenched, and then sent it back hard, half because I was mad and half because I couldn't throw worth shit.

It was an insane pass, too high and arcing too far to the left, but in a few great, effortless strides, Ezra thrust out his hands and closed his fingers easily around the ball.

Some of the PTs gasped in admiration, but Ezra didn't look gratified. He just sent a soft, slow pass to me. I caught it, grudgingly, and sent it back.

After what seemed like way too many minutes of this, Mr.

Sellers told us to break into groups of three to run drills. I scanned the room for a lonely pair of girls to join, but Ezra was lingering close by, and before I could grab hold of a couple of freshmen— any freshmen—Foster loped over.

"Can I be in your guys' group?"

I glanced at Ezra; he was staring at the wall as if it were staring back.

"Yeah, sure," I replied, and tried to extinguish any thought of broken noses from my mind.

Mr. Sellers explained the drill to us, a confusing pattern we were supposed to execute across the length of the gym, one group at a time. He told us all to form three lines under the basketball hoop, and because Ezra, Foster, and I were the ones standing closest to that spot, everyone queued up behind us.

I cursed inwardly. How was I supposed to see how it's done if I had to go first?

"What are we supposed to do?" I hissed to Ezra. He didn't reply.

"All right!" Mr. Sellers clapped his hands. "Let's go, first group!"

I had no choice but to take off across the floor. Ezra pitched the ball to me and then took off running behind me. I missed the ball and had to go back for it, and then I threw it to Foster, who seemed to share my aptitude for sports. Mr. Sellers had said something about people shifting places, so I moved over to the spot where Ezra had been and managed to grab the tip of the ball as Foster chucked it back at me.

"You were supposed to lateral it," Ezra said, slowing to a stop behind us. "And *you*"—he pointed at me—"are supposed to be *there*." He jabbed his finger at the spot where Foster stood.

I stopped, too, football still in hand. "Well, maybe I would've known that if you had explained it to me before."

"Mr. Sellers explained it just fine."

"Maybe I didn't understand the first time."

His face never changed. "Maybe you should've listened more closely."

I opened my mouth to say something I'm sure wouldn't have been very nice, but Mr. Sellers jumped in.

"Ah, well," he said, and smiled good-naturedly. "We can't all be All-Americans, can we, Ezra? Why don't you join Rivers and Kenyon, and let's put Gracie with the Tennysons and try running this one again? And make sure to keep your eye on Kenyon, Ezra. He's our new up-and-comer on the defensive line!"

Kenyon was a particularly thick-looking boy with dark, bristly hair. If there was any person in this room you would peg as an up-and-coming human bulldozer, it would be this kid.

Ezra shuffled off to the back of one of the lines, and Gracie Holtzer made her way to the front, sticking out her bottom lip in an overexaggerated pout. As soon as she reached the front of the lines, however, her expression changed to one of horror.

"Ewwwwww!" she crooned, pointing at something behind me.

I turned around. Foster was standing there, blood dripping down the front of his gray TS gym shirt.

"Dev," he said thickly, two fingers clamping his nostrils together. "Dev, I think I've got a nosebleed."

I sighed.

"So gym wasn't fun?" Cas said at lunch, giving me a grin and then turning to his fish sticks.

I was still riled up about it. "I won't make it through a year in that class. I can't. It's not humanly possible."

"It's kind of your fault for putting it off so long, isn't it?"

I glared. "That's not the type of sound bite I keep you around for."

"It's everyone else's fault and you're perfect?"

"Better." I set about opening my carton of chocolate milk. "I don't get why Ezra's even in that class. You'd think the star player would've taken gym before senior year."

"He needed an elective," Cas said between bites, "so they're letting him take it again. I heard him and Coach talking about it at practice."

"Figures. I need an easy A, too, but no one's going to let me take freshman English again."

"You're not an athlete. We matter more."

"I hate you."

"You love me. You love me so much you're going to give me your chocolate milk."

"We're the only two seniors in the whole freaking school who still eat cafeteria food. You do realize that, right?"

"I like cafeteria food. It's greasy, and more important, it's cheap. No, more important, it's greasy. Come on, gimme the milk."

I took a long, pointed swig from the carton.

"You never mentioned how Ezra's a great big giant asshole," I said, abandoning the chocolate milk and turning to my pasta salad.

Cas laughed, nearly choking on a fish stick. "I thought it was common knowledge."

"The star football player's supposed to be all charming and winning and stuff. Not surly and mean-spirited."

"The talented ones usually are."

"You'd think they'd be grateful that they're talented. It should be the really untalented people who get to be jackasses. At least they have a reason to be angry at the world."

"Well, I guess it's hard for Ezra with all those exciting and unexpected opportunities cropping up everywhere. Like he goes into the bathroom to take a piss and all of a sudden an exciting and unexpected opportunity jumps out at him from behind a shower curtain and scares the living shit out of him."

"At least he's in the bathroom," I said.

"For when all the living shit comes out?"

I grinned. "Exactly."

Cas grinned back and then glanced up at a spot behind me. "Hey, Marabelle."

When I turned, it was to the sight of Marabelle Finch stopped a few feet away from our table. She looked lost in thought, but for Marabelle, that was pretty typical.

"Oh," Marabelle said, looking at Cas vaguely. "Hello."

"How's it going?" I asked.

She lifted her shoulders, a tiny, delicate shrug. "I can't remember what I was going to do."

"Get lunch?" Cas suggested.

"Baby's not hungry," she said.

"Is Marabelle hungry?" Cas's face was deadpan, but his eyes were shining. He thought Marabelle was funny.

"No." She stood there for a moment and then reached up suddenly and grabbed her chest as if checking to see if it was still there. "I've got breasts now. Have you seen?"

"Yeah." Cas bobbed his head, unable to keep from grinning. "Yeah, they're nice."

I kicked out at him under the table as she took a seat.

"I don't like them," she said.

23

"Does Baby's dad like them?" Cas asked.

Marabelle just looked at him. I, on the other hand, swung out harder and connected with Cas's leg under the table. Marabelle and I weren't great friends, but I had sort of a soft spot for her.

I first met her at the library—the town branch just a few blocks away from school. I went there pretty often, and I'd always see Marabelle in the stacks. Thumbing through a periodical or pushing a cart around, shelving books. She was two years younger, and we didn't have any classes together, but we coexisted at the library nicely enough. I would say hi, and she would nod, or she'd check my books out and comment on what I had chosen.

"Do you like working here?" I asked one time as she was leading me to a copy of *Hamlet* for class.

"Well, technically, I don't work here," she said. "But they let me help out." And she promptly found me four different editions of *Hamlet*—"You don't want that one, though. They try to translate it all into normal words and it totally ruins it. The annotations in this one are better." I learned that when it came to information, Marabelle was better than Google.

She was also singularly odd. I guess she reminded me of Foster in some ways. They both seemed to operate on their own wavelength. But whereas Foster excelled at being conspicuous, Marabelle was just . . . quietly eccentric. I wasn't sure if she didn't realize stuff sometimes—like Cas poking fun at her—or if she just didn't care.

"How're your classes going, Marabelle?" I asked as Cas dove back into his lunch.

She wrinkled her nose. "Trigonometry is awful."

"Ah, yeah. Trig sucks. Sorry."

She blinked. "For what?"

"I love that girl," Cas said as we headed to class after lunch.

Marabelle had drifted off in the direction of the foreign-language hallway with one arm wound around the bump swelling beneath her baby-doll dress. "Like, I seriously love her. She's the funniest person I've ever met."

"She's not trying to be funny, you know."

"That's why she's hilarious."

"She's a teen mom. Have some sympathy."

"Oh, so you can have sympathy for teen moms but not for abandoned children?"

I gave him a shove. "You're a great big giant asshole, you know that?"

"Just like Ezra Lynley?"

"Worse. You're not as good-looking."

Cas grabbed his chest. "That's a terrible, horrible lie."

"Come on." I glanced at my watch. "We're gonna be late for Calc."

He clapped his hand to his chest again and stopped dead in the middle of the hallway.

"Oh, stop it. You know I think you're pretty."

Cas shook his head, massaging his chest like some great pain was brewing under there. "It's not that."

"What is it?"

He grimaced. "Senioritis."

I hit him in the arm. "Get to class."

"Good one, right?"

I couldn't help but grin. "*Go.*"

3

Foster was awake by five thirty every morning. School didn't start until eight, and I was still trying to shake my summer sleep schedule, so I wasn't the most receptive to his early-morning clattering.

Usually after a few minutes I would sink back into a nice doze, but this morning my eyes refused to stay shut. My head couldn't find a comfortable spot on the pillow. The covers were too warm.

I flung them back and rolled over. A soft breeze blew through my window, pressing against the shade. Outside I could hear the scuff of sneakers on pavement and a faint intake of breath as a jogger passed by the house. A car door slammed somewhere not too far off. The blender buzzed.

Foster was making a smoothie.

I groaned. It was official: I was awake.

I never saw Foster in pajamas. He was always the last in bed and the first one up in the morning, looking just the same as he had the night before. He must've had more clothes from home than it appeared, but the problem was that they all looked the same. All the crisp new tees, the button-down shirts, the perfectly whiskered jeans that my mom had bought him sat unworn in his dresser drawers upstairs. I felt bad that he refused to let go of his shit from home, but worse for my mom, who—although she wouldn't admit it—scrutinized clothes that other kids were wearing on TV and in the magazines so that Foster would have exactly the right stuff. When he refused to wear it, she said she'd been silly—of course he'd want to pick his own look. But another shopping trip that ended empty-handed said it all: Foster had a look, and it was dingy.

"You want a smoothie?" Foster said when I stumbled into the kitchen.

"It's really early to be using the blender, Foster."

"You know, it's only three thirty on the West Coast."

"Did you wake up at three thirty when you lived on the West Coast?"

"Sometimes," he said. "Doesn't waking up early make the day seem longer?"

To me, the day was twenty-four hours long, and no amount of getting up early would change that.

"You know what today is?" Foster asked when I didn't speak.

"Friday?"

"Uh-huh. And guess what happens on Fridays?"

The Future Science Revolutionaries of America focused their combined mental energies on moving the principal's car one inch to the left? Wait, no—that was yesterday.

"I don't know."

Foster's eyes widened. "You don't know?"

"What happens on Fridays, Foster?" I was getting impatient. Then it dawned on me. But there was no way on earth something so normal could leave Foster's lips. He couldn't mean—

"Football!"

I stared. It had only been three months. There was still so much I didn't know about him. "You like football?"

"I don't know. I've never been to a game in real life."

That was more like it.

"Aunt Kathy said you'd take me."

My mother had a way of volunteering me for Foster-related activities without my knowing. The look on Foster's face said mine gave that away.

"Will you take me?" he asked.

"Sure," I said, because what else was there to say? Things were different now.

Football wasn't as grand in Temple Sterling as in some of those places you hear about in Texas and even in other parts of Florida—twenty-thousand-seat stadiums and a full-scale town shutdown on game nights. But still, it was undeniably important. The football followers were devoted: parents, siblings, aunts, uncles, cousins of boys on the team. Kids like me, unrelated but still wanting to be a part of something. Men, from the guys down at the bank to seventy-year-old Fred of Fred's Service Station, who played on past TS teams, who understood the feel of the stadium on a Friday night, and who migrated there Friday nights since to try to claim a little piece of it back. Football was something everyone had in common—like a mutual religion. We all believed in touchdowns and field goals. We were all baptized in the floodlights.

I wove through the crowd that night, Foster in tow. He grabbed the back of my shirt as we worked our way up to an emptier stretch in the far bank of bleachers, in front of the end zone.

"They look like an army," Foster murmured, and I followed his gaze to the visitors' bleachers, a sea of blue and gold.

After we claimed our seats, I surveyed the crowd around us. A rowdy bunch of freshmen was in front, and there was a large group of seniors behind us—people I recognized but no one I was particularly friendly with. In Jane's time, they put a huge distinction between acquaintances and friends. Friends you could disclose your innermost feelings to and spend a lot of time with. Acquaintances you visited for a quarter of an hour because propriety called for it.

The equivalent of that quarter-of-an-hour visit today was a few smiles, some waves, and a "what's up?" here and there. That's what I received from the seniors, and what I readily returned with as much friendliness as the occasion called for, before turning back to observe the rest of the crowd.

Foster was sitting next to a Goth couple who were so deeply entwined it was hard to tell whose limbs were whose, and to my right, holding a cigarette and looking mildly bored, was Emir Zurivic.

"I was wondering when you'd notice me," he said.

I didn't know much about Emir; only that he had moved to America just a couple of years ago, and that he already knew cooler slang and more obscenities than I had learned in my seventeen.

"You psyched for the game?" I said, because I didn't know what else to say but felt as if some conversation was required.

"Psyched to make some cash. I put a hundred down that we win by more than thirty."

"More than thirty? That's five touchdowns."

He shrugged. "Flat Lake's a shitty team, and that Ezra kid's good."

"Five touchdowns good?"

"You seen him play?"

Everyone had seen Ezra play, and everyone knew he was

good—five touchdowns good. He never missed a pass. Where the average guy could push five yards, he pushed twenty. But I thought about him in gym class, that lazy drawl, *You were supposed to lateral it*, and so I said, "He's all right. Nothing special."

Emir smiled. "I like a girl with impossibly high standards."

I looked out at the field once more. Emir's smiles tended to make me a little uneasy. Somehow frowns seemed more natural on his face.

I couldn't imagine what it must've been like for him, transitioning to Temple Sterling. Emir was the source of many rumors around school, mostly concerning his pre-suburban Florida life. I thought most of them were pretty outlandish, but as Emir looked out over the field, I couldn't help but examine his face for some indication of his past. Like maybe there was some sort of mark people bear if they've seen tragedy in their lifetime. A look around the eyes, some downturn of the lips. But nothing looked out of place on Emir's face, aside from a slightly crooked bar piercing his left eyebrow.

Action started up on the field before I could ponder Emir's past any further. The crowd around us leaped to their feet as the players entered, a wave of TS red and white from one end of the stadium. The cheerleaders had one of those paper banners, which the first few guys burst through with ease. From the other end of the field came the blue and gold, and the Flat Lake bleachers erupted. The scoreboard glowed like the tip of Emir's cigarette, and the game began.

It wasn't a particularly good game. Not too exciting, I mean, because we gained a three-touchdown lead in the first half and maintained it for the rest of the game. It pushed ahead to a five-touchdown lead in the last quarter. Emir was practically beaming at the prospect of his wager.

I let my mind wander through the better part of the game; I had been rereading *Sense and Sensibility*—I called it my favorite, but every Jane Austen book was my favorite every time I read it. The only one I couldn't completely throw myself behind was *Mansfield Park*, because—spoiler alert—the main character has a huge thing for her cousin. I know things were different back then, and maybe it was completely acceptable in their eyes, but the idea of cousins declaring romantic love for each other made me feel a little queasy, especially since Foster had arrived in our lives.

The only other complaint I had about Jane's books, cousin-loving aside, was the getting-together part. They were stories of such unconquerable love, such strong feelings. You follow these characters through the ups and downs of an emotional roller coaster, this breathtaking will-they-or-won't-they, and is it too much to ask for a little more time spent on the I-love-you-and-want-to-be-with-you part? It was the very best part, and I wanted to draw it out. I wanted kisses—good, long, passionate ones. Jane never wrote about those.

She didn't write about high school football, either, so I wondered how I would do it, how to explain the pride Miss Tennyson felt when watching Mr. Kincaid rush ten yards. The crimson glow of TS helmets sparkling in the light of the flood lamps. The faint scent of marijuana hanging on Emir. Would anyone have dared to write about weed back then? Jane would probably be shocked.

Foster didn't talk at all through the entire game. I glanced over at him every so often to make sure he was still breathing, and each time found his eyes glued to the field.

"Did you have fun?" I asked as we joined the crowd flooding into the parking lot after the game.

He replied in typical Foster fashion, not with an answer but with another question: "How do you think they learn to beat up on total strangers?"

"I don't know . . . it's not really beating up, is it? Just tackling."

"But how do you throw yourself at somebody without really hating them?"

"You don't have to hate them. You just have to want them not to win."

He considered this for some time and only spoke again when we were in the car heading home. "That Ezra guy's good," he said, just in the same way Emir had. "He was like a . . . ball magnet."

I couldn't help but snort. "A what?"

"A ball magnet. He was the magnet and the ball was the metal. It just flew to him and stuck every time."

All-American. Four-year varsity starter. Ball magnet. I wondered how the great and powerful Ezra Lynley would feel knowing he had acquired such a title.

"Cas dropped the ball," Foster said after a moment. It was true—Cas had fumbled in the third quarter. "He's a ball dropper."

I couldn't even be indignant. I just snorted again.

4

Foster must've been in some deep contemplation that night; he didn't even think to invite himself to the postgame party until I pulled up to our house and he was halfway out of the car.

"Are you sure I can't go? I'll be quiet and I'll stay out of the way and if you want to get drunk, I won't even tell Aunt Kathy."

My eyes darted to the house to make sure the windows weren't open.

"I'm not getting drunk," I said. "No one's getting drunk. And it's already past your curfew, so get inside."

Foster's curfew was just what mine had been at his age—ten o'clock. At seventeen, I was up to eleven thirty. For a difference of three years, an hour and a half hardly seemed fair, but I wasn't going to push it.

"I'm not even tired," Foster argued, still standing with the door half open.

"Curfew doesn't mean you have to be tired. It just means you have to be home."

"But you need me there to look after you."

I laughed out loud. I couldn't help it. "Get inside," I said. He dutifully shut the door and watched me pull out of the driveway.

House parties weren't my favorite, but because it was the first one of the year, I felt obligated to go. As I made my way over to Martin Lahey's house, I wished it could be more like how it had been in Jane's time: ordering a carriage, wearing a gorgeous gown, having your name announced when you came into the room. Real dancing to real music. Some sense of decorum. In short, nobody throwing up in the bushes. Nobody fooling around. TV and movies liked to dress it up—put a pop-rock sound track under it, too few people, and too much lighting—but they kept the essentials true to life: High school parties are breeding grounds for idiotic people with too much drama and not enough sense. Walking into Martin's house (to be sure, no one announced my name), I recalled the one thing that TV and movies never mentioned, and that a summer away from this had allowed me to forget: If you're not one of those people, these things are damn boring.

I found Cas in the kitchen, standing around with some guys from the team, most of them nursing the classic variety of red plastic kegger cups. Cas's hands were empty, and he threw an arm around my shoulders as soon as I made my way over. He made some comment that I couldn't hear over the music, and I got a few hellos that I could return with only a feeble wave. Had these things always been so loud?

Stanton Perkins seemed to be leading the conversation; he was a huge, square-headed kid who played on the defensive line. His kegger cup was already drained, and he was the only one I could hear clearly over the pound of the Laheys' overtaxed sound system.

"Like I said, it was an okay game," he started up again. "Not our best work, but like that even matters anymore." He shot a meaningful look at Cas.

"I would've liked a little more play," Cas replied.

"I feel sorry for you guys," Stanton said, and as the music seemed to increase in volume, his voice spiked, too. "The whole offense is fucked as long as Lynley's out there."

One of the other guys said something about the interception Jackson got, and the fifteen yards Smith rushed for our fourth touchdown. But Stanton just waved one huge hand and said, "The only guys out there that get a hand on the ball are Wilcox and Lynley, and Wilcox only does because he's the fucking quarterback! Anything else is just a fucking accident!" He downed the dregs of his cup and went on. "Without Lynley, we'd all be better off. Get the team going like it should be. Cas out front and not some little cast-off bitch from Shaunessy calling the shots."

Stanton Perkins was inherently unlikable. You could tell he was one of those people who went around pulling cats' tails and throwing rocks at cars when he was a kid.

I looked to Cas for a response. He just smiled and squeezed my shoulder, guiding me away from the group and saying something about drinks. Only when we had left the kitchen did he say in my ear, "That guy scares the shit out of me."

I nodded. "Future mailbox bomber." Cas laughed but didn't get a chance to answer, because as soon as we made it to the living room, we were waved over by Jordan Hunter.

Not only was Jordan varsity and a straight-A student, but as old clichés go, he was also the coolest guy in school. And he was currently holding court on the Laheys' overstuffed sectional, the hood of his sweatshirt pulled up over a baseball hat, huge mirrored sunglasses reflecting the pool of admirers around him. Under the hood lay Jordan's signature dreadlocks, and under the glasses shone his signature eyes. That was the mark of true cool—the luxury to cover up your best features.

Not that the rest of Jordan wasn't superior; he was an offensive back, broad-shouldered, and cut as all hell. He had perfect skin, and his teeth were toothpaste-ad white.

I was pretty much in love with him, but so was everyone else. It wasn't that burning sort of unrequited love, but a good, healthy regard. It was just so easy to smile around Jordan, and so hard to speak without sounding like a complete idiot.

"Cassidy, my man." Jordan slapped Cas's hand from where he sat on his dual-reclining throne. To his immediate right was a girl named Lauren McPhee, who I had English class with last year, and to his left sat Ezra Lynley, looking bored. The rest of the couch was teeming with people, spilling onto the floor, holding their own kegger cups, and basking in Jordan's glory.

"Hi," I said, when Ezra's eyes caught mine. Cas and Jordan had taken up a conversation about the game.

Ezra didn't reply but rather just stared at me, and I felt the same mixture of embarrassment and indignation that I had in gym class when met with that sneering *You're a senior?*

"We have gym together," I said flatly.

Something like surprise flickered across Ezra's face. "I know."

"Is that Devon Tennyson?" Jordan snatched my attention away in an instant. He pulled off his sunglasses, as if requiring serious visual confirmation, and then jumped to his feet.

A dopey grin took over my face, the kind only people like Jordan are really capable of producing. "Hi."

He threw an arm around me, the most casual, coolest,

best-smelling hug of my life. "Where you been, Champ? I didn't see you all summer. What've you been doing with yourself?"

Admittedly, *champ* was usually the kind of endearment passive-aggressive dudebros called each other, but Jordan claimed it was short for "champion of my heart," and I may or may not have melted a little each time he said it.

"Uh . . . we were in California for a little while," I said when we broke apart.

"California," he said, nodding. "Got to love those beaches. Nothing like some West Coast sun, am I right?" He resumed his seat. "You guys want some drinks? Where's Martin?"

I hadn't seen Martin Lahey all night—as was the way with house parties. More often than not, the host is of little or no consequence.

Without an answer regarding Martin's whereabouts, Jordan went right on.

"D'you see the work our man Ezra did in the first half? Three-touchdown lead and I was there to cover his ass."

He hit Ezra on the arm. "Don't I always say I got your back?"

Ezra barely nodded.

"Shut up, man," Jordan said, and hit him again. "You're talking too much. Let somebody else get a word in."

Not even the smallest smile cracked Ezra's expressionless face. No one was safe from Jordan's charm, but this guy seemed immune.

"There's that sense of humor," Jordan went on. "That's why I love this guy. Such a fucking comedian. Seriously, Ezra, shut up and let someone else talk."

Cas and I stayed with Jordan's inner circle a little while longer, but it gradually grew more and more crowded (as Jordan's stories grew more and more animated), and we resigned ourselves to moving on once more.

We went into the front hallway, where over the noise of the crowd came a cry of "*Cas!*" All at once a shiny-haired figure broke away from the masses and flung herself at Cas. His hand slipped from mine and his arms encircled her. It was Lindsay Renshaw.

She broke apart from Cas and threw her arms around me.

"Where've you guys been?" she said, and squeezed far harder and with much more sincerity than most people afforded in their hugs. "I haven't seen you once this week!"

She pulled back and I got my first good look at her after a summer apart.

Lindsay was a breathless sort of beauty; her cheeks were perpetually tinged like she had just had a nice, brisk morning jog. Wisps of hair were always hanging out of her ponytail, and she always seemed to be in a happy hurry, too busy and too in demand to stand still for more than a second.

And she wasn't like those cheesy popular girls on TV, who push girls off the tops of cheerleader pyramids and scheme to steal other people's boyfriends. There was something so inherently sweet about her that you couldn't help but want to be her friend. That was the way I felt, despite Cas standing just a little straighter now that she had appeared, and the fact that her eyes shone just a little brighter when they turned in his direction.

Jane would have a fucking field day.

"How was your summer?" I said, trying to draw their attention away from each other.

"It was really awesome. I did Habitat for Humanity with my church group."

Of course she did.

"How about you guys?" She smiled at Cas. "How was your summer?"

"Great." Cas's voice suddenly sounded deeper. "Really great. Worked a bunch. But great."

Say *great* again, I thought. Go on, just say it.

"And two-a-days," Cas continued. "Loads of 'em. But the team is really great this year."

Lindsay didn't seem to notice Cas's inferior grasp of synonyms. "I know, the game was incredible, wasn't it? And Devon"—she beamed at me—"I heard your cousin's staying with you. That's so awesome."

I raised my eyebrows. "Have you met him?"

"Not yet. You should totally bring him around to the next party. I'm sure he's a blast."

"Foster's not really the party type. And neither am I, actually." I was pretty good at the quick escape. "I should probably get going."

"I'll walk you out," Cas said.

"It's okay. I'll be fine."

But Lindsay was already glowing at Cas's gallantry, and I knew I couldn't refuse.

"You're staying, though, aren't you, Cas?"

"Sure. As long as you save me a dance."

I opened my purse and tried not to gag myself.

"Come on." Cas reached for my hand, but I stuck it into the purse and rooted around noisily for my keys, even though my fingers had located the Matchbox-car key chain a good four or five times. In that nature, I headed to the front door, and Cas, undoubtedly casting some kind of devastating smile back at Lindsay, followed.

"Where'd you park?" he asked when the front door had closed behind us and the sounds of raucous partying were somewhat quieted. A few more minutes and the cops would probably be here.

"Just down the street. You really don't have to—"

"The only time I don't will be the time you get snatched, and then you'll be dying in an alley somewhere cursing my name, and I'll be haunted for the rest of my life by an all-consuming guilt."

"That was a really well-thought-out answer."

"Thanks. I try."

When I looked over, Cas was smiling at me. It was moments like this when Jane would say something about my feelings for him. I was attached to Cas—that's how she'd put it. It had been the truth for so long that I couldn't really imagine it any other way.

One of my favorite things about Jane's books was the *feelings*— she understood that whole unrequited thing, how it felt to pine, how it felt to hope. But the best part was that sometimes the feelings became requited, and that was undeniably another facet of the allure for me. The heroines dared to love, dared to hope; their hopes are dashed, but then . . . there's the reversal! The revelation in the final act—the person reciprocates. They feel what our protagonist felt all along.

Cas didn't have those kinds of *feelings*. Not for me, anyway. I was almost certain of it. He cared about me, but it was a brotherly sort of affection, one arm perpetually slung over my shoulders in a this-is-my-pal kind of way. And that was okay, most of the time. It was nice. But sometimes . . .

Sometimes I just wanted to kiss him so bad.

I came home in tears on the last day of eighth grade, having walked in on Cas making out with Molly McDowell in the home ec room after school. Molly McDowell had long, curly hair like a

Disney princess, and she played on the volleyball team, and she was always wearing the thing you were trying to get your mom to buy you. Nothing about the situation should've surprised me— obviously someone as cool as Molly and someone as cool as Cas would pull each other into their respective orbits—but it still stung.

My mom poured me a glass of milk, squeezed in a healthy dose of chocolate syrup, and told me that this just wasn't the universe where Cas and I were right for each other, simple as that. Maybe in another time or place, maybe if he were different or if I were different.

"But you don't want to make yourself different for a boy," she said. "You don't want to make yourself different for anyone."

My reply was something halfway between a sob and *You just don't get it.* But my mother persisted.

"Someday someone will like you for you, just the way you are. And as much as you like Cas, this other person will be so much better for you."

That didn't cut it at the time. I sobbed through the glass of chocolate milk, went upstairs, blasted the radio, and hid under the blankets in bed, hating Cas and Molly and the world.

It's silly, but even at this point, even at dumb postgame house parties, even knowing that Cas had now gone so much further than home ec room French kissing with girls like Molly McDowell, the image of them together still grabbed me in the stomach every so often. Just a quick little spasm, somewhere below the rib cage, that made me feel like I was in middle school again, and made me long for that universe out there where Cas and I were together, and hate the one where we weren't.

But I would never admit that. I just smiled back, and we

shuffled down the sidewalk toward my car, Cas with his hands in his pockets and me with my eyes toward the sky. It was a beautiful night.

We reached my car, which was a shameful distance from the curb and sticking into the street at a really awkward angle. I couldn't parallel park to save my life.

"Drive safe, okay?" Cas said as he took the keys out of my hand and unlocked the door.

"Oh, I was planning on driving recklessly."

Cas clutched a hand to his chest.

"Senioritis?" I asked wryly.

"Just picturing the world without Devon Tennyson. The sky's all black and torn open, and trees shrivel and die, and all the top-forty bands break up."

"You notice how we never have conversations grounded in reality?"

He grinned. "I love you."

I got into the car, half wanting to tell him not to say stuff like that and half wanting to say it back.

"Drive safe for real, okay?" he said before I could reply.

"Well, I *was* going to give it a go blindfolded, but I guess I could wait on that. For you."

I knew that was just as stupid as Cas's *As long as you save me a dance.* And I knew that sometimes around Cas my voice turned strange, too, that some sort of gravel jumped into it, like I was trying to sound cool and sexy and cavalier but really sounded just as idiotic as Cas had talking to Lindsay. But I couldn't help it.

He rapped the roof of the car. "Night, Devon." And then he shut the door, moved onto the curb, and watched me pull away.

5

The second week of school is decidedly worse than the first, most especially in senior year. The first week can have its novelties: seeing who changed their hair color, who bulked up over the summer. There are new faces to familiarize yourself with. New privileges to grow accustomed to.

But by the second week, the novelty has worn off. Now you're just back in school, plain and simple—another year that, despite Josh so-and-so's new physique and the fact that we can all park in the senior lot, is discouragingly like the last three.

The only difference, I guess, was that now that the end was so near, it seemed further away than ever. Now the future after high school was hanging vaguely in the distance.

I began my halfhearted quest for extracurricular activities on Monday, hoping to snag something before my next meeting with Mrs. Wentworth. I didn't know if I could handle the cold stare of disapproval from the ACHIEVEMENT lion if I went back empty-handed.

I scoured the student bulletin board between classes. There was the fall production of *Pippin*. Volleyball tryouts. Art Club. The

Enviro-thon team. The Future Science Revolutionaries were looking for someone with a car to join so they could go to the science museum. The school orchestra needed another percussionist.

I didn't fit the bill for much of anything. Most of the time I had a car (when, like all ancient used cars, it chose to cooperate), but I didn't see myself as a revolutionary of any sort, and the last thing I needed was to spend more time with Foster. I was entirely too uncoordinated for sports, and entirely too uninspired for art. Enviro-thon had potential, but just the idea of spending my afternoons dissecting ecosystems and talking about the layers of the atmosphere was enough to make me drowsy.

By the time the bell rang, I had exactly as many extracurricular prospects as I did before my sojourn to the activities board: zero.

Tuesday dawned bright and early, with the sounds of Foster bustling around the kitchen. All I could do was roll over in bed and groan. Tuesdays meant gym class.

During third period, Mr. Sellers led his troop of uniformed freshmen (and two uniformed seniors) down to the varsity field with a giant mesh bag full of balls in tow. He began throwing them to us as soon as we reached the fifty-yard line.

"Partner up!" he yelled, pitching a ball in my general direction. I flung out my hands to catch it and watched it pass right over my head. "We're going to practice passing. Remember how to place your fingers, and let's try to get a little spin on it, people!"

I was standing near enough to Ezra Lynley to give him a glance, but I knew we wouldn't partner again anytime soon; him with me because he was conceited, and me with him because, well, I thought he was conceited.

A swarm of prostitots was already forming around him with a general cry of, "Be my partner, Ezra! Be my partner!"

He glanced around for a second and then pointed to a particularly buxom PT. She had tied up her maroon TS gym shirt in the back so that it was now a midriff top. "You," he said.

I rolled my eyes. The PTs dispersed, disappointed, and then divided into pairs. Ezra walked off, too, but to my surprise the tied-up-shirt girl didn't join him. I followed Ezra's path to a point just beyond where that PT had stood.

Foster was trying to balance his football on his forehead, the way seals at the zoo balance balls on their noses. His shirt was tucked in so unevenly that it had bunched up inside his shorts, giving him the appearance of smuggling a cotton inner tube around his waist.

Ezra reached over and plucked the ball from Foster's face. "Stand there," he said, pointing to a spot about ten yards away. Foster grinned and bounded away.

"Ready!" he said, turning to face Ezra and jumping up and down like an idiot.

"Devon!" Mr. Sellers barked. "Partner up!"

I glanced around. A rogue PT, a straggler, was standing alone. I made my way over to her.

"Come on. Let's be partners."

She looked taken aback, like I had just suggested slitting our palms open and making a blood pact, but, nevertheless, she trotted over to a spot across from me and turned to catch the ball.

She was wearing a particularly thick layer of makeup—dark eyeliner, sparkly shadow, iridescent lip gloss. Her shirt was tied up in the back, too, but unlike the buxom PT, you could see the ponytail holder she used to fix it up.

I glanced over at Ezra and Foster as she retrieved a missed pass, just in time to see Foster wind his arm back and throw a rogue ball. It spiraled up and backward, landing just beyond the visitors' bench behind him.

"Oops!" Foster went galloping after it. I cringed inwardly. Ezra Lynley was a jerk, sure, but he was still the grand prodigy of TS football, and Foster was currently blaspheming his craft.

"That's your brother, right?" my PT asked, following my gaze.

"No, he's my cousin."

"Really? Because he said he's your brother."

"Why would I lie?"

She looked at me unwaveringly beneath sparkly eyelids. "Why would he?"

I was quibbling with a prostitot.

I turned my gaze back to my "brother." He had reached the ball and bent to snatch it up.

Don't throw it back, Foster, I willed. *Don't throw it back.*

Once upright, Foster pulled his foot back, released the ball, and kicked it. It looked like the easiest, most effortless motion.

The ball skyrocketed in a grand arc over our heads and landed somewhere in the bleachers on the other side of the field.

We all stood there, stunned, except for my PT, who chose that moment to lob the ball at me. It bounced dully off my shoulder. I barely even noticed.

Foster broke the silence first, yelling "Sorry!" and jogging back across the field. He emerged from under the bleachers, trotted up to Ezra, and handed him the ball.

"Sorry about that," Foster said, grinning sheepishly.

Ezra looked at the ball like Foster had just handed him a

potato, and then regarded Foster like he was . . . I don't know, someone who had just handed him a potato.

"Kicker," Ezra said.

"Foster," he replied. "But you're close!"

"He can kick." Ezra looked to Mr. Sellers. "Did you see that?"

It was the first time I had seen Ezra express anything more than lazy detachment. Mr. Sellers sauntered over with his arms folded, clearly ready to offer his expert opinion. Foster just looked confused.

The punt was good, I had to agree, but it had to have been a fluke. The wind and the angle of his foot and the weight of the ball must've all teamed up to create it. Maybe there was some sort of special rubber in the sneakers my mother had bought him.

Ezra waved Foster over, knelt, and placed the tip of the ball on the ground. "Have you ever done placekicking?" he asked.

Foster shook his head. I watched as Ezra told Foster what to do, and a sense of uneasiness penetrated my chest. This wasn't right.

Foster backed up a few yards and angled himself. It dawned on me what was about to happen here—Ezra would pull the football away and Foster would fly up and land flat on his back, like in those old Charlie Brown comic strips. Undeniably, it would've been funny, but it was also just plain mean, so I started to move toward them.

"Wait, Foster—"

Then Foster kicked.

It flew rogue this time, flying end over end and landing twenty feet shy and sharply left of the goalposts.

So it was a fluke. Foster looked vaguely interested, but not too concerned. Ezra, on the other hand, was all determination.

"Again," he said. "Let's do it again."

Mr. Sellers jogged over and retrieved the mesh bag of footballs, while Ezra talked quietly to Foster, gesturing to the ground and then to the goalposts.

"I want to see some passing!" Mr. Sellers bellowed as he moved through the partner pairs back to Ezra and Foster.

I spotted my own football a few feet away and picked it up, but my PT had drifted off to join another group. They weren't passing so much as handing each other the ball while gabbing a mile a minute, probably about Ezra Lynley's favorite brand of socks or something equally irrelevant.

I resolved to stay solo rather than be at the mercy of any conversation in that vein. I held the football so I could at least aim it in the direction of one of the groups if Mr. Sellers looked over, meanwhile edging my way around the other pairs to get closer to where Foster and Ezra stood.

Ezra knelt with the new ball and gestured Foster forward. "Try it again."

This time the ball nicked the left goalpost and bounced off into the sidelines.

"Closer." Ezra eyed Foster. "Again."

He lined up another ball. This one did the trick.

That same powerhouse blast, the same cannonball force of Foster's accidental punt, launched this ball cleanly between the goalposts.

"Shit," I heard a nearby freshboy murmur. He punched the arm of the guy next to him. It was Kenyon, the kid Mr. Sellers had called "our new up-and-comer," who received the blow. Kenyon, broader than two Ezras or three Fosters, was standing with his mouth wide open. "Shit, d'you see that?" the freshboy said.

48

Foster kicked four more times, two rogue shots and two that nailed it. Then Ezra demonstrated a proper punt. Foster copied his movements, and his ball landed ten yards past where Ezra's own had fallen.

I watched shamelessly for the rest of the period. It was oddly disconcerting . . . like learning that your dog could tap-dance. After dismissing us for the day, Mr. Sellers, Ezra, and Foster began to confer.

"What did he say?" I pounced on Foster after class. He was the last one out of the locker room. Even Ezra had strolled out with his duffel bag flung over his shoulder a good ten minutes after the fresh-boys had dispersed and a good five minutes into fourth period. He didn't give me a second glance.

Foster stooped down to pull up his socks. His backpack slid forward over his head as far as the straps would allow, giving him the appearance of a turtle retracting into its shell. "He said with some practice, I have a shot at varsity."

Shock and *surprise* were words too weak to describe it. "Varsity? He said *varsity*?"

"Uh-huh."

"But Mr. Sellers doesn't even coach varsity."

"Not Mr. Sellers. Ezra."

"Ezra? Why would Ezra say that?"

Foster shrugged. "Maybe I'm good."

He didn't say it with any sort of indignation, and I felt a little pang, knowing that I would be pissed if someone were that incredulous about me. "I didn't mean . . . it's just that freshmen don't usually make varsity."

"Mr. Sellers said to go to the C team field after school and he would talk to the coaches about me playing."

C team. That made more sense. Well, as much sense as any of this could make.

"Are you excited?" was all I could think to ask.

"Nobody at home cared that I could kick stuff."

I frowned. "But Mom and Dad don't even . . ." Foster was looking at the wall. I trailed off, and when I spoke again, my voice was a little too bright. "How'd you learn to kick like that?"

Foster looked back at me, and the moment was over. "I had a soccer ball. Sometimes I would try to kick it over our garage. I couldn't get it every time. Ezra said if I practice, I'll become consistent."

"Well . . . you're good at it."

Foster smiled. "Apparently."

6

One by one, the players launched themselves at the tackling dummies, shouldering hard with all their weight behind them. There was no denying it—these were fresh*men*.

Foster watched with round eyes.

"I think they'll start you off as one of those," I said, gesturing to the dummies, just to be stupid. He didn't crack a smile.

Temple Sterling's freshman team played on the field behind TS Junior High, just across the street from the high school. Foster hadn't asked me to go with him, but when he showed up outside my eighth-period science class, I figured the invitation was implied.

There were two freshman coaches—Mr. Jones, who was in the math department, and Mr. Everett, who was a volunteer.

Foster's gaze traveled from the tackling dummies to where Mr. Everett was watching the offense run plays. It was strange—as big as the guys were compared to Foster, their actions looked clumsy and slow compared to what happened at varsity practice.

Foster nudged me.

"What?"

"Go talk to him," he said.

"Me? Why would I talk to him?"

"I don't know."

Foster hung back. I couldn't read the look on his face, but if I were him, I'd probably be wishing that I was a little taller or a little stronger or that my shoelaces weren't tied into such loopy bows. Was something as natural as that possible when it came to Foster? If it was, he wasn't owning up to it. He just stood there, eyeing Mr. Everett suspiciously, until Mr. Everett turned and looked right at us.

A smile broke his face. "You must be Foster!" he called, waving us over. "Mr. Sellers said you'd be stopping by." He lowered his voice as we neared, but the smile never wavered. Mr. Everett was probably twenty years older than my dad, but in way better shape. "I heard you've got quite a kick, Foster," he said. "Mr. Sellers was hoping you might come and play for us."

"Do I have to audition?"

I cringed. This wasn't *Pippin*. But Mr. Everett didn't even blink. "If you wouldn't mind. We don't usually take guys after the start of the season, but Mr. Sellers was enthusiastic, and I've heard you've got Ezra Lynley for a mentor."

This was news to me. Foster nodded solemnly. "He said he'd help me train. I'm behind."

Mr. Everett chuckled. "There are pros I'd call behind compared to Ezra."

Foster and I made our way over to the sidelines after Mr. Everett asked Foster, with another dazzling smile, if he wouldn't mind waiting until practice had gotten a little further under way. Foster cast a glance at me that clearly said "stay," so we parked ourselves on a bench. I opened my book, and Foster watched the progress on the field until Mr. Everett came and collected him.

Then it was the kicking game all over again. He did better this time than he had during gym class. He managed to kick quite a few straight through the goalposts.

Mr. Jones came over then and had Foster throw and catch a few long passes to another one of the players. He managed to catch some, but his throws were as pitiful as mine. No matter how you sliced it, there wasn't a quarterback among the Tennyson family.

I heard Mr. Everett and Mr. Jones murmuring about "special teams" and "field work," and by the time they approached Foster with a final decision, I had lost my place in *Sense and Sensibility* and was wishing I was close enough to hear what they were saying.

Whatever it was, Foster's expression never changed. He just bobbed his head and then proceeded over to the bench to pick up his stuff.

"Well?"

"They said their best kicker can't get distance like that."

"You made it?"

A shrug. "I have to be at two weeks of practices before I can play."

At dinner that night, my mom let out a happy shriek. "You're joking. You're absolutely pulling my leg."

"Way to go, buddy!" was my dad's exclamation. "We got a walk-on in the family, a genuine walk-on!"

"I need a physical," Foster said, and then shoved a large piece of meat loaf into his mouth and chewed unceremoniously.

"Well, you just had one," my mom said. "I'll call the doctor's office and have them send the papers over."

"I need spikes," Foster said, through more bites of meat.

"We'll drive up to the mall after dinner," my mom replied.

Foster looked suspicious. "They're expensive."

"Don't worry about that," my dad said. "As long as your feet promise to stay the same size 'til you make it to varsity."

Foster didn't smile.

This wasn't unusual—and if I had noticed it, then my parents certainly had, too. Foster was cool with "Aunt Kathy," forever happy to talk her ear off as often as he did mine, but he hadn't warmed up to my dad yet. I wondered if it was because he reminded Foster of his own father. Older, to be certain, but maybe they sounded the same, or looked similar, and maybe it was just . . . painful, or something. I didn't know, and I wasn't about to ask.

"Ezra Lynley is going to help Foster train," I said, only to break the moment of awkward silence that followed. I figured it would impress my parents, who knew Ezra merely as TEMPLE STERLING'S OWN.

"No way!" Dad said. "How'd that come up?"

Foster just shrugged, so I cleared my throat a little and said, "Remember how we have gym class with him?"

"Sure. You're the lone seniors."

"Yeah. Well, I guess Ezra offered to help him during gym class. Right?" I looked to Foster. "Didn't he?"

Foster was tearing apart the skin of his baked potato. "Uh-huh," he said, and bit into a long strip. I glanced at my mom. She never let me eat the skins when I was younger, and so by habit I never attempted to now.

She didn't seem to notice. "What did he say?"

"We have a secret."

"What is it?" To my surprise, the question escaped from my own lips.

"If I told you," Foster said, "then it wouldn't be a secret."

Mom and Dad smiled at each other, like they were exchanging some secret of their own. "Well, we'll leave it between you and Ezra then," Mom said.

Foster just kept on chewing.

7

We have a secret. I watched part of varsity practice after my meeting with Mrs. Wentworth on Wednesday and thought about secrets. I didn't have any particularly good ones, save a long-term crush on Cas, which wasn't really that great of a secret anyway. Secret crushes went out of style in the seventh grade.

Foster had lots of secrets, and as much as he jabbered, he was good at keeping them. He went to therapy once a week, and what he talked about there was a secret. His mom had been unwell since Uncle Charlie died, and all that had happened with her he kept secret, too. That was one of the things that bothered me about Foster. Not the therapy stuff—that was private. But he hadn't said a single word about her since the moment we left their house in California. It was as if he'd never had a mother at all. He never talked about her, never cried, never complained, and as far as I was concerned, that wasn't normal.

Maybe all his normal emotions took place behind the door of the therapist's office. Maybe for an hour once a week he wailed and yelled and punched a pillow like a regular person. Or maybe whatever it was that happened with his mom squeezed all the normal right out of him.

"It smells like nacho cheese."

I looked up. Marabelle Finch was drifting up the bleacher steps toward me, one arm wrapped around Baby, as always. She'd been doing that since she was two months in and there was nothing there but flat old stomach.

I would say that before Baby really started growing, Marabelle was delicately pretty; fragile, like spun sugar or a glass figurine. But this was her sixth month, and she had fleshed out. Her face was rounder and her body was fuller and she looked more like a real person—like a really pretty real person.

I sniffed my underarm as she sat down next to me.

"It's not you," she said. "It's the air."

So I sniffed the air experimentally. To me, it smelled like afternoon heat and, somewhere below, forty high school guys working out.

"How are you?" I asked.

"Okay. My head hurts."

"You probably shouldn't be outside. It's so hot."

"They do it." She pointed to the field.

"That's different."

Marabelle frowned in faint indignation. "Because they're boys?"

I sighed. "Let's go inside." As we made our way back up to the school, I asked, "Do you want a soda or something?"

"Baby hates soda."

Marabelle had few opinions nowadays that were actually her own. Baby was first and foremost, no matter what, and there seemed to be quite a few things that Baby couldn't abide.

I was browsing the fiction section at the library last spring when I turned down a new aisle and saw Marabelle sitting on one of those library step stools. A cart stood nearby, abandoned.

Her back was straight, and her hands were folded neatly on top of a pile of books in her lap. Her eyes were fixed on one of the upper shelves across from her.

"Hey," I said, and when she didn't move, "Everything okay?"

Marabelle blinked, once, twice, and then shifted her gaze to me. "Yeah," she answered finally. "I just need to check something out."

"Like a book?" I said, and she laughed. Laughed a lot, actually, until her eyes were glistening.

"Not like a book," she said.

We went to the closest 7-Eleven. She stood by the snack counter while I tried to locate the right aisle. Her eyes were closed, and she was inhaling deeply. I thought for a second that she was panicking, but then her face relaxed, her lips curling into a smile.

"What are you doing?"

"It's the best smell in the world," she replied.

"Sorry?"

"Hot dogs spinning on heated rollers."

I didn't even know where to start with that one. "Come on. We gotta . . . just, come on."

She took the test in the bathroom and made me come in to wait with her. I stood at the sink and she sat on the toilet seat, staring at the stick.

It wasn't blue. I know back in the day they used to turn colors, but this one was just supposed to say PREGNANT or NOT PREGNANT. The letters were small but all too clear.

"Huh." I remember being so freaking surprised, one, that

Marabelle had sex before me, and two, that she could sit there holding that life-changing hunk of plastic and just look mildly . . . perturbed. Not sad or scared or anything. Just perturbed.

"It's got piss on it," she said after a long silence. "Can you believe I'm holding something that's got piss on it?"

I took the stick from Marabelle, even though she was right: It did have piss on it. I shook it a few times, as if, like a Magic 8 Ball or something, that would change the answer.

"Maybe it's wrong."

Marabelle didn't say anything. It was so strange. Almost funny. She didn't look upset. Most of all, she didn't look surprised.

"What are you going to do?" I didn't want to ask, but I couldn't help it.

Marabelle looked at me. "What do you think?"

"You . . . I mean, I don't know. Are you going to have it?"

"He's not an 'it.'" Marabelle took the stick from me and threw it into the trash, and then she set about washing her hands. "He's a baby and I'm his mama, and I don't know what else you'd suggest I'd do but have him."

"But you don't have to keep him." It flew out of my mouth. I couldn't stop it. She was fifteen, and she was wearing pink plastic jewelry, for god's sake. She was supposed to be someone's mom?

Marabelle turned to me, hands dripping, and looked me in the eyes. I was taller—she had to tilt her nose up to look at me full in the face. "I'd get rid of you first," she said, and then she left the room.

I had never heard intensity like that from Marabelle before, and I had yet to hear it again since. I couldn't understand how she just *knew* like that, so strongly, without hesitation. I don't think I'd ever been that sure about anything.

Now she was standing next to me at TS High's sole juice machine, staring down the mango-papaya and strawberry-kiwi buttons with a mildly troubled look on her face.

I stuck a dollar into the machine. "Just pick."

She rubbed her stomach. Then she hit mango-papaya.

"How come you're here after school?" Marabelle asked as we shuffled down the hall with juice in hand.

"I meet with Mrs. Wentworth."

"That counselor lady?"

"Yeah."

"She gave me pamphlets about special schools. She was nice. Nicer than my mama was."

"You didn't want to go to one of those schools?"

"Baby'll never be normal if he's not mainstreamed."

I smiled a little. "Why're you here so late?" I asked as we rounded the corner to the main hallway.

"I don't have a license," Marabelle said. "Other people have to drive us around."

"You want a ride home?" My car was cooperating this week, happily parked in the side lot next to Cas's.

"No, I don't mind waiting."

I pushed through the school's front doors and stepped out into the September sun. Foster's first C team practice would be ending momentarily.

And sure enough, there he was, tripping out from behind TS Middle, an enormous duffel slung over one shoulder. My father had had a field day at the sporting goods store the night before.

He waved when he spotted me and picked up his pace to a loping sort of half run.

Marabelle had joined me on the school's front steps and trailed me as I made my way down.

"I kicked, Dev!" Foster said, near breathless upon approach. "I kicked, and I ran sprints, and I caught the ball . . ." He was sweatier than I had ever seen him, red-cheeked and grinning. "Who's that?"

"This is Marabelle. Uh, Marabelle, this is my cousin Foster."

Marabelle gave Foster a slight smile. His grin faded, his eyes raking her midsection.

"We should get going," I said. "See you later, Marabelle."

"Uh-huh." She waved a few fingers and then guided herself down onto the steps.

I started to go, but Foster hadn't budged.

"Are you just going to sit there?" he asked.

"No." Marabelle held up the mango-papaya. "I'm going to drink juice, too."

"All alone?" Foster looked concerned.

She patted her stomach. "I'm never alone."

Foster looked back at me helplessly, and I cleared my throat. "Are you sure you don't want a ride, Marabelle?" I asked.

"No, I'm fine."

I accepted it straight off, one, because she looked quite content, and two, because I don't think Marabelle was capable of lying. But Foster still looked troubled.

"Come on," I said, pulling the strap on his bag to guide him forward. "Let's go."

"Bye," Foster said, stumbling as he looked back at Marabelle.

It was only when we reached the car that he spoke again. "How come she's got a baby?"

"Well, she doesn't have it yet, does she?"

"I mean, how come she's pregnant?"

"How should I know? There's lots of ways to get pregnant."

"Do you think she wanted to?"

"Foster, nobody in high school *wants* to get pregnant."

Foster craned his neck to look back at the front of the school as we pulled out onto the street.

"Where's its dad?"

"Huh?"

"The baby's dad."

Marabelle had never said a word about him, and I had never dared to ask. "I don't know."

"Does she have a boyfriend?"

Whenever I saw her, she was always alone—aside from Baby, that is. "I don't think so."

"She's pretty," he said after a pause.

I glanced over at him. It was true, but still the last thing I expected to hear. "Yeah, she is."

Foster didn't reply.

8

I woke up the next morning to the usual noise from the kitchen. It was hard to tell if Foster was so loud because he was inconsiderate or because trying to do everything soundlessly made him even clumsier than usual. I didn't really think Foster would consciously be inconsiderate toward us—it was just that he had been used to doing what he wanted for so long. It was like eating the skin of the baked potato. There was never anyone there to tell him not to.

I turned over in bed and stared out the window through the crack between the shade and the wall, listening to myself breathe. I was awake, but I wasn't quite ready to admit it until I heard the front door shut. It's a really distinctive sound—the opening and closing of your own front door. Ours was a kind of wooden click. That click drew me out of bed.

I had a blanket thrown over my shoulders and that fuzzy feeling in my mouth you get when you've just woken up and haven't talked yet. I emerged through the front door into the early-morning light to see Foster, dressed in full TS gym uniform, running in big loopy circles around the front lawn.

"What are you doing?"

He didn't break stride. As he turned and jogged back across the yard, he said, "Ezra's gonna run by here any minute. I want to warm up, but I don't want to miss him."

"How do you know he'll run by?"

"He jogs past our house every day at six fifteen."

"Does not." It was immature. But I couldn't believe that someone else our age voluntarily woke up as early as Foster.

"Does so. I see him every morning. And he said if I'm awake"— he pivoted and ran back—"I can run his route with him."

"His route?" I sank down onto the step and wrapped the blanket around me a little tighter.

"Uh-huh. A four-mile route."

"He runs four miles before school every day?"

Foster gave me a withering look. "You don't get that good by doing nothing."

I didn't know what to say to that, so I just ran my tongue around the inside of my mouth (it still felt fuzzy) and watched Foster pivot and run another lopsided circle around the front lawn. It struck me suddenly that it had been exactly three months since he first came. Before this summer, I hadn't laid eyes on Foster in five years. Now it was three months to the day that he had been living like . . . well, almost like my brother. The word made me feel funny, the way it had when the PT used it in gym class. *That's your brother, right?* I was seventeen years an only child.

Another set of footsteps broke the early-morning silence, and just as Foster had predicted, Ezra Lynley jogged into view. His strides were long and even and controlled. He was like a windup toy, perfectly consistent.

He didn't break stride as he neared the house. He didn't even look over as Foster began waving like a lunatic. He just kept running.

Foster looked at me for a second, shrugged, and then went tearing off after him. I could hear "Wait up, Ezra, wait for me!" all the way down the street, until Ezra turned the corner and Foster, lagging somewhat behind, disappeared as well.

School came, and at lunch I went to investigate what Mrs. Wentworth had described at our meeting yesterday as "an extracurricular opportunity." This opportunity came in the form of the school newspaper—apparently they were looking for photographers, and Mrs. Wentworth had made it clear that skill wasn't a prerequisite.

I tracked down the student editor of the *T.S. Herald* in the writing lab. The table that spread in front of Rachel Woodson was covered in papers, books, old copies of the *Herald*, and issues of the monthly TS literary magazine (to which Rachel also contributed). She sat amid it all looking more than a little harried and twice as much hassled, but that was how Rachel always looked.

We had known each other since preschool. I'm not sure when exactly she declared her intention to get into every top-ten university, but she must've known it pretty early on, because even back then she always took great care to color inside the lines.

She called her college plan "the Straight Sweep." It wasn't enough for her just to want to go to Princeton, to be accepted into Princeton, and to attend Princeton. Rachel wanted to be accepted into all of them—Harvard, Yale, Stanford, all the top schools. I guess so she could have the luxury of turning down the places that kids across the country worked tirelessly just to be rejected from.

It was strange. Rachel was absolutely brilliant. She was involved in just about every extracurricular activity you could think of. She had a load of friends and was the best at practically everything. It didn't make sense that somebody so accomplished could seem anything close to pathetic, but still, inexplicably, I couldn't help but feel sorry for Rachel sometimes.

"Are you available after school?" she asked as she typed furiously on her laptop. She barely glanced up at my entrance.

"Uh, yeah."

"Okay. You can have boys' soccer or girls' track. Which one do you want?"

"Huh?"

"We need pictures from sporting events. We'll put 'em in the sports section, but they'll also be good for yearbook." Did I mention Rachel contributed to the yearbook?

"Okay, well . . ."

I'd never seen anyone type so fast before. I had no idea what she was working on, but it had nothing to do with me. Rachel's ability to multitask was nearly frightening.

"Soccer or track?"

"Uh . . . can I have football?"

Her fingers stopped short.

"You want football? Everyone wants football."

"I mean, I guess I could do something else, but . . ."

"What is it about football?" Rachel regarded me through narrowed eyes. "I mean, what is it that's so great about it anyway?"

"It's . . . tradition?"

Rachel looked put off. "It's a popularity contest disguised as violence disguised as recreational sport." She began to type again. "You know, someone needs to do a story about high school football—not the team or the scores or anything, but the *facts*. It's gotten so political."

"Political?"

"The sport itself—*tradition*—is hardly the issue anymore. Kids play football in high school to get money to go to college. It's just a numbers game."

I thought of Cas. "People play because they love it. Because their dads played, and their dads before them . . . stuff like that."

Rachel glanced up for a split second, and when she spoke next, I couldn't tell if it was in condescension or if her sincerity was just as clipped as her personality. "That's a nice sentiment, Devon."

"But . . ." I knew she was just dying to go on.

"But I mean, come on. Look at Ezra Lynley."

"What about him?"

"You don't think there's anything suspicious about a two-year varsity starter for Shaunessy High School—three-time state champions in the last five years—up and switching to dinky little Temple Sterling in his junior year, only *the* most important year in a high school football career?"

"Well . . . I mean, I guess it's kind of weird, but—"

"You know how you get named an All-American?" I didn't, but Rachel didn't give me a chance to answer. "Your stats. Ezra racked up some incredible plays with Shaunessy, there's no doubt about that, but the stats he earned last year at TS blew all of that out of the water. Forty-five touchdowns in one season. Zero fumbles. *Zero.*"

"He's a good player." Even I had to admit that.

"Yeah, but Temple Sterling's a Class Three team. We've got nothing on those Class Six schools—their teams are huge. Ezra's in every play here. He's responsible for every move, whereas at Shaunessy, he'd have to share the limelight."

"So you think Ezra only came here—"

"To improve his stats. To get recognition. To become an All-American, play in the Bowl, and secure his future."

"Wow," I said, but it wasn't the revelation about Ezra. "For someone who hates football, you sure know a lot about it."

"You can't really oppose something until you've researched it properly, can you?"

She turned back to her computer and didn't speak for a few moments. I finally had to clear my throat. "So . . . about the photography stuff . . ."

Rachel blinked at me like she had forgotten I was there. "Yeah. Well, JV and C team are already covered, but I think I could work something out for you with varsity. See me at lunch tomorrow and I'll get you a sideline pass."

"Really?"

No one got sideline passes unless you were an equipment manager or something.

"Uh-huh."

"Cool. Thanks."

Rachel had already resumed typing, and it was like I had never been there at all.

9

There was a C team game scheduled for Thursday afternoon, but as a new player, Foster wasn't eligible to play yet. As I watched the Freeport players warm up, I figured the longer they could keep Foster from being steamrolled under those guys, the better.

My mom had begged me to go—neither she nor my dad could leave work. I didn't bother telling her that I probably would've gone anyway. I wanted to see if they made uniforms small enough for Foster.

Apparently, they did. C team players didn't get personalized jerseys, but I'd recognize Foster anywhere. He stood on the sidelines, bouncing up and down as the rest of the team assembled for warm-up.

The teams took the field and circled up for jumping jacks and stretches, and I let my eyes wander to the crowd. Turnout for C team games was scant compared to that of varsity, but it was funny to think that in just a few years, a lot of these guys would be playing under those famous "Friday night lights" instead of the glaring Thursday afternoon sun.

I was starting to wish I'd brought a soda or something when

someone plunked down next to me. Lindsay Renshaw held out a bottle of water.

"You thirsty?"

She really was perfect.

"Oh, thanks, but—"

"We've got a whole bunch of them." She gestured to a spot a few rows behind us, where a woman and two elementary school–age girls sat, holding umbrellas and resting drinks on a huge cooler. "Woo-ee, it is hot out here." Lindsay wasn't sweating.

"Yeah." I twisted the cap off the bottle and took a long swig. "You, uh, you got a brother on the team?"

"Yup. Number seven, that's Parker."

"What's he play?" Down on the field, the team finished up calisthenics and circled up around the coaches.

"They're trying him as a safety, but of course he wants to be quarterback. More glory. How about you?" Her eyes widened. "Is your cousin here? Does he play?"

"Uh, yeah. Number twelve."

"Awww, he's adorable!"

Huh. I searched Foster for something that might be considered cute. He wasn't shorter so much as scrawnier than the other guys; even the small, thin receivers had a little muscle to them.

Still, despite that, it was hard to make a football uniform look particularly wrong, so I guess he was like any C team player—a pint-size version of the varsity guys, which was pretty adorable.

"He just started," I felt it was my duty to say. "So he can't play today."

"What position is he?"

"He kicks, mostly. Pretty much entirely."

"Really? Wow, that's awesome. My dad says high school kickers are really hard to come by. He used to play, but not for TS. My mom's from here, but he played for Shaunessy."

Something Rachel said struck me: *a two-year varsity starter for Shaunessy* . . . "That's where Ezra Lynley's from, right?"

"Uh-huh. Man, are they *good*. My dad still drives down to see their games sometimes. He saw Ezra play way before anyone here had ever heard of him."

"Back before he was 'Temple Sterling's own'?"

Lindsay let out a peal of laughter. "Ezra's a sweetheart, but those signs in the bathrooms everywhere are pretty creepy, aren't they? Like, I can hardly go with him watching me like that."

I couldn't help but smile.

Rachel presented me with a sideline pass the morning after the Temple Sterling C Team Cavaliers managed a small victory against the Freeport Bulldogs. She forced the long, rectangular pass into my hand on her way through the hall before lunch and told me to meet Mr. Harper, the faculty adviser of the *Herald*, on the field at six thirty. Then, in a flurry of paper and handheld electronics, she was gone.

I wore the pass proudly that evening. It was laminated and everything. I felt like a VIP, parting ways with Foster as we reached the bleachers, flashing the pass at the fence, and continuing on to the field. Foster had plans to watch the game with some of the Future Science Revolutionaries. I think they were going to calculate ball trajectories or something. If not that, I'm sure they would find some other way to make everyone around them feel simultaneously uncomfortable and mentally inferior.

I scanned the sidelines for Mr. Harper and spotted him at the thirty-yard line. He was holding a tripod and had an enormous black camera bag slung over one shoulder.

After I introduced myself, I waited, as any normal person would, for him to hand me the camera. But Mr. Harper handed me the camera bag instead.

He held the camera up wordlessly and took a few shots of the field. For a moment I thought he was demonstrating how to work it, but then he turned and started down the sidelines, camera still in hand.

What were Rachel's exact words? *I think I could work something out for you?* As the players took the field and the game began, I came to realize that I was little more than a glorified luggage rack.

At least I had a good view of the game.

There were a few other photographers on the sidelines, but they definitely weren't for the *Herald*. These were real photographers for real papers. They were commonplace around the end of last season—the team was headed to the Class 3 championship—but this was just a regular-season game. I wondered what the big story was, but it was clear as soon as we got close.

"Twenty-five," one guy said to another as a new play started on the field. "That's him. Watch twenty-five."

As if he knew they were watching, Ezra emerged from the fray in a full sprint toward the goal line. He had the ball tucked under his arm and his head down, shouldering off a particularly large Freeport lineman and darting to the left as another Freeport player threw himself at Ezra's legs. The last of the defenses failed; the final few yards were free and clear. The touchdown was Ezra's.

"And in the second half? When the Freeport guy bobbled the ball and Ezra stole it and did that hairpin turn, did you see that? When he just took off in the opposite direction and Jordan tackled that guy like two seconds before he was going to get Ezra? Did you see it, Dev?"

Foster talked the entire way home. He paused the commentary only when we pulled into the driveway. "Are you going to go to the party tonight?"

"No." I didn't know the host of tonight's soiree, and I wasn't in the mood for a party. My shoulder ached from lugging that stupid bag around.

"Why not?"

"I don't feel like it."

"Do you like those parties? Ezra says he doesn't. He says it's just a bunch of people getting wasted and acting like idiots."

I looked at Foster as we approached the back door. "When were you talking to Ezra?"

"During gym. When we ran the mile."

I had been too focused running my own mile to pay attention to anything else, let alone carry on a conversation.

"We're going to start training for real on Sunday. Not tomorrow, 'cause he has plans tomorrow, but on Sunday."

I wondered what Foster was going to tell me next: Ezra's shoe size, or whether he preferred boxers to briefs. Maybe Ezra's opinion on foreign policy in the Middle East, or what he had for dinner last night.

"Night," I said, heading up to my room before he had a chance to go on. I knew my mother would be happy to listen to Foster expound upon the many talents and opinions of Ezra Lynley. She'd be happy listening to Foster read the nutritional contents of a box of cereal, so long as he was talking to her.

It was endearing, in that way that almost ached sometimes, how much my folks wanted Foster to be okay. And I think even more than I did, they wanted Foster to be normal. For me, being normal meant fitting in. For them, I think, it just meant being happy.

Cas took his car to the coin-operated car wash every Saturday afternoon, sort of a postgame ritual. He had a shitty black two-door he bought used off a senior back in sophomore year, and he absolutely worshipped it.

Everything in the car wash worked on a time limit; the more quarters you put in, the more time you got. Cas had an entire system worked out to get a maximum cleaning with minimum cash, but it was a two-person system. So more often than not, I found myself at the car wash on Saturday afternoon. I didn't mind it; I'd take mine along and we'd wash it, too. But unlike Cas, I knew no amount of ultrashine dry coats could make my old Toyota look any more glamorous and any less used.

After doing the interior, Cas positioned his car in the little open-air garage and I stood by the metal box on the wall that controlled the kind of wash you wanted. There was one knob that you turned to get conditioning coat, rinse, and ultrashine. You had to put in a dollar surcharge, and then every quarter after that bought thirty seconds. Cas swore the entire thing could be done for a dollar seventy-five. This was rarely the case, but it was a nice dream.

"Time?"

The rinse always tripped Cas up. "Twenty seconds."

"Shit. Switch it."

The ultrashine was my favorite. It smelled the best. I turned the knob and Cas blasted away. Soap was still dripping from the tires.

"You want me to put another quarter in?"

"No. I'm going to make it."

"You don't want to have to pay the buck again."

"Time?"

"Nine seconds."

He had only made it halfway around the car.

"You want me to put another quarter in?"

"No!"

I put another quarter in.

Cas finished the ultrashine, and the hose automatically shut off when the clock ran down. "I could've made it," he said, jamming the wand back into its holder. "We wasted, like, ten seconds there at the end."

"Next time."

He pulled the car through to the back lot. Mine was already there, washed, dried, and shining in the sun. I unrolled the windows and turned the radio on as Cas parked and got out.

"I'll be wet-dry and you be dry-dry," he said, and threw me a towel. I was always dry-dry.

I followed him around the car and retraced the tracks left by his towel. My car radio chattered with itself as we cleaned, commercials for laser hair removal and resale clothing stores. I glanced up at Cas periodically as we worked. I loved his faded T-shirts. He'd been wearing today's since the eighth grade. It hung too loose back then, but now it was just the right amount of tight, the screen logo long since peeled away, the color now a perfectly faded shade of blue. A lot of the ones my mom bought for Foster at the mall tried to imitate this color, but Cas's was the kind you couldn't buy for ridiculous mall prices, or any amount of money, really. Cas earned that color with time.

"What?" he said, after we started on the windows.

"Huh?"

A smile split his face. "Why're you looking at me funny?"

"I was just thinking."

"About what?"

I invented fast. "The party last night. You have fun?"

He shrugged and pushed the towel in wide circles across the glass. "It was all right. Boring without you."

Sometimes I hated when he said stuff like that, because it was always just what I wanted to hear, but not with the intention I wanted it to have. "Nothing spectacular happened?"

"Not really. Some people got pretty shit-faced."

I snorted. "Stanton Perkins."

"Yeah. Jordan and Ezra left pretty early, took most of the party with them. Good thing they did, too, or else I would've told Ezra to get his ass out of there. Stanton's angry enough when he's sober."

"Why does he hate Ezra so much?"

"More of the same, I guess. Just in a greater intensity than everyone else."

In a way, Ezra was a true celebrity, disliked just as much as he was admired. Half of the school revered him for taking the varsity football captain title this year, and the other half resented him for exactly the same thing. Cas didn't like to admit it, but until Ezra came, the captainship had been down for him. Ezra was clearly the better player, but people liked Cas—that was the problem. You don't always want what's better. Sometimes you just want what you want, the familiar, the dependable, the accessible. There was nothing accessible about Ezra Lynley.

When Cas spoke again, his voice was strange. "Forty-five touchdowns in one season. It's ridiculous."

"Do you think Stanton's right about him?"

"No. No, of course not. I just . . ." He paused, his towel resting on the back windshield across from mine. "Sometimes I can't help but think it should be me, you know?"

I didn't know what to say, so I just made some incoherent sound of sympathy.

"It's a fucking classic," he said. "It's a TV movie in the making. The charismatic underdog and the brooding prodigy he'll never be able to catch up to, no matter how hard he tries."

"Charismatic might be a bit of an overstatement."

"Shut up. I am so charismatic." He gave the windshield a final swipe. "He's a jackass, sure, but he's better than me. I can't hate him for that, right? It's the same old story, so it's, like, what is there to do?"

I shrugged. "Give it a different ending?"

"You mean, like, push Ezra into a pool of laser sharks?"

"Yes. That's exactly what I meant." I threw the towel at him. "Or you could just . . . be the good guy. Be the one everyone roots for."

"So I should run up and down the bleachers a thousand times, throw the football through a tire swing, and then the big championship game'll come around and Ezra will screw up and I'll save the day? Win Temple Sterling's heart? Get the girl?"

"Yeah. And the girl might even let you keep the laser sharks."

Cas grinned.

10

I took Foster to training with Ezra the Sunday afternoon succeeding Temple Sterling's victory over Freeport Senior High. I didn't want to go, aware that both my mom and Foster expected me to stay the whole time, but I tried to see it as an opportunity to read, take in some fresh air, and appreciate the last of the lingering summer sun.

As we approached the empty varsity field, Ezra came into view. I peeled off toward a bench on the sidelines, not wanting to face a conversation with him, and Foster continued on to where Ezra stood in the middle of the field, a football in hand.

I opened *Sense and Sensibility* to the part where Marianne, our heroine Elinor's younger sister, is sick. It couldn't get any better than this. Mr. Willoughby, distraught at the news of Marianne's sudden illness, shows up at their house intoxicated, begging to see her. It was tense and dramatic and somehow, although two hundred years previous, still totally relevant. It was the drunken text message to an ex two centuries before such a thing existed.

To me, Mr. Willoughby was one of the most interesting characters in Jane's books. First, you think he's great—he comes out of nowhere and has this whirlwind romance with Marianne—but then he turns around and drops her completely, and you feel like he's this truly terrible guy. But then somehow, in that scene where he shows up at the house, desperate to see if she's okay, you almost feel sorry for him. Like maybe you could sympathize with him in some way. Maybe he's not such a bad, villainous person—just a regular person who made stupid decisions. He could've had everything he wanted, but he threw it all away because of the choices that he made. You can't truly hate someone like that. You can pity him, sure, but you can't hate him.

The scene with Mr. Willoughby was as dramatic as ever, but I couldn't help but lose focus. I glanced up from the page every so often and watched Foster and Ezra work. Foster missed the ball the first few times Ezra threw it to him, but he seemed to get the hang of it as they went on. Ezra gave advice at a volume too low to be heard from where I sat, but Foster's voice rang out clear and strong, asking what he was doing wrong and how he should fix it. It was strangely endearing. Foster really seemed to want to learn.

They came over for a break after a while. Ezra downed a bottle of water, and Foster relayed in his typical rambling style everything they had covered thus far.

"... And Ezra said this is just the way he learned, like this is just the same stuff they did! And next we're doing . . . what are we doing next, Ezra?"

"Tackling."

Foster's face fell. "But . . . I thought I wouldn't get tackled."

"Anyone can get tackled."

Foster didn't reply.

Ezra put down his water and edged a little closer to where we were sitting. He wouldn't look at me. It seemed to be a standard

79

Ezra move—denying the existence of anyone who wasn't of importance to him.

"What are you scared of?" he said.

"It'll hurt."

"Yeah, maybe it'll hurt. So what?"

Foster just blinked at him.

"You ever play any board games?"

Foster practically worshipped the Parker Brothers. "Yeah."

"What's your favorite?"

He screwed up his face in thought. "Monopoly."

"Okay. Say Monopoly was a contact game, and every time you passed GO, you got hit upside the head. Would you still play?"

"Why would I get hit upside the head? That wouldn't make sense."

"Why not?"

"'Cause it has nothing to do with the game. It doesn't accomplish anything. At least in football . . ." Foster stopped himself. Ezra nodded.

"You're getting hit for a reason. If taking a tackle means your team gets a first down or a touchdown, it's not for nothing, right?"

"Yeah."

Ezra looked somewhat satisfied, but I knew Foster. He still had that troubled look on his face. This wouldn't be easy.

"But . . . I mean, just knowing that it has a purpose doesn't mean it'll hurt any less."

"Yeah, but won't it feel better to know that your getting tackled helped the team accomplish something? Look. You can kick, and that's great, but they need to know that they can put you in there for a field play and not have to worry about where you're at and what you're doing and whether you'll get steamrolled or not."

This was the most I had ever heard Ezra say. I realized I was staring at him when his eyes met mine for a split second. I turned back to my book.

"Maybe if I kicked, like, *really* good, they wouldn't care," Foster said.

Ezra sighed. "Let's just quit for today, okay? Go grab the ball."

Foster jogged over to where the football lay in the grass a little ways away.

And all of a sudden, Ezra charged. Before I could call out a warning, Ezra had thrown himself at Foster and flattened him to the ground.

The yell escaped my lips a moment too late.

I leaped to my feet and ran over. Ezra pulled himself back up. Foster was still on the ground, looking somewhat dazed.

"What the hell is your problem? You could've hurt him!"

"A lineman could hurt him; that's how they do it."

"He's *little*, you can't just do that!"

"Hey, Dev, you got a Kleenex?"

"I'm trying to help. He's got to know what it's like."

There was a tug at my sleeve.

I looked down. Blood was pouring from Foster's nose.

"Holy shit." Foster was prone to nosebleeds. I'm pretty sure a stiff wind or a crooked look could make Foster's nose bleed. But I glared at Ezra anyway. "Look what you did."

"He's fine." Ezra pulled Foster to his feet. "You're fine." There was something searching in his eyes that made it more of a question than a statement.

Foster cupped his nose with blood-smeared hands and nodded sagely.

I grabbed Foster's elbow—"We're going"—and pulled him across the field.

"Did you see that, Dev? Did you see me get tackled?"

"Yeah, I saw. I was sitting right there."

"I got tackled by Ezra Lynley. When we're adults, and Ezra's gone pro, I can watch TV with my kids and be, like, that's the guy who tackled me."

I looked at Foster, only to see that the face under his bloody hands had broken into a grin.

"Give it up, Foster. He's a dickhead, and you shouldn't let him push you around like that."

"He's not pushing me around; he's teaching me."

When we reached the car, I yanked my door open and slammed it shut behind me with equal force.

It was only when we got home that I realized I had left *Sense and Sensibility* at the field. By the time I deposited Foster and drove back, the book, along with all traces of Ezra Lynley, was gone.

11

Labor Day is really the last sweet taste of summer. One final pardon before all your Mondays become Mondays again. I tried to make the most of it, that weekend of Ezra and Foster's training session.

But now it was over, and Rachel Woodson was cornering me in the hallway between classes.

"Are you pissed?" she said with no preamble.

"What—"

"About the whole camera-bag thing. See, it's not as bad as it seems. You just put it on the application as 'Assistant Photographer' and 'Equipment Manager for the *Herald*.' You could probably wrangle an athletic extracurricular out of it, too, like 'Assistant to Sports Documentation' or something like that. So it's really not that bad, you see?"

"Assistant to Sports Documentation" did sound a lot better than "Camera Biatch."

"I'm not mad."

"Good. Because if I had told you everything, you wouldn't have wanted to do it, since no one wanted to do it, not even a freshman or anything. So it's all for the best."

"Uh, right."

"But what I really wanted to talk to you about was that idea you had for a sports article."

"What idea?"

"About how high school football has gotten so political."

As I recall, that was Rachel's idea, but she didn't give me time to protest.

"See, I really want to make a piece out of that, but I'm just so swamped. I thought maybe you could do some of the groundwork for me, maybe conduct some interviews and stuff? I'll print out a list of questions and everything, and then you can add that to your résumé. I'll even put you in the byline." Rachel said this last part like she was offering me one of her kidneys.

"Oh . . . well, I guess—"

"I want the crux of the article to deal with how much the future of a person's college football career is dependent on his high school stats. I've already sent a load of e-mails off to different sports recruiters and heads of programs from colleges in the state, but I need the student perspective, so I want you to interview Ezra Lynley, okay?"

"Why—"

"No one's got stats like him, and no one's gotten recruited like him. He blows the rest of the team out of the water. I printed you out a list of questions since I didn't have your e-mail." She shoved a sheaf of papers at me, and I accepted them, bewildered. "Speaking of, I'm going to need your contact information. If you could shoot it over to me sometime, I would really appreciate it." I opened my mouth to speak. "Thanks, Devon, you're the best." And she was gone.

I continued down the hall, turning the corner just in time to see Mrs. Wentworth emerge from her office with a large flyer.

"Oh, Devon!" Her face lit up. "Just the person I wanted to see."

She held up the flyer. It described an impending trip to Reeding University in large, enthusiastic Comic Sans font. Under the description were eight lines for names; mine had already been printed in the top spot.

"I spoke with a rep over at Reeding and everything's arranged," Mrs. Wentworth said as she tacked the flyer to the bulletin board outside her office. "We'll head down on a Thursday and stay overnight. You can sleep in the dorms, sit in on classes, everything."

"Great." I wasn't sure how I should feel. I suppose I should've been grateful to Mrs. Wentworth for caring so much, but it was all a little overwhelming. It was September, college was light-years away, and I apparently had a newspaper article to research.

"The best part is, there's a Saturday game that weekend, so you won't even have to worry about missing your extracurricular."

"Oh. Cool." And by *cool* I meant *ugh*.

"See you on Wednesday!" And just like Rachel before her, Mrs. Wentworth was off.

"Devon."

This was getting ridiculous. "What?" I whipped around fast.

Ezra stood behind me, looking slightly bewildered. He held up my copy of *Sense and Sensibility*.

"You left this," he said.

I blinked. "Yeah, I know. I went back to get it and it was gone."

"That's because I picked it up for you."

"I could've picked it up when I went back if you had just left it."

I had no good reason to chastise Ezra. But I was already annoyed.

"I didn't know you were going to go back. I was just . . . trying to help."

I took the book, and we stood for a moment.

"Thanks," I said hastily, and shoved it into my backpack.

When I looked back up, he was staring at me.

"Was there something else?"

"Yeah, uh . . . about what happened Sunday . . ."

"You mean you flattening Foster to the ground?"

"Yeah . . . sorry."

"Why are you apologizing to me?"

"You seemed more upset than him."

I had to admit it: "He was pretty ecstatic about it, actually."

There was a pause.

"I just figured . . . well, he seemed scared. And I just thought it would be better to get it over with so he could see that it's not such a big deal. And a surprise tackle is better than if he just had to stand there facing someone down, you know?"

It sort of made sense. But for some reason I tried to hold on to my indignation. For Foster's sake. Right?

Before I could speak, Ezra frowned. "Why do you have a paper with my name on it?"

I realized I was still holding Rachel's questions. INSIDE TEMPLE STERLING'S OWN EZRA LYNLEY was emblazoned across the top of the first page.

That was embarrassing on so many levels.

"Oh. Uh, Rachel just gave me these. You know Rachel Woodson?"

He just gave me that blank look.

"She wanted me to interview you about . . ." The first question read: *As a high school football player today, do you value personal statistics over team victories?* And the next: *Do you feel as if the focus of high school football has shifted from the team to the individual?*

Man, it was like an essay test. "Football stuff," I finished.

"Okay."

That was not the answer I was expecting. "Really?"

"Yeah. Whenever."

"Um . . . cool. Great."

He gave me a nod and then headed off down the hallway.

Foster bounded up to my locker after school that afternoon with a huge grin on his face.

"Guess where I'm going!"

He was already wearing his football helmet.

"Hmm. Give me three tries."

Foster's eyes were wide. "*Varsity* practice."

"Why?"

"I don't know. Mr. Sellers told me to at lunch."

"Wait, like, you're actually going there to *practice*?"

"I don't know what else I'd be doing," Foster said. "You're going to come, right?"

Of course I would, and of course I did, but not before hunting down Cas. I found him by his locker, chatting with a couple of girls we had math class with. I none too ceremoniously interrupted.

"Can I talk to you for a second?"

"Yeah, sure. Hey, I'll see you guys tomorrow."

The girls walked off, and Cas turned back to his locker to pull out his duffel. "Thanks," he said, giving the strap a pull. It was wedged in there pretty firmly. "It's like you've got this radar or something. You know exactly when I need to be saved. Ashley just kept going on about what nail polish color to wear to Homecoming. I mean, it's, like, ages away."

"She was probably working up to asking you." I joined Cas in pulling on the duffel bag strap. We heaved together and managed to yank it out. "Hey, so why's Foster practicing with varsity?"

"Reggie mentioned that at lunch. I thought it was just a rumor."

"Just confirmed. By Foster himself."

Cas hoisted his bag onto his arm. "Got to be a mistake."

"Why? I mean, he's got a good kick. Maybe they want to try him out."

"No way."

"Why no way?"

We started down the hallway. "The season's already started, for one thing, and anyway, nobody bumps up to varsity their freshman year. They probably just want him to get a little coaching from Whittier since he's inexperienced and stuff."

Marcus Whittier was the current kicker. Since we were a smaller division, there wasn't a whole lot in the way of special teams. Marcus performed pretty much any sort of kicking function necessary.

I stationed myself in the bleachers after Cas and I parted ways, and I watched as Foster joined the rest of the guys for jumping jacks. I left my book open in my lap so I looked less like one of those creepy football groupies and more like the uninterested ride of one of the players. But I kept an eye fixed on the field.

It was just like a normal practice, aside from Foster being plugged into it. He ran sprints. He did drills. He practiced kicking alongside Marcus while the team ran plays. Maybe Cas was right. Maybe they did just want him to get a little extra help.

I waited for Foster outside the locker rooms when practice was over, but it was Jordan Hunter who emerged first.

An easy smile broke his face. "Champ! How's it going?"

That voice. Jordan Hunter could charm snakes with that voice. I grinned stupidly up into his mirrored shades as he sidled up to me. "Good. Great. You?"

"I'm good. Better now that I've got company. Walk me to my car?"

I probably would've accepted an invitation to walk Jordan across the Sahara. "Sure."

We started toward the lot.

"So . . . that was weird, right? Foster playing with you guys?"

"Nah, kid's a natural. And I don't know for certain, but I have it on pretty good authority"—he glanced around and then lowered his voice—"your boy's going to be asked to join varsity."

"*What?*"

"Just what I heard."

"But he just joined C team!"

"He's good. Learns fast. Whittier had that sprain last year and hasn't been the same since. Foster's better."

"But Foster's . . . *Foster.* And what about Marcus? What'll happen to him?"

"He'll still go in for punts and kickoffs. Foster'll do field goals and extra points."

"But why Foster? I mean . . . even if Marcus can't do it, there must be a great kicker on junior varsity."

"Not like him."

I thought about what Lindsay had said at the game: *High school kickers are really hard to come by.*

"But freshmen don't play varsity."

"Ezra did, up at Shaunessy. And we all know Shaunessy could crush our little team."

"Yeah, but that's Ezra. When he was born, he probably sprinted out of his mother and charged the delivery nurse."

Jordan laughed. "It's a wonder he wasn't drafted right out of the nursery."

12

I didn't tell Foster what Jordan had said, in case it wasn't true. But we didn't have to wait long to find out. Foster was called out of gym class on Wednesday and it was made official. He brought home the varsity warm-up jersey that night to show my parents.

I thought they would injure themselves smiling. One of those "be careful or your face will freeze that way" situations.

Foster seemed happy but a little confused about the whole thing. He just kept asking, "But I'm going to get to play, right?"

"If the coach puts you in," I said.

"But he wouldn't want me if he wasn't going to put me in, right?"

"Either way, it's better to be a benchwarmer on varsity than the star of the C team."

"Not if you don't get to play. I want to help the team accomplish stuff. Like Ezra says."

"Just be grateful. This doesn't happen often. This doesn't happen, like, *ever.* You're a lucky guy."

I blanched inside as soon as I said it. Football aside, Foster was a pretty unlikely candidate for "lucky guy."

But he just looked at me placidly and said, "I must be," and there was not a hint of irony or sarcasm or anything.

News of Foster's move spread through school pretty fast. Cas shrugged it off, and I didn't play up that he had been wrong about the whole thing.

"It's cool," he said as we passed through the lunch line on Thursday. "Get a little young blood on the team."

"Young blood? Yeah, you guys are ancient."

"Reggie's almost nineteen."

Reggie Wilcox was the quarterback, a pretty nice guy with a pretty good arm who unfortunately lacked the skills to pass trigonometry.

Usually the quarterback is the lifeblood of a team, and almost always he's the captain. But I don't think Reggie ever had the motivational skills necessary to be captain. He was just a laid-back sort of guy who was good at throwing a ball around and, because of seniority, happened to find himself quarterback. Sometimes I wondered if I would ever be lucky enough to fall into some kind of talent like that.

Before I knew it, it was Friday night. I was down on the sidelines with Mr. Harper's camera bag on my back, and for the first time, Foster was down there with me.

Well, not with me, but with the team. Wearing that TS red and white and stepping onto the field under the floods.

Most of the other guys eclipsed him. He even looked small next to Jordan, who was by no means a mountain. I watched as Jordan clapped Foster on the back and said something that was no doubt devastatingly charming. I was too far down the field to hear, so I just shouldered Mr. Harper's camera bag and craned my neck to get a better look.

Foster went out with the rest of the team to warm up. They seemed to be taking to him pretty well. I guess it's because Foster was just about as nonthreatening as it got; he was small, he was inexperienced, and he wasn't about to take time from anybody on the field. Except maybe Marcus Whittier, of course, but it wasn't as if he were being ousted all together. I knew enough about the dynamics of a team from Cas to know that the future of the team always had to be kept in mind. A star senior lineup was great, but you always had to have an eye on the next generation to see what you'd be left with when that lineup moved on.

The game began after the usual roll call of starters. The roar of the crowd and the coin toss. Marcus handled the kickoff, just as Jordan said he would, and after TS scored in the first quarter, he stepped in for the extra point as well. It seemed they weren't going to sic Foster on Hancock—or rather sic Hancock on Foster—right off the bat.

Hancock was a pretty good team, and Temple Sterling didn't score its second touchdown until the end of the first half. Ezra took a handoff and made a spectacular run down the field, propelling himself into the end zone and raising the score to 13–6.

And then it was time for the extra point. Surely they would send Marcus in. But there was Coach, pointing right at Foster.

Foster trotted out onto the field and got into place. Play started. Marshall Samford hiked the ball. Eliot Price caught it and set it, and Foster ran, ran, and connected with the ball. It shot into the air, arched gracefully, and landed right between the goalposts.

The crowd erupted, and I realized I had been holding my breath.

There were three more extra points that night. Marcus took two of them, but Foster had the last, and he nailed it. It was official: He was a hit.

"Fantastic!" My dad slapped Foster on the back in the parking lot. "You were incredible. Really showed 'em your stuff."

Foster looked past my dad to my mom. "Can I go to the party with Dev?"

Don't get me wrong—I was happy for Foster. But that was the last thing I wanted to hear. No, okay, second to last thing. The last thing I wanted to hear was my parents say yes.

"This isn't fair," I said, after my mom had pronounced sentence.

"Look." Mom lowered her voice while my dad tried to talk to Foster about the game. "This means a lot to Foster. Just this once, please, take him and keep an eye on him."

"If I had asked to go to one of these things when I was a fresh-man, you would've said no flat out."

"You didn't have an older sibling to look after you."

"I'm not his *sibling*."

"Devon." Mom's voice went icy. "You're being unreasonable."

She was right, and I knew it, so I just scowled and said, "Fine," and didn't talk to Foster the whole way over to Frank Ferris's house, because it was easier to take it out on him than on my parents.

"You won't even know I'm here, Dev," Foster said before we got out of the car. "I promise I won't do anything embarrassing."

I felt a twinge of guilt and said, "I'm sure you'll be fine."

"This isn't my first party, you know. I used to go to these things all the time."

"Really?" We trekked up Frank's front walk. From the cars on the street and the silhouettes in the windows, you could tell the place was packed.

"Well . . . they were kind of different. But sort of the same." We pushed through the front door, a sea of people opening up in front of us. Foster smiled. "See you later."

"I'm supposed to look after—" I started, but he melted into the mass of revelers and disappeared.

It wasn't a great party. I didn't locate Cas for the first twenty minutes or so, and when I finally spotted him, it was on the sun-porch with Lindsay Renshaw, a little too cozy on a wicker love seat.

"Hey, Devon!" Lindsay waved me over. "Some game, huh?"

"Yeah, it was awesome."

"Sit with us," Cas said, but he didn't scoot over, because, clearly, there was nowhere to scoot.

The nearest seat was halfway across the room. "It's cool. I've got to go find Foster anyway."

"Oh my gosh! Your cousin!" Lindsay's face brightened. "He's so cute, Devon, and really talented! My dad thought so, too. He said Foster's kick is incredible for somebody so young."

"Awesome . . . I'll, uh, let him know."

"We're going to hit the dance floor in a little bit," Cas said. "You should come with."

One, there was no dance floor, just an awkward space cleared in the living room. Two, I had just about as much social dancing skill as I did athletic prowess. Three, I had no desire to watch Cas and Lindsay grind to crappy pop songs.

"Thanks, but I think I'm gonna go catch up with some people." Tonight's version of the quick escape.

After a circulation of the ground floor, a few hellos, and a little small talk, I was left to hover. Chapter Two of the story of my life: How awkward party hovering looks good on no one.

I was standing in the front hallway when I noticed that Ezra

Lynley was nearby. He was with a group of underclassmen who were desperately trying to engage him in conversation, but he didn't look chatty. In fact, upon closer inspection, it appeared that he was hovering, too. It was only after a few minutes that I realized he was drifting closer and closer to where I was standing.

"Hi," I said, finally, when he was too close to be ignored. "How's it going?"

I hadn't spoken to Ezra since he had returned my book. I can't say Rachel's interview was at the top of my to-do list. But since he had been decent in the hallway, I figured maybe he could be decent at a party, too.

That thought left my mind when Ezra turned and looked at me like he didn't know who I was. I was about to roll my eyes when he said, "Not bad. You?"

A response. Not a particularly effusive one, but at least it was civil.

"Okay. You seen Foster around?" I was considering leaving.

"No. I didn't even know he was here."

"Yeah, he said he'd make himself scarce."

The pound of bass added to the din in the living room as the sound system kicked in. The "dance floor" flooded with people.

"I don't really like these things," Ezra said after a while.

"No?"

"No."

Silence.

"Kind of reminds me of dances in middle school," I said. "You know, the ones where the vice principal would go around with the ruler, making sure there was 'room for the Holy Ghost'?"

"I never went to those."

The sea of dancers rippled a little. I spotted Cas in the middle of the room with Lindsay. They were gyrating to the beat. There was no room for the Holy Ghost.

A dull ache hit my stomach. Don't get me wrong. Cas had dated before, but—as bad as this sounds—I had always felt vindicated by the fact that Cas's relationships never lasted long.

But this was *Lindsay Renshaw.* Lindsay Renshaw wasn't the kind of person you go out with for two weeks and then get bored of.

I knew that one day Cas would fall in love, and then it would be all over but the crying. Someone else would be dry-dry at the Saturday afternoon car wash, and I would be minus one best friend.

I didn't notice Ezra staring at me. "So . . . do you . . . dance at all . . . anymore?"

"Excuse me," I said, and walked off.

I went across the room, picked up a cup, put it down, circled the couch twice, and then hurried off as fast as I could to the bathroom.

Cold water. A little peace. I splashed my face with water from the tap and hung there over the sink for a moment, letting the beads roll down my cheeks and land in the basin.

"Are you drunk?" a voice said.

So it was only temporary peace.

I whipped around and ripped the shower curtain back. There sat Foster, fully clothed, in the empty bathtub.

"What the hell are you doing in here?"

There was a rubber duck balanced delicately on his head. It didn't move as he spoke. "Just sitting."

This was one of those moments. Those Foster moments. Early-morning smoothies and the like. I squeezed my eyes shut hard.

"Why is your face wet?" he asked.

I grabbed a towel.

"Did Cas make you cry? I'll punch him."

I wasn't crying. "No one's punching anyone."

"I'm sure somewhere someone's punching someone else. Like in a prison, or at a bar, or during a war, or something."

"Foster." I was weary of this. "Get out of the bathtub."

"There were a guy and a girl in here earlier. They talked about condoms and stuff."

This was too much. I turned back to the sink and flung the towel back onto its holder. "Foster, you shouldn't be in here. You can't just listen to people's conversations like that."

"They weren't talking the whole time. I think they made out some, too."

"You have to learn to keep your nose out of other people's business and to keep your mouth shut. People don't say stuff like that."

I could see Foster's expression in the bathroom mirror and it didn't change at all. The rubber duck didn't move a millimeter.

"I do."

"Normal people don't."

"I'm just being honest."

"Well, don't be, Foster. Don't be honest. Be normal."

He and the rubber duck stared at me unwaveringly. "Are you drunk?"

I slammed the door shut on my way out.

13

My mom took Foster to therapy on Saturday mornings. The sessions were usually an hour, but they were late coming back the morning after the Hancock game. I found myself wondering if Foster had extra things to talk about. What were the chances of him coming through the front door with puffy eyes and pockets full of Kleenex? Maybe he was telling the therapist that I was kind of a jerk the night before. Maybe he had a breakthrough or something.

That word, *breakthrough*, conjured up images of a wall of suffering, a fortress of inner turmoil, being leveled by a bulldozer. Was that what it was like? Did Foster even have a wall to knock down in the first place? He didn't seem depressed or scarred. No pent-up rage. No crying spells. What did they even talk about in there?

Before this summer, the last time I had seen Foster was five years ago, at his father's funeral. Uncle Charlie and my dad were ten years apart—my dad was older—and we hadn't seen him much since he moved to California with Elizabeth, right before Foster was born. They came to a couple of Christmases when I was little—I faintly remember Foster as a baby—and then they stopped coming. Uncle Charlie was too sick to travel, and anyway, I think they were too poor to afford the tickets. My dad flew out to be with him right before he died, and my mom and I joined him for the funeral.

Foster was nine at the time, and I was twelve. We were the only kids there. Elizabeth's only family was her mom, who I was told died a couple of years later.

I knew that this was a truly somber occasion; my dad had lost his brother, his only sibling. But I didn't know enough about Uncle Charlie to miss him personally. They lived so far away and visited so infrequently that the only way I can really remember his face now is how it looked in his coffin.

I don't know what kind of person Elizabeth was before her husband died. I vaguely remember her from some of those early-on Christmases: stringy hair and watery eyes. That was the one thing that stuck in my mind—happy or sad, Elizabeth always looked close to crying.

We went back to California five years after Uncle Charlie died, and Elizabeth looked at us with those very same eyes, only now there was this vacancy to them. She clasped my dad in a hug, my mom, and then me, but it lacked warmth. Her arms were frail, and her face had these hollows in it.

My parents never said it outright: *Elizabeth is on drugs.* It was always "Elizabeth's issues" or "Elizabeth's addiction." But I was old enough to know that Elizabeth certainly wasn't hooked on phonics.

"Come say hello, Foster!" she had called into the depths of the house.

And Foster emerged—taller, thinner, and paler than when I had seen him at Uncle Charlie's funeral. I thought maybe it was the result of adolescence—losing that childhood rosiness he used to have. But there was something else. His eyes looked a little like

Elizabeth's. They weren't as vacant as hers, but there was some distance there that I didn't remember from before.

And now, today, the morning after the Hancock game, Foster emerged through the doorway, another version of his ever-changing self. It was clear why they were late.

Foster's hair was cut. His scraggly hair was gone, and in its place was a very respectable, oddly stylish crew cut.

"You like it, Dev?" Foster threw himself down on the couch next to me.

"You look . . ." I said "different," but I meant *nice*. From the neck up, Foster looked . . . well, he looked like a freshboy.

"Why'd you change it?"

He shrugged.

"He said it was time for a new look," my mom told me in the kitchen after Foster had retreated to his room. "A *varsity football look*."

The *varsity football look* went over well at school. Jordan rubbed Foster's head between classes, saying, "I like it, man, I like it. We should rub your head for good luck."

And there was Foster, grinning. "I thought about doing dreadlocks, but that's sort of your thing."

Jordan laughed. The girls around Jordan (for there were always girls around Jordan) laughed, too.

The look even made an impact on Tuesday's gym class. We started off with more football exercises and Mr. Sellers's usual call of "Partner up, everybody!" Foster would go to Ezra, and I would be stuck with a PT, as per usual.

But not today. Today a particularly enterprising PT grabbed

Ezra by the sleeve before he could move an inch and said, "Partners! We're partners!"

"Look at that," I said to Foster. "They're mobilizing against you."

Foster grinned. And then there was this cough. A cute little "ahem." Foster and I turned, and there stood Gracie Holtzer, with her flawless hair and her tied-up tee and her disconcertingly perfect eyeliner.

"Do you want to be partners, Foster?" she said.

I glanced over at the group of PTs and freshboys assembled nearby. The PTs looked amazed, and the freshboys looked aggravated. This wasn't a joke. This was the queen bee working without the approval of her drones.

"Uh, I'm going to be partners with Dev this time," Foster said.

Gracie wore a look of mingled shock (for being rejected) and awe (for being rejected). I expected the look to morph into a scowl or some expression of disgust, but Gracie's lip just sank into a pout, and she said, "Okay. But next time, all right?"

"Sure."

"You could've gone with her," I said when Gracie retreated.

He shrugged. "She's not really my type."

"You have a *type*?"

"Sure. Don't you?"

"I guess." I hadn't really thought about it before. I had one boyfriend, in the eighth grade. I don't think boys' personalities, brains, or bodies are fully developed enough in the eighth grade to be able to classify them as "types." And, honestly, I didn't think Foster's personality, brain, or body was fully developed enough to *have* a type.

"So what's your type?" I asked as Foster pulled a football from Mr. Sellers's net bag.

"I don't know."

"How can you have a type but not know what it is?"

"I mean, I know it when I see it."

I chewed on that for a moment. "So, have you . . . seen it? Lately?"

"Maybe," he said, and then with a "Think fast!" he chucked the football in my general direction, and I had no choice but to follow it as it sailed on by.

I met with Ezra after practice that day. Rachel had taken to flooding my in-box at least twice a day with little updates and queries about the article. The sooner I could give her some useful information, the sooner she'd get off my back.

Foster bummed around on the field while Ezra and I sat in the bleachers. I figured the whole interview would go more smoothly without Foster buzzing around asking what Ezra had for breakfast this morning or, even worse, awkward Foster–style questions, like how many times a day does Ezra go to the bathroom or when was the last time he made out with someone.

I watched as Ezra pulled off his jersey and shoulder pads, and I dwelled on that last thought for just a moment. He was wearing a white T-shirt underneath that clung to him, and his hair was damp with sweat.

"So." My voice was loud and unlike my own when I spoke. Ezra took a seat and started packing his equipment into his duffel bag. "Uh . . . how many schools are recruiting you?" It wasn't Rachel's first question, but I wasn't about to start with a journalistic sucker punch.

"Four."

"That's it?"

"What, four isn't good enough?"

"No, it's just, everyone says it's, like, twenty or something."

"I narrowed it down."

"So there were twenty at one point?"

He shrugged.

"Which one are you going to pick?"

"Whichever one has a uniform color that I look good in."

His face hadn't changed. But was that a joke? It had to be a joke. "Ha. So is that why you came to Temple Sterling?"

"Not exactly," he said, and didn't go on.

I wasn't sure what to say to that. I could only think of what Cas had told me and of Rachel's questions about football and politics. *A shift from the team to the individual.*

"I know what people say," he said after a moment. "It's not enough to be good. You have to have some kind of . . . like a fucking *agenda* or something."

"So that isn't the case?"

His eyes darkened. "No, that isn't the case."

"So why did you come here?"

"That's nobody's business."

"But if it's not some . . . agenda . . . then why can't you say?"

"I can say. I just don't want to."

Sheesh. "Okay."

There was a pause.

"Sorry." Ezra made a face. "I don't . . . I guess I'm not very good at talking about myself. Or just . . . talking in general . . ."

I didn't know what to say to that, either, so I just made a sound of assent and then looked out at the field. Foster was absently kicking the ball around, trying to punt it and catch it. At this moment, he backed up to catch a rogue ball, which hit him on the head.

I thought for a moment about how young he was and, even more, how young he acted. "I still can't believe he got bumped up," I said without thinking, and, surprisingly, Ezra followed this non sequitur.

"He's good."

"I know he made it through the first game okay, but I'm kind of afraid someone's going to crush him out there."

"I'll look after him."

I glanced over at Ezra. "You'll be busy making touchdowns."

"Yeah, but that doesn't mean I can't keep an eye on him. And Jordan's the best defender on the team, and one of the only people who can stand me, so Foster'll have him, too."

I felt awkward. "People can stand you."

"General opinion is that I'm a giant asshole."

My face flushed. "Well . . . you're nice to Foster."

He didn't speak.

I thought about what Foster had said at dinner about him and Ezra: *We have a secret.* "*Why* are you nice to Foster?"

"Is this part of the interview?"

"No . . . I think I got all I need for Rachel," I said a little too heartily, getting to my feet. "Thanks."

"You hardly asked anything. I didn't mean to—I mean, I don't mind answering questions. I'll try to give better answers."

I looked down at Rachel's sheet.

"Yeah, well, it's mostly . . . I mean, these questions are kind of idiotic, I'm not going to lie."

"Like what?"

I read him number seven, about *the ethics of statistics mongering.*

"Statistics mongering?"

"I know. Like fish mongering, only for your athletic future."

Ezra smiled a little. A slight upturn of the lips.

"Maybe I can just send them to you or something, and you can, like, answer them on paper. No talking necessary."

He nodded. "Yeah, okay."

"Cool. Well . . . see you." With that, I went down to the field to retrieve Foster.

14

When I went to pick up Foster from practice the next day, I found him on the front steps of the school with none other than Marabelle Finch.

"Hi." He ducked his head through the window. "Can we give Marabelle a ride?"

Like I would really deny the pregnant girl a ride. "Sure."

"Great." The grin that lit his face was electric. He went over to Marabelle and helped her up.

"So where do you live?" I asked when Marabelle was strapped into the back and Foster had taken his place in the passenger seat.

"Oh, I'm not going home. I'm helping out somewhere."

I followed Marabelle's directions. "Somewhere" turned out to be a powder-pink building near the freeway, with an enormous, sparkly sign out front that read MISS VICTORIA'S SCHOOL FOR LITTLE BEAUTIES.

"Are you sure this is the right place?" It flew from my mouth before I could stop it.

"Of course." Marabelle was already angling out of her seat belt.

"Well . . . have a good day," I said.

"Oh, please, come in," Marabelle said. "The girls love visitors."

"Um . . ." I looked over at Foster, who nodded eagerly. "Okay. Sure."

Marabelle headed into the building as fast as she could, and Foster and I lingered for a moment after parking the car and looked up at the giant sign. It showed a sparkly crown, a scepter, and a pair of ballet shoes.

"Little beauties?"

Foster shrugged and headed after Marabelle.

It was as if someone had spewed pink all over the interior of Miss Victoria's School for Little Beauties and all over Miss Victoria herself, who clasped my hand and smiled with hot-pink lips, exposing ungodly bright white teeth. She was probably midfifties and had masses of bleached blond hair teased into an updo.

"I'm Miss Victoria, but you can call me Miss Vicky," she gushed, and then turned to Foster. "And what is your name, handsome?"

"Foster."

"Foster, what an interesting name."

"It's my mom's maiden name," he said, and I couldn't help but stare. This was the first time I had ever heard him mention her.

"Well, come on in. Welcome to the School for Little Beauties." Miss Vicky led us down a little hallway that opened into a large (pink) dance studio.

"So is this like a ballet school or something?" I asked.

"Oh, honey, no." Miss Vicky had that old-time Southern dialect.

Marabelle entered the studio from what seemed to be a dressing room, followed by six or seven little girls. They were all wearing pink tulle skirts, but they weren't doing ballet. They strutted behind Marabelle and swished their hips. Marabelle swished along with them, a sort of creepy, runway-walk Follow the Leader.

"This is a beauty pageant school. These girls compete in pageants all over the country. See Tiffany over there? Wave for us, Tiffany."

Tiffany looked like a china doll I had when I was little. Brown ringlet curls and perfect tiny features. She waved and smiled, exposing missing front teeth.

"Tiffany won Supreme Ultimate Beauty last month at the Southern regionals. She's our very best."

"She's cute," I said, and couldn't help but feel as if I were appraising an armchair or something.

"When she puts her flipper in, she's even cuter. But Tiffany hates her flipper, don't you, sugarplum?"

"What's a flipper?" I whispered to Foster, like he would know the answer.

But he surprised me. "It's fake teeth they make them wear."

"How do you know that?"

"Marabelle told me."

Miss Vicky overheard us. "Oh, Marabelle was our very best, our very, *very* best, student here at Miss Victoria's. She won Supreme Grand Beauty three times at Fabulous Faces. I was so delighted when she came back to work with our girls." She dropped her voice. "Some of the parents questioned the example she would set in her *current situation*, but I said, there is no way I'm letting my very best student go. And these little girls don't know where babies come from, so what does it matter?"

"Okay." Marabelle clapped her hands. "Let's see our swimsuit walks."

We sat and watched the whole class, from the swimsuit walks to the choreographed dance routines. I must admit, the whole thing was slightly unsettling. But Foster didn't even seem to notice what was happening. He never took his eyes off Marabelle. And a couple of times I thought I saw her smiling in his direction.

This was singularly odd.

"Thanks for coming." Marabelle walked us out the door after the five-year-olds had broken for the day.

"Do you need a ride home?"

"Oh, no, there's another class in a little while."

I looked to Foster to say something, but he was just staring out at the highway.

"Uh . . . thanks for having us," I said. "It was really . . . interesting."

Marabelle's eyes flicked toward Foster. "See you at school," she said after a pause, and then retreated back into the building.

I shoved Foster. I couldn't help it.

"What?" he squawked.

"Why didn't you say something? She was waiting for you to say something!"

"I didn't know what to say."

"Foster, you have something to say for every minute of every day."

"I panicked."

Once again I was reminded of how little I knew about Foster. "Have you ever had a girlfriend?"

"Sure."

I eyed him as we got into the car. "For real?"

"Uh-huh. We made out and everything."

"Liar."

"It's true! Have you ever had a boyfriend?"

"Sure." My eighth-grade boyfriend was Kyle Morris. Future cymbal player in the high school band.

"And you made out and everything?"

"*Foster.*"

He eyed me. "Are you still a virgin?"

"*Yes!*" I screeched. "And don't tell me you're not or I'll drive this car off the road right now."

Foster just laughed.

I sent Rachel's questions to Ezra that night. I started the message with "Hi!" and then thought the exclamation point seemed a little too excited. So I put "Hi," but then that looked oddly glum. So then I wrote "Dear Ezra" and erased it, closed my laptop, squeezed my eyes shut, and wondered how or why my greeting to Ezra possibly mattered at all.

Then I opened my computer again and wrote, "Ezra, here are Rachel's questions. Get back to me whenever. Devon." And sent it. But I forgot to attach the questions.

Not five minutes after I succeeded in *actually* sending the questions, there was a *ping* signaling a message back.

Ezra had changed the subject to "I think Rachel Woodson hates me." I cracked a smile. The body of the message just said "Will get back to you soon."

I was sitting in bed not long after, slogging through a set of calculus problems, when there was another *ping*.

I could hardly believe it as I scrolled through. Ezra had answered all of Rachel's idiotic questions. Not just answered them, but answered them seriously and with thought, with the authority of someone who knew what he was talking about.

I fell back against my pillows when I was finished reading. Ezra was far and away the best football player in our school. That he made All-American said that he was one of the best high school football players in the country. What must it be like to have a path so clearly delineated for you? To have talent and a passion that guide your future like that? It seemed so foreign, and unlikely, and yet it made me feel weirdly . . . adrift.

Ezra wasn't asking colleges if he could go there—colleges were asking him. And what about me? No one was knocking down my door. Why was that?

I wouldn't say that I was *lazy*, necessarily. I had always done what was expected of me. I checked off all the boxes. Showed up on time. Passed every class. But I wasn't . . . well, I wasn't Ezra. I didn't have a talent like that. But I didn't have the work ethic to make up for it, either. I guess Ezra had both.

I wrote him back. Just a quick "Thanks" and a smiley face. And Ezra replied with a "No problem" followed by a reciprocal smiley face. I almost laughed, thinking he should've used one of those slanted-mouth emoticons to indicate how he actually looks in real life. Then I remembered my calculus homework, vowed to put in the extra effort, and started back in on it.

15

"Did you talk to him?" Rachel Woodson strode past me in the hall on my way to American History the next day, slowing just a notch to indicate that I was meant to walk with her.

"Sorry?"

She was typing on her phone, thumbs tapping furiously. "Ezra. Have you conducted your interview with Ezra?"

Conducted my interview. Rachel made this venture sound a lot more legitimate than it ought to have sounded.

"Yeah, actually—"

"Why haven't you sent me your write-up yet?"

"Uh, he sent me some . . . expanded thoughts on some of the . . . more critical issues. I just need to compile them with my interview." Now *I* was making it sound more legitimate than it ought to have sounded.

"Oh. Okay." I think this was what passed for pleased with Rachel.

I decided to take this opportunity.

"Hey, Rachel?"

"Yes." She was really flying on that phone.

"Do you . . . I mean, would you mind, maybe, helping me out with some of my college stuff? You know, like, looking over my application materials, and maybe giving me some pointers?"

She actually glanced over at me for a second. "My schedule's pretty tight at the moment."

Understatement of the year. "I know. I just . . . well, you're the best at it, obviously, so I just thought if anyone could help me, you could." I wasn't sure if Rachel was immune to flattery, but I was about to find out.

"How many schools are you applying to?"

"Just one, right now."

The look on Rachel's face told me that that statement may have ranked among the saddest things she'd ever heard.

"I'll add some others," I said quickly. "But this one . . . it's a good one: Reeding University."

"You want to go there?"

"I mean—yeah?"

She raised one eyebrow.

"Yes," I said, definitively, though I had very little to back this up.

I had gotten a postcard from Reeding in the mail, and I liked the picture. It showed an old building with white siding and black shutters, a porch running along the front. Some students were sitting on the porch steps, grinning at one another in that kind of not-so-candid candid way. OFFICE OF STUDENT AFFAIRS, the text read in little letters below them.

The back of the card proclaimed Reeding's small class sizes and its history of diversity and its study-abroad program. ACHIEVE YOUR GOALS, it read. START YOUR FUTURE.

That was the kind of thing that normally made me roll my eyes.

It was like that smug lion on the wall of Mrs. Wentworth's office. BE BETTER THAN YOU ARE RIGHT NOW.

But there was something about this postcard that I latched onto. I couldn't tell Rachel what, or why, because I hardly knew myself.

There was a pause, in which Rachel did not type, or check the Dow, or e-mail the Secretary of State, or do whatever it was she happened to do on that phone. Maybe she knew. Maybe she was just taking pity on me.

"Send me your résumé and meet me in the writing lab at three," she said. "I have fifteen minutes between meetings."

What could Rachel Woodson possibly accomplish in fifteen minutes? I was about to find out.

"Your résumé is terrible," she said.

"Okay. Yes. Constructive criticism. Let's do this."

"You know that the point of a résumé is to make yourself sound good, right? Where are your special skills? Where are your awards?"

I won a writing award in fourth grade. My essay on the subject of "pay it forward" won me a one-hundred-dollar gift card to Target. Ignoring a stunning opportunity to *actually* pay it forward, I bought a bike with pink and purple streamers coming out of the handles.

I didn't tell Rachel this anecdote. Something told me she wouldn't find a fourth-grade writing award amusing. That bike really did kick ass, though.

I watched over Rachel's shoulder as she gave my résumé an overhaul. At the end of roughly seven minutes (I honestly think she was timing it), she had burrowed deeper into my academic career than I had ever really thought to, grilled me on each of my extracurriculars, and recommended two ACT manuals so I could retake the test, because "obviously" I would want to raise my science score.

"You don't have any volunteering," she said. "You need to volunteer."

"Like . . . where?" I flashed suddenly on Lindsay, building houses with her church group. She would know where.

"A community center. A hospital. A library, hospice care, the Humane Society. Doesn't matter where. Find a kid and read a book to it."

Rachel must've sensed the look of mild panic on my face, because she shut the laptop abruptly. "What was your best class?"

"Freshman English."

"So it's all been uphill since then."

I would've smiled if my academic future weren't hanging in the balance.

"Who'd you have? Chambers? Mackenzie?"

"Chambers."

"Ask her if you can volunteer as her TA."

"TA?"

"Teaching assistant." She didn't add "*Geez, Devon,*" but it was heavily implied.

"I know what *TA* means, it's just . . . isn't that for college?"

"Everyone needs help making copies and stapling handouts. Go. Tell her I sent you."

I almost asked if that would work, like if Rachel had some version of cred that worked on teachers like the kind that worked on nightclub bouncers. But then I realized if anyone could get me past the velvet rope to a teacher's good side, it would be Rachel.

"Okay. Great. Thank you."

"Uh-huh. Thank me when you graduate."

"Right. I'll set a phone alert for May."

"From Reeding. Thank me when you graduate from Reeding."

"You're funny."

"I never joke." She looked at me. "You could actually pull this off. I see you around. You're good at talking to people. There's something about you that people like. You could capitalize on that if you actually gave a shit."

"I . . . give a shit. It's just that you give enough shits for, like, two dozen people."

Rachel smiled. "That's what I'm talking about. Use that. And don't take it for granted. Not everyone . . . not everyone has such an easy time of it."

I didn't know if Rachel was referring to herself. She didn't give me a chance to wonder. "I have a meeting," she said, and that meant ours was over.

16

Rachel was right. I went to Mrs. Chambers the next day and easily secured the TA position. She flung a packet of handouts at me and pointed me in the direction of the photocopier.

She also invited me to sit in on the section of freshman English that occurred during my study hall and set me up with "office hours" when the freshmen could come to me with questions or to look over their papers.

"Grammar, syntax, and, please, if you notice anything clearly copied and pasted, give me a heads-up. I mean, I've had people who haven't even bothered to change the fonts."

"If I see any Comic Sans, I'll let you know."

Mrs. Chambers smiled, and I felt the weird sensation of having a sort of camaraderie with one of my teachers.

My first "office hours" weren't exactly thrilling. I didn't get to bust a plagiarizer. I didn't get to do much of anything, because, in fact, no one showed up.

Sitting in on freshman English again was kind of strange—like a time warp. A lot of it was the same, except I was three years older, and I could now call exactly who died at the end of pretty much everything we read.

The freshmen in the class were a lot like the ones in gym—some of them may actually have been the same ones from gym—but they seemed a little more subdued. Maybe it was those bright red TS gym shirts that amped them up.

Foster wasn't in the fourth-period English class, but that was fine, because I saw plenty of Foster already. However, in the weeks that followed, I was finding that to be less and less the case. Football, of course, was taking up a lot of his time, but there was something else that I couldn't ignore—something growing between him and Marabelle.

I'd see them having lunch together in the cafeteria, or talking in the halls between classes. Foster liked her—I could tell. Marabelle, on the other hand, was harder to read. She seemed to enjoy Foster's company, but there was definitely a kind of reserve about her. At least from what I could see as I spied on them in the hallways.

At the same time, Lindsay and Cas seemed to be hanging out more and more, and with enough enthusiasm on both sides to make me feel pretty dejected. With every giggle-infested flirt session that I was forced to witness, the prospect of the upcoming trip to Reeding became that much more appealing.

It would be my escape. Devon Tennyson's Escape from Temple Sterling. Like a Disney World ride or something.

At least that's how I had come to think of it until I saw the sign-up sheet on the College Info bulletin board.

The other lines for signatures had remained empty since Mrs. Wentworth put up the sheet. The trip was next week, and I was almost assured that it would just be me and her.

But there were more names today.

Maria Silva. Lauren McPhee. Perfectly acceptable.

But then, underneath those names:

Cas Kincaid.

Lindsay Renshaw.

Jordan Hunter.

Ezra Lynley.

What. The hell.

I cornered Cas between classes. "Why are you guys visiting Reeding? Their football team is a joke."

"It's a safety school. Any TS guy could get on that team, easy."

I just stared.

"Okay, fine. It's on the beach."

"It's on the Atlantic, Cas. It's too cold to swim!"

Cas put his hands on my shoulders. "It's like a free vacation, Dev! We thought it would be fun."

"But you hate Ezra."

"I don't *hate* him. And it's not like I told him to sign up. He was just hanging around when Linds and Jordan and I decided to go."

"Linds?"

"Yeah. Lindsay. You know."

Oh, I knew. A cute nickname was the first mile marker on Gag Highway, heading straight to Relationshipville. And making up the names of fake roads and cities to express your unhappiness was probably the first step to insanity.

I wanted to cry. Reeding was supposed to be *my* trip to *my* school. But it seemed I had little say in the matter.

✦   ✦   ✦

While seemingly everyone around me was creeping toward Relationshipville, and I was wishing myself to Reeding, something was
brewing at home. Not conflict—in fact, the opposite of conflict.
My parents were so proud of Foster and his football achievements
that they wanted to throw a party for him and all his new friends.

I was wary of this idea from the get-go. For one thing, it was
awfully hard to throw a party that would attract TS high football
players and their associates without having alcohol, and Foster was
hell-bent on inviting his friends from the football team as well as a
few guys he managed to bond with during his incredibly brief stint
on the C team. He also wanted the Future Science Revolutionaries
of America to come, and, of course, Marabelle had to be there.

"Oh, only half will come," my mom said when we went shopping for supplies. "That's how these things always work out."

"What about the girls?" I said, as Mom priced paper plates. "Me
and Marabelle will be the only girls!"

"Foster's only fourteen, honey. He doesn't have a lot of girl
friends. If it'll make you feel better, invite a few of your friends, all
right?"

I grumbled that it was such short notice that no one would be
available. But everyone I asked could come. Even the charming
Miss Renshaw, who Cas urged me to text.

I also forced Foster to get Gracie Holtzer's number from one
of the freshboys, and he invited her. I could hear her squealing on
the other end of the line from across the room.

"That's great. She'll bring her entourage," I said.

Foster just made a face.

Seven o'clock Saturday evening rolled around and the house
was empty. The dining room table was loaded down with food. I
was wearing my good jeans, and Foster—lo and behold—had put

on one of the shirts my mother had bought for him at the start of summer.

My parents had closed themselves off upstairs for the evening, but my mom kept coming down, nervously flitting around the dining room, rearranging stacks of paper plates, and checking the level of ice in the freezer. Like somehow an invisible crowd had depleted the supply in the ten minutes that she was gone. Foster sat on the couch, flipping through TV channels and looking as blank and Fosterlike as ever, though with that strange new haircut and freshboy shirt. I hovered in the doorway, watching him for a moment. For some reason . . . my stomach was in a knot. I ached for a knock on the door. Someone would come. Someone had to come.

I swallowed hard. No one would come.

"Foster?"

"Uh-huh." He paused on an infomercial.

"We could watch a movie or something. . . . We could play any game you want."

Foster glanced up at me. He looked so different with the hair out of his eyes.

"They'll come, Dev."

I nodded and then went into the dining room and rearranged some stacks of paper plates. What can I say? It was hereditary.

There was a knock at the door at a quarter to eight. I bolted to the front hallway. Foster didn't move from the couch.

"Hi." Marabelle stepped into the foyer.

"Hey. Foster's inside. You're the first one here."

To my primitive high school self, being the first one at a party was almost as embarrassing as hosting a party with just one guest.

But Marabelle just smiled. "Someone has to be first." And then she floated into the living room.

I was about to shut the door behind her but then I realized there was someone else on the front stoop: Ezra Lynley.

"Where'd you come from?"

"I drove Marabelle."

"You guys know each other?"

He nodded.

"Um . . ." It was only slightly less embarrassing to have a party with two guests. "You want to come in?"

"No, I figured I'd just stay out here for the evening."

That was a joke. I was almost sure of it this time. I smiled a little and held the door open, and Ezra entered our house. I followed him into the living room and watched as he plopped down on the couch with Foster and Marabelle and took the remote from Foster's hand.

"Not fair," Foster said.

"I'm the oldest," Ezra said, and flipped channels.

"But I'm the host."

"Devon's the host."

Foster wavered a moment and then said, "Fine."

And then there was another knock at the door.

"Oh my god, that's Ezra Lynley's truck!"

"I knew he'd be here. He and Foster are like *best friends*."

I cleared my throat. "Uh . . . hi."

Gracie Holtzer turned and her entourage snapped to attention behind her. "Hi, Devon!" she said, and smiled pink lips and bright white teeth at me. Maybe she had been one of Miss Victoria's Little Beauties. She certainly commanded the hallway like a runway.

"Oh wow, you look really cute, Devon. I love your jeans."

"Uh, thanks. Cute . . ." I scanned her outfit. Insanely tight jeans and a baby-sized T-shirt with a brand name emblazoned across the chest. So no one would have to ask her where it was from, I suppose. "Shirt," I finished lamely, and held the door open for them. "Come on in."

The entourage flooded the foyer and spilled into the living room. The sound level instantly doubled.

This was unexpected. Now there were two guys and a whole lot of girls. More specifically, there were two guys and a whole lot of PTs.

Another minivan pulled up. At first I thought it might've been the C team players, but as soon as they emerged into the porch light, it was clear these were Future Science Revolutionaries. They were loaded down with all kinds of strange contraptions.

"Potato gun," one said, and grinned at me as they pushed into the house. "I wonder where the kitchen is," I heard another say as they angled into the living room.

I followed quickly.

17

Turns out, Foster threw a pretty good party. It was like watching him kick that first day in gym—strange and disconcerting. He schmoozed with the varsity guys. He joked with the PTs. He held court in the living room with Jordan Hunter. But all in his own Fosterlike way.

I didn't mind being the host. I refilled the ice trays and reloaded the paper plates and got drinks for people, and there was something oddly gratifying about it.

As the party progressed, I couldn't help but keep an eye on Ezra. It was his proximity to Marabelle that was particularly intriguing; not so much physical proximity—though they both shared the couch with Foster and Jordan—but there was a familiarity between them that I hadn't seen between Ezra and anyone else, even Foster.

"Do you think it's going good?" Foster asked while I was in the kitchen depositing more French onion dip into an already-twice-depleted bowl.

"I think it's going great."

"We're going to have a *Rock Band* competition. You should play."

"Maybe."

Foster headed off with the dip and I began refilling some bowls of chips until there was a rustle behind me.

"Hi." It was Ezra.

"Hey." A pause. "Uh . . . do you need a drink or something?"

"Some juice would be cool, if you have it."

I set about extricating a couple of cans of fruit punch from the overstuffed fridge.

"So, um . . . have you and Marabelle known each other long?" Subtle, Devon. Super subtle.

"A little while."

I nodded, and a terrible thought struck me for the first time, one that I couldn't suppress.

When I looked up next, his eyes were on me. "What is it?"

My face grew redder by the second. "I was just wondering . . . I mean . . . you couldn't be—I mean, you're *not* . . ." I gulped. "Are you?"

Ezra just looked at me. "Baby's father? No."

Silence. I was inside out with embarrassment.

"She's my sister," he said.

"*What?*"

A shrug. "Stepsister, really."

I was in disbelief. And rest assured, I can't convey pretty disbelief. I'm sure I was all bulging eyes and gaping mouth. "I . . . I had no idea."

He nodded.

How could I have missed this? I had known Marabelle for a while now, but never gleaned any connection between her and Ezra. I quickly scanned back through recent encounters with Marabelle, hoping I hadn't said anything horrible about Ezra to her.

"So, uh . . . who married who?"

"My mom, her dad."

"Where's your dad?"

"I don't have one."

"So you came from, like, a sperm bank or something?" Ugh. I lacked a filter sometimes.

"No, I just—"

"I get it. Sorry. That was stupid."

Ezra just looked at me.

"Hey, Dev!" And then Cas appeared in the doorway. I turned, and he strolled into the kitchen and gave me this huge hug. I was still holding Ezra's drinks, almost too surprised to hug back.

"How's it going?" I managed.

"Good." Cas kept an arm around me as he turned to Ezra. "Hey, man." He extended a hand. Ezra looked at it for a moment and then shook it, his face expressionless. A brief, yet incredibly awkward, silence followed.

Cas broke it. "Sorry I'm late, Dev. I couldn't get off work any sooner."

"No problem. Uh, Lindsay's not here yet."

"That's cool." Cas's voice was strange. Like too cheerful, and he was still touching my waist. "I wanted to see you anyway. Can I help you carry something?"

"I got it." Ezra took the drinks from my hands, and there was another moment of silence. I would almost swear that both of them were trying to look taller.

"See you," Ezra said after a pause, and then left the room.

Cas rolled his eyes and dropped his hand from my waist. "You're welcome."

"For what?"

"Saving you from Ezra. Guess I got your radar, too, huh?"

I pulled some ice out of the freezer. "I was fine. We were just talking."

"Ezra doesn't talk. He just scowls and gestures indeterminately. It's how his creators programmed him."

I didn't speak.

"Oh come on. That's funny, right?" When I glanced at Cas, he was looking at me strangely. "You don't *like* him, do you?"

"No," I said. "Of course not. I just . . . I don't need you to save me."

"Okay." Another awkward pause. "All right. So . . . Jordan said they're going to play *Rock Band* soon."

"I heard."

"You coming in?"

"Yeah. In a minute."

Cas drummed his fingers on the counter for a moment and then left the kitchen.

I patrolled the first floor for a little while after that, picking up empty soda cans and plates. When I made it into the living room, the video game competition was in full swing. Jordan was strumming the plastic guitar alongside Gracie Holtzer, who missed every other note because she was too busy ogling him. Needless to say, he crushed her.

"Champ!" Jordan exclaimed when their song was over. "You next?"

I was happy to remain a spectator. "Nah, I'm good."

"Where's your cousin at then? I want to take him down."

Foster was nowhere to be seen, and Marabelle was conspicuously absent, too. "I'll look for him."

The din from downstairs was somewhat dampened in the

upstairs hallway. The door to my parents' bedroom was shut at the end of the hall, as was mine. But Foster's door was slightly ajar, and I could hear voices.

I couldn't resist. I moved closer.

Marabelle stood in the center of the room, surveying the posters and the football gear and the bedspread.

"I like your room," she said.

"Aunt Kathy picked out most of the stuff."

"Like this shirt?" Marabelle flicked Foster's collar.

"Mine are falling apart. They're all from, like, the sixth grade."

Marabelle moved toward the desk, picked up a book, and looked at the cover.

"How come you live with your aunt and your uncle?" she asked as she thumbed through the pages.

"How come you're pregnant?" Foster countered.

"Because I had sex. Answer my question."

"Because they're my godparents. Why did you have sex?"

"I thought it'd be fun."

"Was it?"

She shrugged and sat down on the edge of the bed. After a moment Foster—having clearly appraised the situation—sat down next to her. Close, but not too close. Mentally, I applauded him.

"What happened to your parents?" Marabelle asked.

"They got sick," he said after a moment.

"Both of them?"

Foster nodded. "In different ways."

"Did they die?"

"My dad did."

"And your mom?"

"She's still sick."

"Can they fix it?"

"She could fix it," Foster said. "If she wanted."

"What do you mean?"

He didn't reply. Instead, he reached over and put his hand on Marabelle's stomach. A smile spread across his face. "Creepy. It's sloshing around in there."

"It's not *creepy*," Marabelle said, clearly affronted. "It's beautiful!"

"You're beautiful," Foster said, and I couldn't believe my ears. Was this my cousin? Was this Foster flirting? As in, *flirting*?

She eyed him for a moment and then, as she tossed the book on the floor, said, "I'm not having sex with you."

"I don't want to." Foster looked taken aback. "I mean, I want to . . . eventually . . . with somebody. And it could be you, if you wanted. But not right now. Or even, you know, like, a while from now."

Marabelle smiled. "Just checking."

Silence.

"You want to play a game?" Foster said, finally.

"What kind of game?"

"Zip Lip. You zip your lips up. First person to talk loses."

"What do we do while we're sitting here not talking?"

"Whatever we want."

Marabelle's eyes shone. "Okay."

Foster zipped his lips shut. Marabelle did the same. They looked at each other for a moment. And then they kissed.

I stepped away from the door. It was a private moment, but it was also a shock to me. I had never thought of Foster as having . . . well, *sexuality*. He talked about liking Marabelle, and there was the girlfriend he said he "made out and everything" with back home, but talk was one thing. He just seemed so young. I had never thought of him as wanting to kiss someone or wanting to be with someone.

"Just to be clear," Foster said when they broke apart, "that's not how Zip Lip is usually played."

Marabelle grinned. "I win."

18

You'd think I'd have been happy that night at the party because Lindsay never showed up, and Cas got stuck talking to Gracie Holtzer and her entourage for the duration. I should've been happy because the party was a big success. But instead, something in me felt like a slightly flattened football in the bottom of the bag in gym class. A little forlorn. A little dejected.

It may have had something to do with the fact that Foster kissed someone at that party, whereas I—three years older and I'd like to think a little more socially adept—had never kissed anyone. Ever. I hadn't even been on a date since Kyle Morris and I went to the movies in eighth grade. And as scandalous as holding hands during a PG-13 movie felt at the time, I'm pretty sure it doesn't count as a real date if your mom has to drop you off at the food court.

But the party was really the last hurdle before the Reeding trip, and that was enough to pull me out of any little, temporary gloom. We were supposed to meet at school bright and early on Thursday morning that next week, overnight bags packed, ready to pile into Mrs. Wentworth's nine-seater van.

I wouldn't say I got *stuck* sitting in the front with Mrs.

Wentworth for the drive. But I got stuck sitting in the front with Mrs. Wentworth for the drive. Figures. I guess I was the only one actually interested in Reeding anyway.

Except for Lindsay, it seemed. She sat right behind us, between Ezra and Cas, and kept poking her head into the front seat with little tidbits of information, such as South Carolina's state flower or the percentage of students at Reeding who go on to grad school.

When Lindsay wasn't acting as a veritable Reeding guidebook, she was talking to Cas. Although it might be classified as masochistic, I couldn't help but watch them out of the corner of my eye.

Ezra was listening to music, but every so often Lindsay would pull one of his earbuds out and include him in the conversation. He'd respond to her in a friendly enough fashion, but whenever Cas jumped back in, the faintest flicker of something distinctly resembling dislike would flash across his face.

About halfway there we stopped at McDonald's for a late breakfast; the guys ate an obscene amount of food, and almost everyone fell asleep afterward, save for me and Mrs. Wentworth. When I checked compulsively in the backseat, I saw that Lindsay had rested her head on Ezra's shoulder. He was dozing, too, and he didn't seem to mind being Lindsay's human pillow. It surprised me—not only because of Lindsay's choice of headrest, but also because Ezra was one of the last people you'd call cuddly.

We passed through the gates of Reeding University around eleven, and there it was: My postcard laid out before us for real.

There was the Office of Student Affairs, the porch where the postcard kids had sat. There was the Student Union, and the dorms (originally built in 1920, most recently remodeled in 2009, according to Lindsay on the ride up), the science building, the theater. There was a chapel, tucked away among a grove of trees.

They definitely had the curb-appeal thing down. But it was more than that. . . . It wasn't just buildings and landscaping. It was the people. Clumps of students studying in the shade or walking together between buildings, talking animatedly. These people were ACHIEVING THEIR GOALS. They were STARTING THEIR FUTURES.

And just being there, seeing it, it was as if something had opened up inside me. All of a sudden I wanted that, too; I wanted it for myself.

Mrs. Wentworth had scheduled the trip pretty much to a tee. On the bright side, it didn't leave much time for Cas and *Linds's* free vacation. But it was also a hell of a lot to take in. We ate in the cafeteria, did a campus tour, and met with admissions counselors.

The trip was accomplishing everything Mrs. Wentworth had in mind for me. I was in love with Reeding. I wanted to write better college essays. I wanted to score higher on the ACT. I even—albeit briefly—considered trucking the Future Science Revolutionaries to the science museum just to pad my résumé. Assistant to Sports Documentation wasn't looking so bad now.

At the end of the day we stopped off at the bookstore.

"Ooh, Champ." Jordan squeezed my shoulders as I perused a pile of Reeding hoodies. "You're going to look great here next year."

Just hearing someone say it out loud sent a little surge of excitement through me. "Blue does work well with my coloring."

"And red and black'll work with mine." He lowered his voice. "Don't tell Wentworth, but I've got a verbal agreement with Georgia."

"No way!"

"Now, if I can just get Ezra there, it'll be perfect. A defender's only as good as the guys he's defending, you know?"

I glanced across the store at Ezra, who was scowling at a display of key chains. He poked at one, which then fell off the display. He leaned down to get it, and when he straightened up, he bumped the rack and jostled several more onto the ground.

I couldn't help but smile a little.

"Why are you such good friends with him?" I asked, watching Ezra scramble for the key chains.

He shrugged. "Why are you such good friends with Cassidy over there?"

Cas, meanwhile, was following Lindsay around the place, picking up and then putting back down every book, souvenir mug, and pencil she touched.

"Why are any of us friends with the people we're friends with?" Jordan went on. "They've got qualities we like—maybe some we see in ourselves. Maybe some we want to see in ourselves."

"What are Ezra's . . . qualities?"

"What aren't Ezra's qualities, baby? He's got 'em all."

"Most people tend to think he's kind of a jerk."

"I've heard that before, but those people don't get Ezra. It's just that he's so . . ." He screwed up his face in thought. "He's so fucking concentrated. He's like . . . like baking chocolate. You ever eat the baking chocolate when your mama makes cookies?"

"Yeah. It looks just like regular but it tastes disgusting."

Jordan laughed. "Okay, so maybe Ezra's not like baking chocolate. But you know what I mean? When you cook it up, it's full of flavor. But by itself, it's too . . . intense to be understood. Ezra's just a really intense dude. You got to *get him* in order to really . . . get him."

"So how did you get him?"

Jordan's eyes shone. "You've seen him take to that field, Champ.

No one's immune to it. It's like watching one of the masters, like fricking . . . da Vinci, painting or something."

"Lofty," I said, and he grinned.

"You know what I mean, though."

"Yeah, but you can be good at something and still suck as a person."

"It's not just that. How Ezra approaches football is how he approaches everything else. Just so damn . . . committed, and thoughtful, and . . . I don't know." He shrugged. "I'm not trying to write a book about him here. I'm just saying, that's the kind of person you want on your side, isn't it?"

I nodded, because it was, and then Jordan continued. "But enough about him. When are we going to talk about *my* good qualities?"

"Would you like me to list them alphabetically?"

"Yes, start with A for 'attractive in the face.' And then B for . . . 'but damn his ass is fine.' And C is for . . ."

"Capable," I said.

"See, you could've said cute, but I'm glad you didn't. I'm not just a piece of meat, you know."

"Oh I know," I said, and linked my arm through his, and we continued around the store until Mrs. Wentworth called us away.

That night I was tucked away in a sleeping bag on the floor of a student dorm room. The room's residents had stayed up late to tell me all about Reeding life, and although they were asleep now, I was too jazzed to shut my eyes.

I imagined myself living at Reeding for real. I would have a dorm room like this, with a bulletin board and a minifridge and a roommate. I would eat breakfast in the cafeteria, and walk to class with a messenger bag slung over my shoulder, and study in the shade of the oak trees, and I would be so *collegiate.* I would have opinions on current events! I would accomplish academic goals! I would have a purpose and a . . . a path to something. I didn't know what that something was yet, but I knew that there was definitely a Something. Forget "advanced breakfast with a minor in cable television." I suddenly wanted . . . more.

The minifridge hummed. The Reeding girls stirred slightly. Eventually, I nodded off.

The next day, we went to a financial-aid seminar and sat in on a philosophy class, and then the trip was just about over. We had yet to see the beach, but I could hear Jordan angling for it as we all stowed our bags back in Mrs. Wentworth's van.

"There's no game tonight, so there's no need to rush. Maybe we could have a little free time," he said. "And maybe we could check out the beach? I mean, it *is* an aspect of Reeding life."

Mrs. Wentworth had that shine in her eyes, that Isobel shine I recognized at our first meeting. After a moment she said, "I'll give you an hour. But then we've got to hit the road."

My family vacationed on the Gulf, so I wasn't used to the Atlantic. Charcoal-gray waves hitting the brown sand. I was right—it was too cold to swim. But everyone managed to make the most of it. Cas, Jordan, and Ezra tossed a football around. Maria, Lauren, and Lindsay lay out on the sand and soaked in the sun. And I sat a bit removed, on a bench overlooking the beach. I had my notebook out, hoping for a little inspiration for a better college essay. One that could actually take me here.

Footsteps came up behind me after a little while. I thought it might be Mrs. Wentworth, but when I turned, it was Ezra standing there.

I hadn't noticed him leaving the game of catch. "How's it going?"

He shrugged.

"Do you . . . want to sit down?"

"Are you working on something?"

"Just essay ideas." I slid down the bench a little, and Ezra sat down next to me. "College stuff. You probably don't have to mess around with much of that, right?"

"Not really."

"Must be nice." I closed my notebook. Last night's revelations about college were still fresh in my mind, but the reality of it all had flooded in as well. I would never wear that collegiate messenger bag and study under the trees if I couldn't get into Reeding in the first place. As much as I knew I had to do more before, I felt an even greater sense of urgency now.

Ezra didn't speak, so I went on, as much to fill the silence as to relieve some frustration. "Trying to sum yourself up on paper can be kind of demoralizing."

"Why?"

"I don't know . . . you have to boil yourself down into, like, bullet points. And unless you have awesome, college-relevant bullet points, you're kind of screwed. It'd be so much easier if you had something that you're good at that you could just show them. Like football, or dancing, or . . ." I shook my head. "Not to undercut all the work you've put into it or anything. I'm just saying, I wish I had spent more time on, like, cross-country running, or . . . plate-spinning, or something."

"You spin plates?"

"Oh, I'm a plate-spinning wizard," I said.

Ezra's lips twitched.

"How come you never smile for real?" I asked.

"My teeth are crooked."

"Are not."

"Are so." He flashed his teeth, and sure enough, the bottom front ones didn't stand quite straight. "All the kids in elementary school made fun of me," he said. "No one would serve me in restaurants. I had to wear a brown paper bag with two eyeholes cut out of it, and small children would run screaming at the sight of me."

"Shut up."

"It's true."

"Why don't you ever smile?"

"I do."

"Not when you win. You never smile when you're playing. When Cas gets out there, it's like he's having the time of his life. But you never look happy."

"I'm not Cas."

I could feel my face flush. Sometimes I couldn't help but talk about him. "But don't you love it?"

"Football?"

"No, plate-spinning."

Another twitch of his lips. "Yeah, I love football. I can't say I have any strong feelings one way or the other about plate-spinning."

"So why don't you look happy when you play? You're the best at it. You'd think you'd be the happiest guy in the world."

"When you love something, you can't be happy all the time, can you? Like, that's why you love it. It makes you feel all kinds of things, not just happy. It can hurt, it can make you fucking mad, but . . . it makes you feel something, you know?"

All at once I flashed on Cas kissing Molly McDowell in the home ec room. Had he ever loved something like that? I watched him throw the ball to Jordan, the late-afternoon light shining on his back, and was suddenly transported to when he had skinny shoulders and pale skin, and we'd walk to the pool together in elementary school. Those days when we were young enough to carry kickboards and wear those hideous neon goggles that left red rings around our eyes. It was before I begged my mom for bikinis, before time and two-a-days made Cas's shoulders broad. When it was just him and me. There had to be an alternate universe out there where that feeling never went away. Where it was never him out there and me up here. Where he never went places that I couldn't follow.

I realized Ezra was looking at me.

All he said was, "I think I'm gonna go back."

"Okay." I had no desire to leave. So I just turned back to the water. Ezra's footsteps retreating got lost in the sound of the waves hitting the sand.

19

I threw my bag down inside the kitchen door that night and bellowed, "I'm home!"

My words were swallowed up in the depths of the house. The place felt empty. The lights were off. I was alone.

Or so I thought.

"Devon?" My mom appeared in the doorway. Her expression was serious, and it stopped me in my tracks on the way to the fridge in the pursuit of post–road trip snacks.

"What is it?"

"Come to Daddy's office. We need to talk."

Dad's office was on the ground floor. It had a big picture window looking out over the backyard. I stared out into the darkness as my mom took a seat and my dad, already behind the desk, shuffled a few papers.

"What is it?" I asked again. A gnawing feeling grew in my stomach. I tried to smile.

There had been a conversation like this before, in which they first proposed the idea of Foster coming to live with us. Only that time we were in the living room, and there were cookies, and something about my parents' demeanor was vastly different. My mom was staring out the window now, her arms folded in front of her, her lips pursed. She looked . . . sad.

Dad spoke. "You know that when we agreed to take Foster, we did it on the assumption that this was a . . . a temporary situation. We're Foster's godparents, but his mom still has the legal right to decide what's best for him, whether it be staying here or going back to live with her."

All at once, the bottom of my stomach dropped out, and this awful, terrible rush of blood swelled from the back of my neck to my cheeks, up through the top of my head. Foster couldn't go back there. Foster would implode there.

In an instant, in the tiniest head of the smallest pin, I was concentrated like Ezra. I was ready to fight for Foster.

And then my father spoke again. "We've been in contact with Elizabeth, and with Foster's social worker, and"—he took a deep breath—"honey, Elizabeth's surrendered her rights as Foster's mother. She's going to let us adopt him."

"Adopt?"

"Yes. Adopt."

Adopt. Adopt. Adopt. If you say any word enough, eventually it loses all meaning.

I blinked, and the only thing I could think to ask was, "Does he know?" After Dad answered yes, I sort of lost the ability to concentrate. My mind was going in too many directions.

I closed the office door softly behind me and climbed the stairs to my room, my parents' reassurances still floating around in my head and that *adopt* still pounding in my ears. My heart was racing, and each beat said the same thing.

I was relieved. I was hopelessly relieved, but at the same time, so incredibly pissed off. I hated Elizabeth, and I hated the world, too, because if I was meant to have a brother, why couldn't I have gotten him the normal way? None of this was right. If I was going to have a brother, I didn't want him just because Elizabeth was a fucking coward.

I should've been better. But sometimes all you can really stand to do is think about yourself. Sometimes it's the only way to cope. The only way to make sense of something as colossal and intimidating as the world is to make it about you. I slammed my bedroom door and fell across my bed wondering if my parents would be able to help me with college now that Foster would be their responsibility, too.

And then . . . then I thought about Foster, and all that selfishness washed out on a tide of guilt. It was one thing to put a kid up for adoption straight out of the gate. But who spends fourteen years with her kid and *then* decides she doesn't want him? *Whoops, sorry, no—I'm going to need to return this one.* Like some sort of cosmic user error. Return to sender.

I dragged myself out of bed. I had to see Foster.

I knocked on his door, and he answered with a perfectly clear, perfectly composed, "Come in."

I opened the door and there lay Foster on his bed, wearing his bright red TS helmet.

I tried to make my voice sound normal. What do you even say in this kind of situation? How do you even start?

"How's it going?"

Ugh. An auspicious beginning.

Foster seemed unfazed. "Okay."

"What . . . uh . . . I mean . . ."

"It's cool, Dev." Foster looked at me through the helmet's grille. "It's not like it's a surprise or anything. She called and talked to me, and it's okay."

I sat down on the edge of the bed. "Do you . . . want to watch TV or something?"

He shook his head.

"We could call Ezra."

He turned his face up to the ceiling. "Okay. But you have to call him."

"What do you want me to say?"

A shrug. "Tell him the truth."

I got Ezra's number from Foster and dialed him in the hallway. It rang, and rang again, and in the space between rings I had another panicky moment of "what the hell should I say?"

"Hello?"

"Uh, hi. Hello. Is this Ezra?"

"Yeah."

"It's Devon. Devon Tennyson?"

A pause. "What's up?"

"Foster." Gahhh. "I mean, Foster was wondering—and I was wondering—"

If only phones had an Abandon Ship! function that you could press in the instance of a really awkward conversation. Though I guess the End button functions pretty similarly.

"It's Foster's mom," I said after a moment of regrouping. "Has Foster ever told you about his mom?"

"Yeah."

"Well, she's . . . my parents, they're . . ." Swallow, breathe, think.

"He's going to be staying with us. Permanently. It's, like, being made official, and we just found out, and . . . and Foster and I were wondering if maybe you would just want to come and . . . hang out. For a little bit, because . . ."

Why? *Because we need you?* I couldn't say that, so I let my "because" fizzle out, and it was silent on the other end of the line.

Then,

"I'll be right there."

And he was. Not ten minutes went by and there was Ezra Lynley, pulling up in front of our house in a shiny pickup truck.

We all sat on Foster's bed and watched *Bill & Ted's Excellent Adventure*. Foster made me sit between them.

After a while, Foster took off his football helmet, snuggled down into his pillow, and shut his eyes. I shifted around a little, very aware of every time my sleeve would brush up against Ezra's. It was a small bed with three people in it.

I could tell Foster was asleep, and suddenly—even though we weren't—it felt like Ezra and I were alone.

Something switched on in me, some awareness, and it turned into a need to make conversation.

"What are your schools?" I said, eyes fixed on the television screen.

"Sorry?"

"You said you narrowed it down to four schools. Are they like a secret or something?"

He rattled off the names. All big universities, all within a one-state radius.

"They're close by," I said.

"They're good football schools. But yeah, they're close, too. I just . . . my mom . . ." He didn't finish. His gaze moved to Foster, as if maybe mentioning moms in Foster's presence was taboo or something.

But Foster's breathing was still deep and even. No internal alarms went off at the sound of the word.

"Thanks for calling," Ezra said after a pause.

"It was Foster's idea," I said, even though—if I recall correctly—it was mine.

Ezra nodded.

"I'm sorry this is happening to you guys," he said. "If there's anything I can do to help . . ."

"You are." I said it before I could even think about it. "Helping, I mean. You are helping."

Ezra nodded, and we turned back to the TV, and I must've fallen asleep shortly after. When I next opened my eyes, it was very dark outside, the movie was over, and both Ezra and Foster were gone.

20

The game the next day was against Independence High School. Usually day games were a lot of fun—something about them was a little more cheerful, more relaxed than night ones—but today's was something else. Today's game was the first time Mr. Harper ever let me hold the camera, and this is why:

Mud. A lot of it. And a healthy downpour to boot.

It had been raining since the previous evening. After waking from my nap, I wandered downstairs and found Foster watching TV and eating popcorn with my parents. Ezra was gone, and the rain had settled in.

By the time a sea of umbrellas piled into the stands and the Cavaliers entered the stadium, the place was muddy as hell. You could hardly read the numbers on anyone's jersey by the end of the first play.

Independence had a good team; just a few minutes before the end of the first half, Temple Sterling had yet to score. We were inching down the field, the offense getting clobbered, and Mr. Harper was snapping away while I held an umbrella over the two of us and shouldered that demon bag.

Play started up, third and seven, and Marshall hiked the ball. There was a flurry of mud, and a figure took off, the ball cradled in his arms. He whipped around, sliding past defenders and hotfooting it down the field with a clear path to the end zone. I had never seen Ezra run the ball that way, and it wasn't until he ran right by us that I realized it wasn't Ezra—it was Cas.

That's when Mr. Harper leaned down for a picture and a whole fleet of defenders barreled past, spraying mud right into his face. He shoved the camera at me, and that's how it came to be that I captured Cas's victory in the end zone through the lens of the camera.

"Gimme that," Mr. Harper barked when he had somewhat cleared the mud off his glasses.

The stands were cheering as Coach sent Foster in. Uniform wet but still pristine, he joined the ranks on the field.

I was a little worried about him. There had been no rumblings from the kitchen early this morning, and he was subdued coming back from therapy.

On the field, it was the usual: the snap, the set, the kick. The ball flew, arched . . .

And bounced off the left goalpost. Missed.

Foster returned to the sidelines. A couple of the guys slapped him on the back, but it was no consolation.

Temple Sterling lost by eight. Foster was silent on the ride home.

"It was rough out there," my dad said from the front seat. "Must've been awful hard to see."

No reply from Foster, so I forced a "yeah."

At home, my mom asked Foster to leave his cleats outside the back door. He threw them down, showering caked mud everywhere, slammed the back door, and then stomped to his room.

My mom started to follow him, but I spoke. "I can do it."

She looked skeptical. "You want to talk to him?"

"Yes." I know she had every right to be surprised, but I was still indignant. "He's like my . . ." I still couldn't say *brother*. "He's like . . ." I gave up. "I'll talk to him."

The door to Foster's room was open. He was lying on his bed with his back to the door.

"Foster?"

"Go away."

"What's wrong?"

"*What's wrong?*" He sat up, his eyes fiery. "I let the team down!"

"Everybody misses once in a while. Look at Marcus. He misses lots of times."

Foster didn't speak.

"Look, you did your best, okay? That's all that counts."

"If it had been my best, the ball would've made it!"

"Okay, yeah, but either way, the team still would've lost by seven, so it doesn't really matter, does it?"

"You don't know what you're talking about, Dev. You don't know anything about anything!"

I blinked. "Well, I'm sure I know something about something."

I had out-Fostered Foster. I didn't think it was possible.

He threw himself back down on the bed. Conversation over.

21

Believe it or not, there was a party that night. Gale-force winds and all. Losing parties—although they were few and far between these last two years—tended to be rowdier than winning parties. There was more to get drunk over, I guess.

The evening's party was at the home of Amber McIntyre. Her house was huge and several miles outside town—ideal for a riotous losing party. And it wasn't all a loss, anyway—although Independence beat Temple Sterling, Cas had scored his first two touchdowns of the season. In this way, the game was a triumph of sorts—for every member of the team who didn't like Ezra.

Foster and I made our way through the rain, only moderately soaked by the time we reached Amber's front door. I glanced over at him before we went in. He hadn't said much of anything since this afternoon.

"Are you sure you want to go in? I mean, we could just go home . . . watch a movie or something."

Foster shook his head. "I want to be here."

So in we went and parted ways in the foyer.

There were a ton of people at the party. I met up with a few girls from math class, and they eagerly showed me the formal dining room (giant), the game room (extravagant), and the conservatory. (Which seemed unnecessary. Really. It was like the freaking house from *Clue*.)

I went into the kitchen to grab a soda after breaking from the math girls. I hadn't seen Cas yet, and I hoped he would be hanging around the beverages.

I didn't see him. I did, however, see Lindsay. She was standing right in front of the drinks table.

I decided I wasn't thirsty anymore.

"Devon!"

It was too late to turn back now.

"Shame about the game, huh?" she said when I neared.

"Yeah."

Silence.

"So, uh, I was actually hoping to run into you."

"Oh?"

"Yeah. Me and Lauren and Maria were thinking about driving into Gainesville some weekend to go shopping for Homecoming dresses. Do you want to come?"

"Um . . . sure. Sounds fun."

"Awesome! It'll be a total girls' day." She paused, and her eyes scanned the room for a moment. When she spoke next, her voice was slightly lower. "Also, about Homecoming . . ." She took a deep breath. "There's sort of someone I'm hoping will ask me. I think you know who I mean."

Did I ever. But I wasn't going to bite. I would never bite on this one.

"I was kind of thinking . . . maybe . . . if it's not, like, totally loser-ish, you could maybe mention to him that I don't have a date yet . . . and you know, maybe sound him out a little? I know you guys hang out and stuff."

"Why don't you just ask him?"

"I don't know. . . . I would, I just . . . I want to gauge his interest first, you know?"

I did know. The question was, why didn't she? Cas had a crush on Lindsay that you could probably see from space.

"So you'll help me?"

"I guess, yeah. Sure."

"That would be so great! Thanks, Devon!" Lindsay's face split into a radiant smile, and, damn her, she was so freaking adorable all I could do was smile back.

She headed off with her drink and left me to get the soda I didn't really even want anymore.

"You guys friends?"

I almost jumped. I hadn't seen Ezra come up.

"No. Yeah. Well, I mean, how close is anybody really?" I said, even though it was a completely inane space-filler.

"She's really sweet," Ezra said, as he glanced off in Lindsay's direction.

"Yeah." I had never really heard him say something nice about someone before.

There was a pause.

"Are you . . . having fun?" he said, and then his mouth made a weird twist, like maybe he thought that was a completely inane space-filler.

"Not really. Are you?"

"No. I was going to leave soon. People act like asses when we lose."

"Are you upset? About the game?"

152

He shrugged. "They were good."

I got jostled toward Ezra as a few linebackers pushed through into the kitchen. It was getting pretty crowded in there. After all, that's where the bar was set up, and most people wanted to be in the room where the alcohol lived, at least long enough to obtain some.

"Do you want to go somewhere else?" Ezra asked.

"Yeah, okay."

We made our way out into the hall and toward the living room. But it was even more crowded in there. At the center of the room, standing on a coffee table, was a clearly drunken Stanton Perkins. He had one beefy arm slung over Cas's shoulders.

"A toast!" Stanton yelled. "To Cas, for fucking *showing them how it's done!*"

The crowd let out a cheer. Cas raised a bottle of something, let out a massive whoop, and then took a swig. The crowd cheered again.

I glanced at Ezra. "Does it bother you?"

"What?"

"No one runs a freaking parade down Main Street when you get a touchdown."

"No, they just hang my picture in public restrooms."

I smiled a little.

Ezra gestured in Cas's direction. "He's, like, your best friend, right?"

"Not so much recently. He's always with Lindsay."

An odd expression crossed Ezra's face. "They're not together, you know. They're just . . . hanging out."

I nodded. "There's no agreement between them."

"That's a strange way of putting it."

"But it's true, right? One person says they like the other person and the other person reciprocates, and then they have an agreement."

"To be attached."

I looked at him. That's just how Jane would say it. "Exactly. That's it exactly." A pause. "I know he likes her. And she just practically begged me to ask him to ask her to Homecoming. So . . . an agreement of mutual like is impending."

"Really?"

"Uh-huh."

It was quiet for a moment. When I glanced at Ezra, he had another strange look on his face. He opened his mouth like he was going to say something, but then Jordan strode up.

"Hey, Champ. Can I borrow Ezra for a bit?"

"Sure."

Ezra glanced at me. "Are you . . . will you be okay?"

It was a weird question. Of course I would be okay. But I knew what he meant. Something told me that before Jordan, Ezra was no stranger to being alone at parties.

"Super duper," I said, and then grimaced. "Yes. Yeah."

Ezra's lips twitched, an almost-smile, and then he headed off with Jordan.

22

My "office hours" for English the next week saw something new: an actual person come for actual advice.

I was drawing in the margins of my history notes when she came in—a tiny freshman girl with thick, dark eyeliner and straight hair, wearing a hoodie that was big enough to swallow her up.

"Mrs. Chambers said you help people with papers," she said as a greeting.

I closed my notebook. "I do," I said, even though that may have not been the exact truth—I hadn't helped anybody yet.

The girl flung herself down in the desk next to mine and handed me some pages. "I failed this. She said if I rewrote it, I could get points back."

I flipped through the paper. It was an analysis of *The Great Gatsby*, the first major writing assignment of the semester. "You know, it doesn't count as four pages if the last two don't have writing on them."

She made a face. "I don't know how to write like she wants. It's annoying. I just . . . don't think like that."

"Like what?"

"I don't know."

"Like the metaphorical resonance of fancy shirts and stuff?"

She cracked a smile. "Yeah. Who cares?"

"Daisy cared."

"Don't even," she said.

Now I smiled.

Her name was Alex, and together we broke her paper down bit by bit. What the thesis statement was. What could be expanded. What made no sense whatsoever. Maybe this was how Rachel Woodson felt looking at my résumé—I knew what to move where and what could be fixed. But all I could do was guide her and let her fix it herself.

It was late by the time we finished. She had a solid outline to work from. Enough to get her started.

"You'll be here next week, too?" she said.

"And the week after that, and the week after that."

Alex nodded. "Good."

Rachel ambushed me in the hall the next day. "Did you see it?"

"See what?"

"The issue is out. The issue with our article."

"Our . . ."

She held up a copy of the *Herald*. There, on the very first page, under "*by Rachel Woodson*," it read "*and Devon Tennyson*."

"Wow," I said. "I'm really in the byline."

"You're really in the byline," Rachel said. "I think it turned out well. Maybe we could collaborate again."

"Uh . . . sure."

"Awesome. Your input would definitely be valuable to future

pieces." She forced the paper into my hand. "I'll be in touch!" she said, and then hurried off.

I looked down at the paper. On the front was a large picture of Ezra, and underneath . . .

DOES HE DESERVE IT?

Ezra Lynley is hailed as the champion of TS football. But is it talent, or just cold, hard strategy?

Ezra Lynley, 18, tall, broad-shouldered, and inaccessibly handsome, spoke to correspondent Devon Tennyson about his time in the Shaunessy High School lineup and his move to the Temple Sterling team, denying any sort of a statistics "agenda."

I blanched. Maybe he wouldn't see it. Maybe he wouldn't read it.

But the *Herald* was everywhere. Everyone had a copy. That picture of Ezra in midair over the end zone, his hands clasped around a football, was plastered all over the school.

And then there he was in the flesh, on the bleachers before practice, with the *Herald* spread out before him.

Bummer.

Ezra looked up as I approached. "'Inaccessibly handsome'?"

"I'm really sorry."

"Everyone's entitled to their own opinion."

"Yeah, but I don't think that stuff. Statistics mongering and all that, I mean . . . well, it's just ridiculous."

"Really?"

I recalled all my former indignation on Cas's behalf, and what I said to Emir at the season opener: *He's all right. Nothing special.* I didn't feel that way now. I had seen Ezra with Foster. He was kind to him. He was patient and loyal, and he was funny if you actually paid attention. There were good things about Ezra. He was just . . . quiet about them.

I sat down next to him. "Your achievements are your achievements, and you shouldn't let anyone try to . . . to cheapen them."

"I wasn't planning to."

"Oh. Well, good."

Ezra glanced at me. "But thanks."

"Yeah. No problem."

"At least you got one of those college bullet points you were talking about. Your name on a hard-hitting piece of journalism."

I made a face. "I'd rather it wasn't. Rachel's got a style straight out of the *National Enquirer*. I hope she didn't write her college essays like that." I twisted my voice. "'*Do I Deserve It?*—Ace student Rachel Woodson hunts for admission to your university.'"

Ezra snorted and then grimaced, and it was quiet for a moment. "So, uh, did you write the 'inaccessibly handsome' part?"

"No, I definitely didn't." I realized how that sounded and then felt compelled to go on. My shoes suddenly became incredibly interesting. "But, I mean . . . it's true."

"You think I'm handsome?"

I tried to sound casual. "Sure, I mean, who doesn't? Those PTs in gym practically salivate every time you walk into the room."

"PTs?"

"The, uh, the girls in gym. They obviously appreciate"—I gestured vaguely to Ezra's body—"all this business."

He smiled a little as he looked back down at the paper. "What about the 'inaccessible' part? Kinda makes me sound like a badly zoned restroom."

"It's true, though. A few details here and there aren't bad. You're not exactly forthcoming."

"I told you. I'm not great at talking."

"You're talking now."

He shrugged. "You're easy to talk to."

Something fluttered around in my stomach at that. A lone butterfly, agitating me for some reason.

Ezra's voice was strange when he next spoke, a few notes higher than usual. "So Homecoming's coming up."

"Yeah."

"Would you . . . maybe want to go with me?"

His face was turned away from me, as if he were extending the invitation to the goalposts.

"Well . . . yeah. Sure."

He glanced over at me. "Really?"

"Why not?"

"Cool. Okay. That's cool. I, uh, I'm also having this thing afterward. . . . I mean, Jordan is trying to get me to have this thing, this party. . . . Maybe you could come to that, too."

"A double invitation. Ambitious."

"If you wanted to, I mean, you don't have to—"

"I'll be there."

"For real?"

"For real."

23

"And then," Foster said in the car after practice, "we ran the fake-out play. I go in, so the other team thinks we're going to go for a three-pointer, you know? But then we don't! Instead of putting it down for me, they pitch it out to Ezra and Ezra runs it and it's, like, *touchdown!*"

We had gone to the McDonald's drive-through and were now parked in the lot of the neighboring combination Taco Bell/Pizza Hut. Parking sort of defeated the purpose of hitting the drive-through, but I wanted one of those vanilla swirl ice-cream cones, and they were hard to eat while driving.

"And what are you supposed to be doing while all that's going on?" I asked, and then caught a lone dribbler running down the side of my cone.

"Trying not to get crushed. That's what Ezra said."

"That's good advice."

Foster looked over at me knowingly. "He asked you. To Home-coming."

"He did."

"And you said yes."

"I did." I smiled a little. "So?"

"So . . . cool. Right?"

"Right."

"I got a date, too," Foster said, and then crammed a handful of fries into his mouth.

"Oh yeah? Who?"

He chewed and then said thickly, "Gwin Holtzer."

"Gwin Holtzer?" I repeated. "Don't you mean Gracie?"

"I mean Gwin. Gracie's older sister."

"Older sister? How old?"

"She's a sophomore."

"Geez, this is a big deal. You skipped a whole class of Holtzer. You must be a hot commodity."

Foster didn't speak. When I glanced over at him, his eyes were fixed on the window, his brow furrowed.

"What about Marabelle?" I said after a pause.

"Oh, she's not going." He was trying to sound nonchalant, but that made him sound even more . . . chalant.

"So . . . Gwin it is."

"Gwin it is."

Apparently, Homecoming was on a lot of people's minds. Cas followed me in the cafeteria line the next day, grabbed a tray and a carton of milk, and said, "So what color's your dress?"

"I haven't gotten it yet."

"Let me know when you do. We don't want to clash."

It took me a moment. "We?"

"You and me. Who else?" Cas grabbed two side salads and put them on each of our trays. "Move down, you're holding up the line."

I slid my tray down toward the entrees. "I . . . I thought you were going to ask Lindsay."

"Why would I do that? I always go with you."

"I know, but—" I had told Lindsay I would sound him out. So I forged ahead. "I was supposed to—she wants to go with you. She told me. And anyway, I sort of . . ."

"Sort of what?" His smile widened. "Don't tell me you already have a date."

It was the way he said that word. *Date*. The hint of incredulity. Like the idea of me having a date was absurd.

"Yeah, actually. I do."

"Who?"

"Ezra."

The smile vanished. "Ezra?"

I had reached the cashier. I handed her a five and avoided Cas's eyes.

"Uh-huh. He asked me."

Cas recovered that easy smile, but I could tell he was troubled by the prospect as he paid. "So, what, are you guys, like, dating now or something?"

I shrugged. I didn't really know if a Homecoming date meant the possibility of future, nondance dates. But something about that look on Cas's face, uncertainty tempered by that cocky smugness, made me want to tell all kinds of lies about me and Ezra.

I headed off to a table, and Cas was right on my heels. "When did you even start liking him? You said he was an asshole."

"I got to know him better."

"When?"

"I don't know." I dug into my lunch. "Maybe when you were spending all that time with Lindsay."

"What does Lindsay even have to do with this?"

"You like her, right?"

Cas looked uncomfortable. "Yeah, I like her."

"Then what are you doing asking me to Homecoming? If you really like somebody, you don't go and take somebody else to a dance."

"We always go together, Dev."

"Yeah, well, that's before we had . . . prospects."

"Prospects? What does that even mean?"

"I don't know." I tore open a package of salad dressing and applied it vigorously to my salad. If this were Jane's time, Cas would be *Mr. Kincaid*, and he would understand what I meant. "People we like. We've both got people we like."

"So you do like Ezra."

"Maybe." I didn't even know if this was true. But I wasn't about to tell Cas that.

"Great." There was a pause. "Well . . . maybe I will ask Lindsay."

"Maybe you should."

"Okay." He looked at me for a second, as if daring me to change my mind, and then he picked up his tray and left.

24

The new assignment in freshman English was to compare a work of literature to its movie adaptation. It was the awesome kind of freshman comp assignment that I dearly missed. Freshman-year essays were the best. Senior year and all you're left with is critical analysis and footnotes and works-cited pages. Heaven forbid you actually have fun with it.

A PT of the highest degree—I recognized her from gym class— came in for my "office hours" that next week. She was the one who had so eagerly claimed Ezra as her partner before Foster got the chance.

"Mrs. Chambers said you would read these," she said, holding a sheaf of pages in front of my face.

"Sure. What, uh, what'd you compare?"

"*Emma* and *Clueless.*"

I blinked and looked up at her. "For real?"

"It said movie adaptation," she said shortly. "It didn't say *which* movie adaptation."

I looked at the title page, which told me (1) that this girl's name was Amanda Jeffers and (2) that Amanda Jeffers wasn't messing around. The title could've been written by Rachel Woodson herself—*Emma vs. Cher: Austen's Heroine Transformed in Twentieth-Century American Cinema*.

If I'd had a seat belt, I would've needed to buckle it. Amanda Jeffers took me on one wild literary ride. Her paper was well thought out, structured, clear, insightful. It was also seven and a half pages long, whereas the assignment called for only four.

I looked up at her after I finished. "Wow. You must really like to write."

Amanda shrugged.

"This is really good."

"What can I change?"

"I mean . . ." I had no idea. I couldn't even criticize her formatting. I wouldn't admit it out loud, but this paper was beyond me.

"I want an A," she said, as if I hadn't heard her. "So what can I change?"

"I would give you an A," I said. "I wouldn't change anything."

"You can always change something. You can always do better."

I looked down at the pages. "I guess . . . maybe you could condense the part about Emma's reflections."

She nodded curtly. "And?"

"And . . . you could integrate your transitions a little better?" This was something English teachers had always told me.

"Great." She took her paper back, her lips pursed as she scratched some notes across the top. "Thanks."

Then she picked up her backpack and left.

We went, Lindsay, Lauren, Maria, and I, to a mall in Gainesville the next weekend. The charming Miss Renshaw wasn't exactly at the top of my hangout list, but at the same time, I knew I didn't have any right to ill will against her. Cas had asked me instead of her, and I had turned him down. Part of me felt justified in doing so, but part of me felt exceedingly guilty, and still another part felt that irrational longing that accompanies any third-degree crush, that chronic "what if?" What if we did go together and this was the one singular night that would suddenly make him realize that he was in love with me, and I threw all that away just because Ezra Lynley asked me first?

But Homecoming dresses, not neurotic inner monologues, were the order of the day, so off we went. We started at your typical department store, at your typical department store sales rack, and after about ten minutes' looking, entered the dressing rooms with an armful of dresses each.

My first dress was terrible. Lauren picked it out for me, and I would have felt bad telling her I thought it was ugly, so I tried it on anyway. As per any shopping trip, everyone told me it was "totally cute" and made me look "absolutely gorgeous." All you had to do was string together a couple of nice adjectives and you could use them on any dress, regardless. How the dress actually looked took a backseat to this whole operation.

But Lindsay truly did look "absolutely gorgeous" in every dress she tried on. Downright freaking beautiful, whereas I looked increasingly clownlike.

After a while, we assembled outside Lauren's dressing room to review the dresses and pick our favorites.

"I like this one," Maria said, holding up a green taffeta thing. "And Marty looks good in green, too."

"Yeah, and it's a lot easier to match than some of these," Lauren said, waving her arm at a couple of the more uniquely patterned (read: hideous) dresses.

"Who are you going with, Lindsay?" Maria said, setting the green dress aside.

Lindsay's face tinged red. "I don't actually have a date yet."

This was news to me. After my chat with Cas, I figured he'd beeline it to Lindsay to ask her out on bended knee.

"So ask somebody," Lauren said. "Why not?"

Lindsay shrugged.

"And you and Ezra are going together, right, Devon?" Maria said.

High school news always travels fast. I wasn't used to being newsworthy, but I guess securing the hand of the varsity football captain was something to talk about.

"That's the plan," I said.

"What do you think of this one?" Lauren held up a sparkly blue minidress. Maria and I praised it accordingly, and Lauren looked expectantly at Lindsay.

But Lindsay was looking at me. I could see her face in the mirror as I held up an awful pink-and-white satin thing I was actually considering buying (it was 45 percent off!). There was something strange about her expression.

Lauren jiggled the hanger. "Lindsay?"

"Huh?"

"What about this one?"

"It's cute," Lindsay said, and her face automatically burst into a smile, wiping away that odd expression. Whatever it had been, it was gone.

We stayed at the mall for most of the day. I ended up getting that 45-percent-off satin creation. Lauren snagged a dress, too, but Lindsay resolved to keep looking, despite trying on any number of things that looked as if they had been made for her. I'm pretty sure if you cut two asymmetrical holes in a trash bag and stuck it on Lindsay, we'd all be wearing trash bags next season.

Our shopping day culminated in a fast-food marathon at the food court. After we partook in some fried food and some idle gossip, Lindsay declared she needed dessert. Lauren and Maria declined, but before I could, Lindsay jumped up and said, "Come with me, Devon! Let's look at all our options."

She slipped her arm through mine as we made our way around the fast-food circuit.

It reminded me of a scene from *Pride and Prejudice*—Elizabeth and Caroline taking a "turn about the room." Except Lindsay was no Caroline, scheming and conniving. Lindsay was just . . . Lindsay. A happy little ray of sunshine in a cut-glass bottle.

"So what did you end up thinking of Reeding?" she asked as we passed the Sbarro en route to Dairy Queen.

I had to admit it: "It's pretty great."

"I loved it, too. I was really thinking I'd go somewhere big, like Alabama or University of Florida. But when I saw Reeding, I knew it was the place. It's the perfect distance from home, it's gorgeous, the classes seem awesome. . . . I have to apply there, and if I can get a scholarship, I'm definitely going. How about you?"

I nodded, wondering if Lindsay, too, had imagined herself with a messenger bag. "Same."

"Oh, Devon, this is so great." Her eyes widened suddenly. "We could be roommates. Do you realize that?"

Roommates. With Lindsay Renshaw. Lindsay in a towel and shower shoes. Lindsay and her unrelenting barrage of charm and cheer. Could I handle that?

What's more, could I handle Lindsay seeing me in my shower shoes? I looked over at her.

Hardly believing the words were leaving my own lips, I said, "I . . . yeah. I mean, yeah. That would be cool. Right?"

"Oh my gosh, I just got really happy." Lindsay squeezed my arm. "Devon—well, okay, this is kind of cheesy, but I've always wanted us to be better friends. I see you around with Cas, and you just seem . . . I just always wanted us to be closer. So this would be so awesome."

Cas. Yes. Lindsay and Cas, potentially dating. Lindsay and me, potentially rooming. I would have to buy noise-canceling head-phones. Or build a cinder-block wall around my side of the room. Either way, Lindsay couldn't be denied. And she looked so happy right now, and it was oddly infectious, so I was kind of happy, too, regardless.

"Awesome," I replied, and part of me meant it.

25

We were still working on football in gym class, doing flag football scrimmages. The flags posed a problem for the PTs, because the flag belts covered up the strip of skin between the tops of their shorts and the bottoms of their shirts. This was prime real estate, so they compensated by tying up their shirts a little higher.

We were dividing into teams in class on Tuesday when Mr. Sellers called Ezra over. He was standing with Mr. McBryde, the varsity head coach, a little ways down the field.

"Wonder what they want," Foster murmured as we both watched Ezra go. Mr. Sellers and Mr. McBryde were speaking in tones too hushed to be heard from where we stood, and when Ezra reached them, Mr. McBryde put a hand on Ezra's shoulder.

"I know what it is," someone crooned. It was the slightly pathetic PT, the one who had lobbed the football at me the day Foster's kicking talent was discovered. "My daddy's a cop. I know what it is."

I didn't know what her daddy's being a cop had to do with it, but most everyone was listening, even the ones—like me—pretending not to. Foster was staring straight at her, as if daring her to say something bad about Ezra.

"Some kid crashed his car. Some kid from . . . like, Lake Falls or something? He got drunk and crashed his car and died."

"What does that have to do with Ezra?" My voice was strangely wooden when it left my lips.

"Well, he was a football player." She said it as if it were the most obvious thing in the world. "He was, like, the captain or something. And we're playing them this week." Her eyes gleamed. "Maybe they're telling Ezra not to crush them because they feel bad."

I stared at her for a moment. What an obnoxious person.

Then I turned my gaze to Ezra. Mr. McBryde still had his hand on Ezra's shoulder.

Ezra didn't look as if he'd just received the news of a death. His face was as neutral as usual. His eyes, though . . . in his eyes there was a brightness that I had never seen before, and not a good kind. I could tell from where I stood that something wasn't right.

Maybe it wasn't a death. Maybe it was the Bowl. Had he been kicked out of the Bowl? Disqualified as an All-American? Maybe they got wind of Rachel Woodson's crappy article and somehow believed all that statistics-mongering stuff.

"I bet it's not that," Foster said, glaring at the PT who had spoken. "I bet they just need him for an interview or something. I bet it's not that at all."

The PT gave Foster a scornful look and turned back to her friends.

I moved closer to where Foster stood. "You're probably right," I said, but I didn't know how much truth there was to it.

Ezra didn't return after his conversation with Mr. Sellers and

171

Coach. Instead, he turned and headed toward the team locker rooms. They had their own building, a little, one-story cinder-block setup right next to the field.

I looked at Foster. We both peeled away from the class and headed that way, careful to keep out of Mr. Sellers's sight line.

Foster went straight into the locker room. I paused for a moment. I didn't know exactly when Ezra's business had become our business, but somehow it had. So I followed.

"Ezra?"

I had never been in the team locker room before. The only difference I noted was that they didn't have shower curtains, which was weird. And, of course, the wealth of urinals, which was gross.

Ezra was standing at an open locker, his back to us.

"Is it true?" Foster asked. "Was there an accident?"

"Yeah." Ezra turned. He was holding a practice jersey. His eyes were dry. "Yeah, Lake Falls' captain died."

"Oh no." Foster voiced what I couldn't. My insides felt frozen. "How?"

"Car accident. They think he was drunk."

"Did you know him?" Foster asked.

"We did a couple of camps together."

"Were you friends?"

A pause. "Yeah."

"Shit," I said.

"Do you want to cry?" Foster said.

"*Foster.*" Scolding Foster came natural in almost any situation.

"I'm just saying, a lot of guys don't think it's, like, socially acceptable to cry. But you could cry if you wanted. Because that's stupid."

Ezra looked at me for a split second. "I'm fine."

"We could go to our house if you want," Foster continued. "I have the *Bill and Ted* sequel."

"It's all right. I'm okay." He dropped the jersey in the bottom of the locker. "You guys go ahead. I'll be right out."

We both lingered. Even though Ezra sounded okay, something in his eyes betrayed his words.

"I'm fine," he said, and there was resolution in his voice. "Go on, okay?"

"Sure." I pushed Foster ahead of me. "See you out there."

The news spread quickly throughout the school, and by the end of the day, almost everyone had heard what happened. Lake Falls was just one town over from Temple Sterling. A lot of people had friends there, and some people, apparently, knew the boy who had died. His name was Sam Wells, I learned in my seventh-period math class. He was a senior and a three-year varsity starter, and he had already committed to Florida State.

"Oh, Devon." I passed Cas and Lindsay in the hallway after last class. Lindsay threw her arms around me. "It's just awful, isn't it?"

I hugged back—what else could I do?—and said, "Yeah. Terrible."

"I can't imagine." She pulled away. "I just keep thinking about the guys on their team. . . . What it would be like if we lost our captain . . ."

Her eyes welled up with tears. Cas closed her in a hug. I averted my gaze.

"We're supposed to go to the visitation," Foster said when I picked him up after practice. "Out of respect. That's what Coach said. It's Thursday afternoon. Will you take me?"

"Of course."

"I don't have a suit."

"You could wear one of Dad's, I guess," I murmured, pulling out onto the street. "I don't know if it'd fit, but you could always try."

"I don't want to wear his clothes," Foster said.

"Why not?" When I glanced over at Foster, his face was turned to the window.

It was quiet for a moment, and then, "Because they won't fit," is all he said.

He settled on a dress shirt and tie for the visitation. I didn't dress nice, but I wasn't planning on going in. I didn't have a sufficient enough connection to Sam Wells to make being there feel right.

The parking lot was packed, and the only spot I could get was way down the street. I looked over at Foster after I put the car in park. He was staring at the dashboard.

"Are you okay?" I asked.

He nodded, and after a moment, he got out of the car and headed toward the funeral home.

I had been waiting only a little while when Ezra came barreling down the sidewalk.

He slowed to a stop as he reached the parking lot in the distance, stood for a moment, and then turned swiftly and headed right back down the street in my direction. For one wild second I thought he was coming to my car, to see me, but he didn't even look up as he walked past.

He was parked farther down the street. In my side mirror I could see him approach his truck. He didn't get inside, though. He just stood, his hands braced against the doorframe, head down.

I leaned closer to the mirror to get a better look; he seemed to be talking to himself.

I don't know why I did what I did, but I got out of the car and headed down the street.

I don't think he heard me coming, but I could hear him as I approached. Muffled but still discernible, Ezra was counting.

"Fiftysevenfiftyeightfiftyninesixtysixtyone—"

"Ezra?"

He straightened up fast, almost tripping over the curb behind him. And when he looked at me, it was that thing he did . . . like it took a moment for him to recognize me. But it was different from the way it usually was. This time he seemed preoccupied, almost as if he wouldn't recognize anyone who crossed his path.

"What are you doing here?" he said.

I didn't know if he meant "here" at the visitation or "here" on the sidewalk. "I drove Foster," I said, a sort of blanket statement.

"Why aren't you inside?"

"Why aren't you?"

"I don't want to hear about him. He was a fucking idiot."

"*Ezra.*"

"He was. And you know it, and I know it, and everybody knows it, and we'd just have to stand there and listen to people talk like it was so fucking tragic. But it wasn't tragic. Tragic deaths aren't avoidable, and Sam's was."

I didn't know what to say, and I wasn't sure what Jane would say, either. Although romance was definitely a hallmark of her work, her books weren't without tough truths—sometimes things don't turn out the way you want them to. Sometimes there's loss. Sometimes your sister marries a douche bag. So maybe she would simply admit that there was some merit to his statement.

"Sorry." He looked back toward the funeral home. "I probably sound like a dick."

"I'm not much of an authority on what dicks sound like," I said without thinking. "Limited personal experience."

One corner of Ezra's mouth lifted, for about half a second.

"What . . . what were you doing?" I gestured to the car, like somehow that indicated Ezra's odd behavior. "The . . . counting?"

He just shook his head, and then it was quiet.

"I'll go in with you," I said. "If you want to see him."

"I don't. Is that bad?"

I swallowed. "No. No, I don't think so."

"It's too much." He shook his head again. "I don't . . . I can't . . ."

Ezra trailed off, and when he looked at me, I thought he might cry. I was seized with an instant need to stop that from happening. I could make another lame joke, but my mind drew a blank.

I had never lost a friend before. A couple of grandparents when I was a baby. An uncle I hardly knew. But I didn't know what it was like to lose a friend, even one you weren't so close with. There were all these people in my life I wasn't so close with, and even the loss of one of them—a Rachel Woodson or a Maria Silva—was unimaginable to me.

I stepped off the sidewalk, moved toward Ezra, and closed my arms around him. He didn't hug back right away, and I felt dumb for the first few seconds, but then he circled his arms around me and held me close. He was taller than me, just the right height to rest my face in the crook of his neck.

"You okay?" I asked, finally, without letting go.

"Uh-huh." I could feel his voice resonate in his chest.

"You sure?"

"No." A pause. "Maybe we could just stay like this for a little while longer."

"Okay."

And so we stood. And it wasn't so much a hug as me trying to put into action what I couldn't put into words. I wanted Ezra not to look so heartbroken. I wanted him to feel as safe as he made me and Foster feel.

Ezra drew several deep breaths, and then he began to count again.

I didn't stop him. I didn't question it. I didn't understand, but in the moment, I didn't feel the need to. I just wanted Ezra to be okay.

We had been back from the visitation for some time when I found Foster hanging out under the kitchen table.

It was not uncustomary to find Foster in weird places, like sitting in an empty bathtub or the laundry basket or the coat closet. But lying under the kitchen table was a new one. So I went and sat down on the floor, wrapped my arms around my legs, and leaned back against the dishwasher. It was running, and loud swishing sounds filled the room.

"He looked like he was asleep, Dev," Foster said after a long time. "Sam Wells? He looked just like he was sleeping. There were so many people there they filled up three huge rooms."

"I guess he was important to a lot of people."

"If you died, what would you want them to say about you?"

I knew this was one of those Foster questions that needed no answer, so I let him go on.

"I mean, would you want people saying all this nice shit about you, or would you want them to tell the truth?"

"The truth?"

"The real stuff. Sometimes you talk too loud. And you get pissed off for no reason. And sometimes you're judgmental about people who don't deserve it."

I didn't get mad, half because Foster was working through something, and half because it was the truth.

"And just because you died wouldn't mean that stuff wasn't part of who you were. But people wouldn't talk about the real stuff."

"They want to focus on the good things," I said.

"The good things didn't kill him." He paused. "He was really stupid, Dev. But you can't say that. You're not supposed to say that."

I didn't speak.

"If Ezra died, would you still call him a dickhead?"

"Don't say stuff like that."

"You always say that. You always tell me what not to say, but I'm just telling the truth and I don't see what's wrong with that. If Ezra died, I'd want you to keep on calling him a dickhead if that's how you felt about him. Just because a person dies doesn't mean it should change the way you feel about them, or the way they really were. Just because they're gone doesn't mean that they weren't a bad person or that they never fucked up."

It clicked. Like a lightbulb, or something less cliché.

"Foster—"

"Don't talk about my mom. Don't say one single word."

"What if it's just to tell the truth?"

It was his turn to be silent. His mouth was twisted into a frown, his eyes locked on the underside of the table.

"If she died, we wouldn't forget what she did to you. Ever. We could even hate her a little bit if we wanted, even if she died."

Foster swallowed and didn't look over.

It was quiet for a long time. And then, "He could've helped her."

The dishwasher shut off and the silence was pressing. "What?"

"Your dad could've helped her. Before she got so bad. Just because my dad's dead doesn't mean he couldn't have helped her."

"I don't think they knew. . . . I mean, I don't think anybody knew how bad it had gotten."

"If he cared, he would've known."

I couldn't speak for my dad. But I knew that grief had something to do with it. Maybe he should've called more. And maybe by the time they realized something was wrong, it was too late.

But who was I to tell Foster about grief? What did I really know?

It took a moment for me to collect enough words for a sentence: "I don't really think you should blame him for all of it." I swallowed, my throat suddenly tight. "I don't think . . . I mean, will it help?"

Foster's voice was hoarse. "It's easier. Than blaming her."

I nodded, and we sat in silence.

26

The unpleasant PT in gym class was right—we were set to play Lake Falls the Friday after Sam Wells's visitation. I don't think anyone really knew how to handle it. Could it be the same as a normal game? Could the cheerleaders still cheer? Could the crowd still rumble, still chow down on hot dogs, still yell and carry on?

It appeared that they could, because they did. There was a moment of silence for Sam Wells before the game. But when the moment was over, everything seemed to go back to normal.

Our team took the field with its usual look of determination, but something was different about play tonight. It was sloppy.

And somehow the sloppier the team got, the better Ezra got; he darted around defenders faster, he pushed himself further. He was playing a spectacular game, and by the end of the first half, Temple Sterling led by four touchdowns. Lake Falls, despite Temple Sterling's sloppy playing, hadn't even come within twenty yards of its end zone.

Mr. Harper was taking sideline shots of our players and of theirs—the sports section would be organized a little differently this week, I'm sure. Some tribute to Sam or something. The courage of a team going on without its captain.

Which was, in a literal sense, what Temple Sterling was doing: When the team went back in at the half, Ezra was held on the side-lines.

"Put me back in." I was close enough to hear Ezra arguing with Mr. McBryde.

"You're out for the time being."

"Why?"

"If you don't like it, you can sit out the rest of the half, all right?"

"Are you kidding me?" Ezra threw his helmet to the ground. I had never seen him so mad. In fact, I had never seen him mad at all. On an emotional scale of one to ten—one being catatonic and ten being full-on daytime soap opera—Ezra usually hovered somewhere around a three.

"Look." Mr. McBryde got right in Ezra's face, his voice dangerously low. "If you don't want to cooperate, you can sit out the next game. Despite what you seem to think, you can be benched like anyone else."

"It's not like that." Ezra was struggling to control his voice.

"You can leave, Lynley." Mr. McBryde was steely. "We've got a game to play."

"And I was playing it!" Ezra burst. "I was the only one out there playing it! Don't you see what they're doing?"

Mr. McBryde picked Ezra's helmet up and shoved it into his chest. "Check yourself," was all he said, and then he stormed away to consult with the defensive coach.

The offensive coach, Mr. Evans, went over to Ezra. I could hear him talking quietly about how important it was to be "classy" in a situation like this, and how he was concerned that it might look as if they were abusing Lake Falls' situation to pad stats.

Just as Rachel had said. Politics.

"Ease up," Mr. Evans said. "Everyone's gonna get a little play tonight, okay? It's only fair."

Ezra didn't speak. He just clutched his helmet and refused to meet Mr. Evans's gaze.

With Ezra sulking on the sidelines, Lake Falls scored twice in the third quarter and twice again in the fourth. A two-point conversion made the score 29–28, Lake Falls. Our coaches pulled the greener players out after Lake Falls began to score, but Ezra never went back in.

With just seconds left on the clock, it was clear that Temple Sterling's only option for a win was to go for the field goal. It was long, but Foster had kicked from farther before. Coach slapped him in, and with a momentary glance back in Ezra's direction, he ran onto the field.

Play resumed. They snapped the ball, and the line took off and collided with Lake Falls'. Foster strode forward and connected. The kick looked good, arcing end over end on a straight path toward the goalposts.

But it fell short.

And the clock had run down. The team went over to shake hands. All but Ezra, who stood with his back to the field.

I carried Foster's bag for him as we left. He trotted alongside me as usual, but there was no running commentary of "Ezra caught that pass, did you see that pass, did you see his touchdown?" Foster was quiet.

Until we reached the car, at least, when he looked at me and said, "Sam was just like any one of us. Like Jordan or Marcus or Reggie, and then that would be us out there."

I nodded and the "yeah" stuck in my throat.

We were parked next to Ezra's truck. I didn't realize he was behind us until I heard his bag hit the flat bed.

"Good game," Foster said.

"We lost."

Foster shrugged. "They beat us."

Ezra snorted.

"Something wrong?" I asked.

"Yeah. He missed that kick on purpose." Ezra's eyes were fiery. "We would've won the game, but you fucked up on purpose."

"I didn't," Foster said.

"You did. Don't bullshit me. You did."

Foster just stood, staring at Ezra like he was a stranger.

"Foster, get in the car," I said after a moment, trying to keep my voice calm. "Go on."

I dumped his bag in the backseat and stood until Foster had closed himself in the front. Then I pulled Ezra around the other side of his truck, out of Foster's sight. The last few stragglers were trailing from the stadium, but all in all, the parking lot was pretty quiet.

"What the hell is your problem?"

"He lost the game."

"Yeah. He made a bad kick. It happens. Not everyone's a fucking All-American, Ezra."

"This has nothing to do with me being All-American!" It was an explosion. An M-80 lighting up the night sky. "He could've made that kick; he's done it a hundred times!"

"Maybe he was nervous."

"He doesn't *get* nervous!"

"Well, maybe it was for the best, right?"

"For the best? When is losing for the best?"

"When the other team needs a win! Their captain died, Ezra, and they had to go out there and play their first game without him."

"Oh, so we should just let them win. That'll make them feel better. We're clearly the stronger team, but since Sam got drunk and ran his car into a tree, we'll give them this one. Is that what you mean?"

"That's not what I'm saying—"

"Nobody *deserves* to win because something shitty happened to them. You deserve to win because you're better than the other team, and we're better than them, we could've beat them straight out, *I* could've beat them straight out!"

"I'm not saying we should've handed them the game," I said, struggling to maintain civility like the best of Jane's heroines would.

"Well, we did. Foster did, with that kick."

"Don't say a fucking word about Foster." That was what flipped a switch in me. I couldn't keep it back any longer. "He didn't do anything wrong. You were the one acting like an idiot out there! All along, you say it's not about winning, it's not about stats, but the minute you get benched you fucking lose it. And you're all about humility, and modesty, and yet you're so conceited you think you can save the game single-handed. But that's not true, and they lost, and you lost, and you're gonna have to deal with it and leave Foster the fuck alone, because he's never done anything to deserve being treated badly by anyone, especially you."

Ezra didn't reply. He just stood there for a moment, and then he got in his truck without even a glance in my direction. The door slammed, the engine turned, and he was gone.

27

Jane talks about *exertion* in some of her novels. It didn't quite mean back then what it does today; nowadays you think of the body—of pushing your muscles to the limit, of working your brain as hard as you can. Physical and mental exertion. But Jane's exertion was of the emotional variety. In *Sense and Sensibility*, when Elinor finds out that the guy she's in love with is engaged to someone else, she works her hardest to exert herself around others, to make sure that her true feelings—her true sorrows—go unexposed. She practices exertion in a way that means she acts as if everything is just fine, so that no one would suspect her of the kind of pain and heartache that was considered inappropriate to feel when someone else's fiancé was involved.

All the way home that night, I practiced exertion. I didn't cry a single tear. And I didn't say a single word.

Only when we had pulled into the driveway did I look over at Foster. "I thought you played really well," I said, and my voice came out perfectly even.

He shook his head. "I could've done better. We all could've done better."

"He's a jerk, though. He's just . . ."

"He shouldn't have talked to you like that."

"He shouldn't have talked to *you* like that," I said, and I stared hard at the garage, hoping that Foster wouldn't notice how shiny my eyes had gotten. "You guys are supposed to be friends. Friends don't do that."

"Maybe if they're going through something. Maybe then they do."

"Don't stick up for him. I know he's, like, your role model or whatever, but just . . . don't."

"He's not." Foster fumbled with his seat belt. "You are."

I didn't know what to say. A thanks was in order, but I didn't think I could muster it without exploding into embarrassing tears. So I just nodded and blinked even harder in the direction of the garage.

We parted ways in the kitchen. Foster went to greet my folks in the living room, and I went upstairs. I didn't feel like talking.

Once in my room, exertion was no longer necessary. I cried.

I woke early the next morning with an undeniable heaviness in my chest.

I was mad at Ezra for acting in a way that I didn't understand, but I was mad at myself, too, for how I had acted. I felt justified, but at the same time . . . was I? There was something so un-Jane-like about what I had said and how I had said it. I could've stayed cool and composed and rational. I could've . . . maintained propriety. But instead, I called Ezra Lynley conceited and said "fuck" a lot.

It was a weird mixture of embarrassment and also feeling like . . . like I had ruined something. Like Ezra and I had both ruined something, but I wasn't even sure what it was. I just kept thinking about standing outside Sam Wells's wake with him. How we stood there together for such a long time, and how even though it wasn't a happy embrace, we still . . . fit together right.

After a while spent thinking along these same lines, I heard the front door open and close.

I got up and headed downstairs.

I stood in the living room and peered through the front window. Foster sat on the top front step. No loopy circle laps on the lawn today.

I looked at the clock: 6:14.

And true to his schedule, Ezra came jogging down the street. Something in my stomach seized at the sight of him. Would he stop for Foster? What's more, would Foster even join him?

He didn't pass our house—I was almost sure he would. Instead, he slowed and walked up the front path, stopping in front of Foster.

I couldn't hear what he said, but Foster shifted over and Ezra took a seat next to him.

They sat there for a little while, their backs to the window. And then they got up and took off. Running side by side down the street.

I went and showered. I made some toast. All the while pretending as if I wasn't keeping an ear out for Foster.

"What did he say?" I couldn't help but ask when he walked through the door.

"Nosy," was Foster's reply. His hair was damp with sweat, and his face was red. "He apologized," he said.

"And you forgave him? Just like that?"

He shrugged, shifted back and forth for a moment, and then said, "I told him he should come in and talk to you."

I laughed. "Don't do me any favors."

"He didn't want to."

"I'm sure."

"But not 'cause he's not sorry. . . . It's just more awkward, you know? Because you're a girl."

"So?"

"So it's more awkward if it's a girl. And if there's like . . . feelings and stuff."

"Feelings and stuff?" I repeated.

He shrugged again.

"Forget about it. I don't want to talk to him," I said, even though it might not have been the truth.

Foster just eyed me for a moment, like he knew that was the case, and then he turned and went upstairs.

I hated gym that week. The football unit had ended, and we were starting basketball. Too many things happen at once in basketball; you're supposed to run and dribble and pass and shoot a big round ball into a teeny-tiny hoop ten feet off the ground. Not my sport. But it wasn't just basketball that made gym suck. It was seeing Ezra.

I knew what Foster meant, as much as I hated to admit it— there were feelings. I wasn't quite sure what those feelings were, but I was pretty sure that if there were none at all, it would've been a lot easier to just go up and talk to him. But instead, I felt compelled to stare in the opposite direction any time Ezra neared me in the gym.

Halfway through passing drills, a PT flung a ball at Ezra, and it bounced right past him toward my general vicinity. Instead of doing the human thing—picking up the ball and giving it back to them—I spun around quickly to head off in the other direction. And promptly took another rogue basketball to the face.

You wouldn't think it would hurt that badly, but I imagine it was what being slapped would feel like. I squeezed my eyes shut for a moment, cupping my face with one hand, and there was that terrifying second where I was pretty sure I was going to burst into tears. Involuntary crying, like when a baby hears a loud noise.

But I managed to keep it together, and when I opened my eyes again, Gracie Holtzer and several PTs had materialized in front of me. Gracie wrapped an arm around me.

"Are you okay? Does it hurt? Madeline, go punch James."

I watched as a tall, lanky PT went over to the stocky defensive end I knew only as Kenyon and punched him in the arm.

"That's for hitting Devon," Gracie called.

"Geez," Kenyon said. "It was an accident."

"I'm sorry, what now?" Gracie said, and her expression was deadly.

"Sorry," Kenyon mumbled.

"That's better." Gracie looked at me. "Let's see." She pulled my hand away from my face. "Oh, that's not so bad. Just a little pink. You want some cover-up? Or ice? Ice and then cover-up?"

Those were the least of my concerns, because it was then that I realized Ezra was right behind us. I needed to get out of there.

"It's fine, I'm fine," I said to Gracie. "Thanks, I'm just going to go. . . ." And I booked it to the girls' locker room, where it was safe. No flying basketballs. No awkward confrontations.

I examined my face in the mirror. I was indeed a little pink around the eye. I touched the skin there and winced. Just what I needed. A gym-class souvenir.

"Are you okay?"

I jumped and spun around. "God, you startled me." I hadn't seen Ezra approach in the mirror. Too distracted by my own reflection.

"Sorry. Just . . . wanted to see if you were okay."

"I'm fine. You shouldn't be in here."

"You went into the guys' locker room once," Ezra said. "If you recall."

I did recall. But I had no idea what to say to that. So silence settled in, yet Ezra made no move to leave.

"We don't have to talk about the game," I said, finally. "Foster said you didn't want to."

"That's . . . that's not what I said."

"So what did you say?"

Ezra didn't speak. He just frowned at a sparkly pink Victoria's Secret duffel bag on the bench to my right.

Something flared up in my chest—annoyance, or frustration, or both. Obviously he was capable of expressing himself. He came through loud and clear in the parking lot after the game. So why was he silent now, why did the burden of talking have to be on me? It wasn't fair.

"Let's just pretend none of it happened," I said shortly. "Press reset or something."

"Reset?"

"Yeah. Wipe the board clean. Move the chains back. Whatever."

"How far?"

"What?"

"How far do we move the chains back?"

"I don't know, Ezra, how about far enough that you can go back to acting like you don't know who I am when I see you in public—will that make you feel better?"

Surprise flashed across Ezra's face. "I don't . . . that's not . . ." But he didn't finish. He just looked to the duffel bag, and the duffel bag sparkled aggressively back at him. "What about Homecoming?" he said, finally. "Do you still . . ."

Oh yeah. A whole night of stony silence with Ezra was just what the doctor ordered. "No," I said, and maybe it was harsh, maybe I sucked in that moment, but I was irritated and . . . residually embarrassed, and I couldn't stand the idea of this awkwardness permeating an entire evening.

Ezra just nodded. No protest there. He was probably relieved.

I crossed over to my locker, opened the door, pulled my gym bag out, and started rifling through it, signaling the end of the conversation. Dismissing Ezra. He stood there for a moment longer, and maybe he would've said something if I had turned back around. But I didn't, and he didn't. He just left.

I sank down onto the nearest bench. My face still hurt, but there was some other hurt now, too—that shitty feeling of having broken something between us. I felt it fresh.

I hated gym class. I stewed in that at lunchtime.

"So then Jenna said 'carbon,' and I said, 'magnesium,' and we were all, like, wow, you're not even listening." Cas stared at me from across the table, two red trays and a whole host of greasy food between us. "Are you okay?"

"What?"

He waved a chicken nugget in front of my eyes. "You seem kind of out of it."

"I'm fine."

We hadn't talked much since the Homecoming incident. Whenever we had disagreed over something in the past, the protocol was to act like there was no conflict and everything was fine, and in that way, everything would be fine. It usually worked, but today was different.

"Look, Dev, about the Homecoming thing . . . if you want to go with Ezra, then that's cool."

This was the last thing I wanted to hear at that moment, since I had just effectively crushed the notion of Ezra and me going together. All I could do was snap: "I'm so glad I've got your permission."

"I'm just saying, I'm cool with it."

"I don't care if you're cool with it or not."

He frowned. "Why are you being weird?"

"I don't know." I threw my sandwich down. "I don't know. I just . . . I don't care about Homecoming." I pushed back from the table. "Excuse me." I grabbed my tray, dumped it in the trash, and took off.

28

I went to the grocery store that evening to pick up a couple of things for my mom and to get some of my own shopping done, too. Embarrassing things, like panty liners and dandruff shampoo, that you really only want to buy when you're by yourself.

The "feminine products" aisle always weirded me out, because inevitably the store paired pads and tampons with diapers, baby food, and condoms. Like everything pertaining to the uterus should be stored in the same aisle.

It was empty when I approached. I grabbed an embarrassingly large package of pads and began to make my escape. Until . . .

"Champ?"

I froze, right there in the middle of the aisle.

Hastily I grabbed the first thing from the shelf I could to hide the pads and wheeled around to face Jordan, shifting the basket behind me. It banged against the backs of my thighs as I took a few steps to distance myself from the brightly colored packages. I knew it was foolish. Like, I'm guessing Jordan was not entirely unfamiliar with the existence of periods. But if I didn't want to buy that shit at the store with my mom, I certainly didn't want Jordan Hunter there for it.

But Jordan just gave me an easy smile. "Hey." He looked entirely unconcerned at meeting me here.

"Hi." It came out as a squeak. I cleared my throat. "How's it going?"

"Not too bad. Just picking up a couple of things for the fam." He indicated a sticky note pressed to the handle of the cart, clearly a shopping list. I took a quick glance at the contents of the cart: some boxes of cornflakes, a carton of milk, a dozen eggs. Standard fare, except for the little black rectangular box resting atop a package of spaghetti. I knew what they were, and I knew at once why he was in the aisle.

Jordan noticed me looking and cupped a hand around his mouth and said in a loud whisper, "Those aren't for the fam."

"Adding rogue items?"

"I'm a free agent," Jordan said with a smile.

Proud of myself for producing successful banter, I glanced down at my own basket and realized what it was I had grabbed to obscure the pads. I nearly choked. Adult diapers.

I tried, if possible, to force the basket even farther out of sight. Jordan hadn't seemed to notice.

"So," he said, as he began to push his cart down the aisle. I walked alongside. "Missed you at the party last week."

"Yeah . . . yeah, I was busy." I hurriedly shoved the adult diapers into an empty spot on a shelf as we passed and grabbed an economy-sized shampoo bottle instead. We turned into the cleaning-supply aisle, and Jordan slowed in front of the fabric softener.

"How's Foster?"

Inquiring after my family. Jordan had class that Jane would appreciate. "He's all right."

"Hope he wasn't too down about the game." He picked up a tub of softener and tossed it into the cart.

"Well . . . I think he felt like he could've done more, but I guess you always feel that way if you lose."

"Yeah, that's usually the case."

We turned onto the frozen foods. It was quiet as Jordan stared at a selection of microwavable snacks.

"Jordan?"

"Yeah."

I couldn't help but ask it. The Lake Falls game—and all its surrounding drama—was on my mind. "Do you think Lake Falls deserved to win?"

Jordan didn't speak for a moment. Then he said, "Depends on how you mean it. Do you mean, do I think they deserved to win because of what happened to them? Or do I think they deserved to win because they're a better team?"

"I don't know. Both."

He glanced over at me. "No, to the first. Yes, to the second."

"They don't have a very good record. You don't . . . you don't think Temple Sterling's a better team?"

"Damn right I do. But it doesn't matter what I think; it matters what happens on the field. And that night we sucked. So that night they were the better team."

"But if they had put Ezra back in, you might've won."

"It was a rough call. They pulled Ezra at the half because it looked bad. . . . There has to be some deference in that kind of a situation, you know? And if Lake Falls had scored six and we scored fifty-six, we'd look like a bunch of assholes. But try telling Ezra in any situation—let alone *that* situation—not to score, and he'll tell you to fuck off, pardon my language."

"But why didn't they put him back in when Lake Falls started scoring?"

Jordan smiled wryly. "Because of the fit he threw. If any one of us acted that way, we'd be out for sure. They hold us all to the same standards, even the game-changer."

This was the question that I really ached to ask: "But why did he act that way?"

"I won't make excuses for him," Jordan said after a pause. "I don't know where his head was at. Well, maybe I do, a little, but it's not my job to try to make it up to you."

I stared into the freezer case. My own reflection stared back, and behind that, several brands of frozen pizza. "Make what up?"

"Come on now. I know about after the game."

Busted. "Ezra told you?"

"Ezra hasn't said much of anything to anybody since that night. But your cousin sang like a bird at practice."

I gave a breath of laughter. Somehow that didn't surprise me.

"He thought Foster missed that kick on purpose," I said. "I know Foster would never do that."

"I bet Ezra does, too."

I didn't speak.

"Hey, you know what?"

"What?"

"One of these days we're going to sit down and have a nice conversation that has nothing to do with Ezra. We'll talk about movies or politics or some shit like that, and lemme tell you, Champ, it will be *delightful*."

I smiled.

"Come on, let's check out."

He put an arm around me, and we strolled to the checkout counter.

29

Homecoming week in Temple Sterling was much like you would imagine—a dash of small-town America (the Homecoming game) mixed with a good dose of the twenty-first century (cue the R-rated hip-hop music and X-rated hip-hop dance moves in the school gym).

We played the Homecoming game the afternoon of the dance. We typically played Priory High School, a long-standing rival. The varsity team beat Priory this year, as it had last year, and this set a nice tone for the rest of the evening. I know Foster was psyched about the whole thing. I wasn't particularly psyched to be his chauffeur, but that was what my Homecoming evening had seemingly been reduced to.

I pulled my dress out of the closet that evening and laid it on my bed. I even took the ballet flats I had gotten (60 percent off!) out of the box and put them on the floor under the dress.

"You're still coming, right?"

I turned. Foster stood in the doorway.

"I'll take you and Gwin. But no . . . I don't really feel like it."

"Are you going to put on the dress to drive me and Gwin?"

"No." I scooped it up, put it back in my closet, and shut the door definitively. "No, I'm not."

"Come on." Foster stepped into the room and sat down on the edge of my bed, picking up the ballet flats. "It'll be fun. And it's your last Homecoming. You don't want to miss your last Homecoming, do you?"

I didn't. Did I? I can't say I had any grand feelings about Homecoming in previous years. The shoes were generally uncomfortable and the music too loud, but it was an opportunity to slow dance with Cas and make fun of everyone else's idea of formal wear.

Suddenly I was flooded with the desire to be there. Why should I be cheated out of a dance just because I didn't have a date? Why shouldn't I go, just because Ezra and I weren't going together? I could have a good time alone.

Foster went to change, I donned the dress, and we left together to pick up Gwin.

The gym was decked out in its usual Homecoming garb; this consisted of twinkly lights, folding chairs, and a big plastic tarp they put over the hardwood to keep it from getting scratched. Inevitably the tarp would get twisted up during an overzealous conga line, and more than a few people would trip over it.

The place was packed. Foster and Gwin departed in the direction of some underclassmen, and I was left to scan the crowd for a familiar face.

Rachel Woodson appeared as if out of nowhere with a giant camera in her hands. She was impeccably dressed—not a hair out of place—and she shoved the camera in my face.

"Picture for the yearbook?"

"Uh . . ." I'd rather not.

"Come on." She poised the camera to shoot. "Smile."

I forced a smile. The flashbulb lit up the place and left stars in my eyes.

"Thanks, you're the best!" And Rachel Woodson was gone.

I swear I didn't regain my vision for the next two cloned pop ballads, and it was only when I took a seat in one of the folding chairs lining the room that I could finally blink them clear and enjoy a full view of the place.

I hadn't been sitting long when the crowd parted slightly and revealed them.

Lindsay Renshaw was wearing a cream-colored dress made of a soft, liquidlike fabric that danced around her legs. I don't know where it was from, but it definitely wasn't found on the half-off rack at a department store. She stood perfectly still on high-heeled shoes, hair shining in curls that cascaded down her back. She was beautiful, and everyone knew it. I knew it. There are lots of pretty people, but you meet so few truly beautiful ones in your lifetime. It was almost as if some glow radiated off her that was absent in the rest of us, some sparkle that couldn't be bought or imitated.

They weren't dancing, but she was standing close so as to be heard over the music. He was wearing a black suit with the jacket open, a crisp white shirt, thin black tie. His head was bent and her lips were right by his ear. My stomach spasmed.

It was Ezra Lynley.

He was . . . gorgeous. They were gorgeous together.

Mechanically, I left my seat, went into the bathroom, and closed myself in the corner stall. I pulled out my phone and thought about calling someone, but who was there to call? And what would I even say? It was just the kind of unpleasant surprise you had to share with someone, but I didn't have anybody to share it with.

Eventually I left the bathroom and headed outside. I had stuck a book in my purse, so I sat down on the steps to the gym and opened the book and stared at the words without absorbing them at all.

It was a crappy surprise, and I had too much pride to admit that it hurt. I had assumed that Ezra wouldn't go to Homecoming, nursing the foolish but nonetheless consolatory hope that he wouldn't want to show up with anyone but me.

And yet here was Lindsay. Swooping in. Interfering with my prospects yet again.

But had Ezra ever even been a prospect? Jane would point out that there was never an agreement between us. He never said out loud that he liked me. But there was something in his eyes at times that I would almost swear said something more. Some deeper sort of regard.

"Dev?"

Wherever I was, Foster had a way of finding me.

I closed my book as he sank down onto the step next to me. "Loud in there, huh?" he said. "And hot."

"That's how these things usually are."

I glanced over at Foster as I spoke. He looked like a different person. It wasn't so much the clothes or the hair or the new physique, but his face. The Foster I met at the beginning of summer looked . . . hollow. This Foster was filled up inside.

"Gwin seems nice," I added after a moment.

"Gwin needs to get a fucking *e* in her name."

I looked out across the parking lot. "Don't talk like them."

"Who?"

"The football guys."

"You want me to talk like the Future Science Revolutionaries?"

He twisted his voice. "*Gwin* is a positively arcane name, defying convention with its unusual choice of vowel."

I actually laughed. "Just talk like Foster."

He shrugged. "I miss Marabelle."

"Why didn't you ask her?"

"She wouldn't have come. She would've said that she can't be my date without Baby being my date, too, and Baby's not old enough to go to school dances."

"How do you know that's what she'd say?"

"Because that's what she said." Foster gave a sheepish smile.

"I'm sorry."

He gave another halfhearted shrug. "At least I've got Gwin. She's . . . nice."

I smiled. Foster was so transparent.

"She actually . . . she really wants to go to Ezra's party. After the dance?"

I had forgotten. Once again, the pathetically egocentric part of me had thought maybe he wouldn't want to have a party anymore. "And?"

"And . . . I think I should take her."

"You mean you think I should take you both."

"You could come to the party, too. We could all go together."

"Why would I want to go to a dickhead's party?"

For once, Foster didn't contest it. There was a conflicted look on his face; he didn't have to say anything for me to know.

I sighed heavily. "It's cool if you want to go to a dickhead's party."

"Dev—"

I stood up. "I'm heading back in. You should come, too. I'm sure all the girls from gym will be clamoring for a dance."

They were. I kept an eye on Foster in the hours to come. He hardly sat down once. I also kept an eye out for Lindsay and Ezra, so I could avoid them if necessary. But I didn't see them again.

I did see Cas, though. Blue suit, shiny shoes, and a great big grin aimed right at me. There was no avoiding him.

"Dev! Wow, you look great!" he said as he crossed the floor toward me.

It didn't even cross my mind until this moment; if Lindsay was with Ezra, then . . . "Who are you here with?"

Someone turned. A glittery pink production number.

Gracie Holtzer.

Cas snaked his arm around her waist and beamed at me.

"Devon, hey!" Gracie gushed. "Oh my god, you look so cute!"

"Thanks." I was numb. "You, too."

"Where did you get your dress?"

I mumbled the name of the store, but I had already lost her attention. She was looking at some point in the crowd, and all at once broke apart from Cas and ran to some other PT out there, presumably to gush about how cute they both looked.

I looked back at Cas. He was still grinning.

I pulled him out into the hallway before I could muster any words to convey my disbelief, and even then, all I got out was, "Gracie Holtzer?"

"Yeah. She's cute, right?"

"Gracie Holtzer?"

"Yes. Can we go back in? This is a good song."

"Do you realize you're here with the *little sister* of the girl *Foster's* here with?"

Cas just stared.

"It's fucking illegal, Cas. She's only fourteen!"

"Chill out. We're just having fun."

I wanted to cry. I punched his arm instead. "Why do you have to go and act like such an idiot? Why couldn't you have just gone with Lindsay?"

"I didn't think you wanted me to go with Lindsay."

"I never said that! In fact, I told you to go with her! And even if I hadn't, why would you let what I think stop you?"

"I don't know . . . it wasn't all you . . . because then Gracie asked me, and I just figured that way everyone would be happy."

"Except for Lindsay!"

"But you don't like Lindsay."

"Since when has that ever kept you from going out with some-body?"

Cas looked uncomfortable. "It's different with her."

"How?"

"I like her. A lot."

"Yeah, so?"

"I don't know." Cas's eyes raked the bank of lockers next to us as he fumbled with the carnation attached to his jacket.

And all at once I knew he felt that same thing I had felt at Frank Ferris's party. It had to be. It was knowing that he would be in love one day. Knowing that someone else would be dry-dry.

He looked at me. "Can't you just say it?"

"Say what?"

"Say that you like me more than just friends."

It was like a punch to the gut, sudden and powerful. "Why would I say that?"

"Because it's true, isn't it?"

"You're not being fair," I said.

"Why? You like me, don't you?"

"How do you know that?"

"Dude, everyone knows it." He looked at me like it was all so *obvious*. "We're friends," he said. "We always have been. And I want . . . I don't know. To fucking . . . protect your feelings, or whatever. Because I know you have them. I do. And so does everyone else, so just . . . why can't you just say it?"

All of a sudden, like an out-of-body experience, I saw myself saving tables for us in the cafeteria. Grabbing an extra side of something I knew he liked as I went through the lunch line. Calling him before bed—it really was always me who called him, wasn't it?—making him playlists for Valentine's Day and pretending I didn't care that he never gave me anything back. All those times I sat in the bleachers at practice: faithful, hopeful, deluded. Cas was a lot of things to me, and maybe I was a lot of things to Cas, too, but he didn't love me. All at once, I realized that truth that my mom, chocolate milk in hand, was trying to get me to see in eighth grade. I couldn't change myself to get Cas to like me. I couldn't change Cas, either. And even if I could—would I want to? Would I want someone I had to *make* love me?

And all the while, Cas stood there as "Everyone knows it" hung between us, and I could see it on his face—this obnoxious confidence. And I knew that he knew, that he had known all along, and here he was, *pitying* me. Poor Devon and her feelings.

I could feel my cheeks flushing, white hot tears of embarrassment pricking my eyes. If I blinked, they would fall. So I didn't blink.

"It's not true," I said. "Everyone's wrong."

"Dev. Come on."

"Cas," I said. "Geez. You're usually pretty full of shit, but tonight you're, like, *especially* full of shit."

"Why are you acting like this?" he said.

I wanted to yell. Rail long and hard at Cas, but I was just as mad at myself. So I let my hands relax. Took a breath. And patted him on the cheek and said, "I'm sure Gracie misses you." And then I turned and walked into the gym.

30

Jordan met me inside the door. Cas was right behind me. The last thing I wanted to do was stay in Cas's presence, but Jordan cornered us both, slapping hands with Cas and putting his other arm around me.

"Next dance is mine, okay?" he said in my ear. "Nice suit, Kincaid," he called to Cas over the pound of the speakers. Cas just gave him a nod, avoiding my eyes, and disappeared back into the crowd.

When the next pop ballad broke through the speakers, Jordan came and led me out onto the floor.

"Are you okay?" he said, when we began moving to the beat.

"Uh-huh." I was scanning the crowd for Ezra and Lindsay over Jordan's shoulder, hoping desperately not to see them but looking all the same.

"I told him not to go with her."

"I didn't know they even liked each other."

"Just because you go to a dance together doesn't mean you like each other."

Doesn't it? Ezra had asked me. That meant something, or so I had thought. So I had come to hope, at least. Then again, Cas and I had gone to Homecoming together since freshman year, and that meant nothing at all.

"She's way too young anyway," Jordan continued.

"Lindsay?"

Jordan gave me a funny look. "Gracie." There was a pause. "You were talking about our man Ezra."

There was that twinge again. "No, I wasn't."

"Now let's not go telling lies. This is your pal Jordan you're talking to."

"My pal Jordan," I murmured. "Champion of my heart."

"No, you're the champion of *my* heart."

"Can we be each other's champions?"

"Yeah." He smiled. "I'd like that."

I returned the smile as best I could, but then my attention was drawn over his shoulder again. I thought I caught a twirl of cream-colored fabric in the crowd.

"I told him to talk to you, you know," he said after a moment. "I told him a million times. But I counsel a lot of folk, and they don't always take my advice. I don't know why. I'm very wise."

I smiled a little. "You are." I swallowed. "Lindsay's . . . Lindsay's great, though." That was the thing. She was. And they looked . . . picture perfect together, like someone's dream notion of a high school dance. They could print that shit, sell it. I'd probably buy it myself.

"She is," Jordan said. "So are you."

I just *humph*ed.

"Nah, come on. Give yourself some credit."

"If I'm so great, why don't you go out with me?" I couldn't believe my own daring, but I felt close enough to Jordan to say it.

"Oh, I would. But I'm set down for someone else. And I have a feeling you are, too."

Jane would love Jordan. I loved Jordan. I wondered who his lucky person was. They must've been magnificent.

I rested my head on his shoulder. This was closer dancing than propriety called for, but Jordan was my friend, and I needed someone's shoulder. We swayed back and forth to the music.

As per all school dances, eventually the deejay announced the last song and then flashed the lights to signal the end of the dance. I piled into the car with Foster and the highly perfumed Gwin and drove them, with a heavy heart, to Ezra's house.

Foster directed me there, and I pulled up in front of the place. The street was already packed on both sides, so I kept the car running while Gwin gathered up her many layers of tulle and searched the backseat for her purse.

"It's sparkly and it's shaped like a cupcake," she said. "I had it in the gym, didn't I, Foster? You saw me carrying it out, didn't you?"

I didn't register Foster's reply, because I was too busy staring up at Ezra's house. Rather, up at the lush, sprawling lawn that led to Ezra's house. Tall oak trees, a brick path, and then the monster-sized home.

It was grand. It deserved grandiose descriptions, but none came to mind. All I could think was that I didn't know a person could be so rich and manage not to act like it.

"Mom and dad said twelve o'clock," I told Foster, when Gwin finally located the sequined cupcake and extricated herself from the backseat. "Be out here waiting at a quarter 'til, because I don't want to have to park."

"No problem!" Foster said, and with a wave, he escorted Gwin up the brick steps.

I didn't go home. I didn't feel like hanging out for an hour and then going right back, so I went to a diner, settled in with a milk shake, and read some Jane. Edward Hopper could've painted me. *The Glamorous Life of Devon Tennyson.*

I made it back to Ezra's house at the appointed time and double-parked out front, waiting for Foster. Eleven fifty. Eleven fifty-five. I called him twice, but the cell service was shitty.

I sighed and pulled the car down the street in search of a parking space. I didn't know what else to do. Foster had cut loose, apparently, and it would be my ass on the line if we were home later than it already was.

I kept my head bent low as I neared the house, rounding the corner to the backyard. This was possibly the worst social act a high schooler could commit.

In reality, no one looked twice at me. No one gawked or pointed or said anything at all, really, but mentioning that fact wouldn't have made me feel any better. I was plunging headfirst into a pure and unbending sea of embarrassment of the very worst high school variety:

I was crashing a party. But it didn't really count as crashing if you were just picking up someone, right? And, technically, I had been invited. But, technically, the invitation had probably expired in the locker room when I killed the idea of Ezra and me going together.

Don't be noticed, I thought. No one look at me. No one talk to me. I'll just find Foster and leave and never speak of this night again. I'll burn this awful dress for good measure.

"Devon!"

Damn it.

Marty Engelson, a pretty natural choice for linebacker, cut

through the crowd and ran at me, lifting me off the ground and hugging me hard. When he put me down, there was a huge grin on his face. He was a happy drunk.

"*Devon!*" he yelled again, and I cringed. "*Baby! Where you been?*"

"I'm just picking up Foster."

He grabbed my hand. "Come see the guys. Everyone's been missing you."

"I've really got to get home."

"You been party-hopping? Heard there's a great one down at the Holiday Inn. That's where we're headed after this. Had to stop by Ezra's, though—good party, except it'd be a hell of a lot better if he'd just let us in the fucking house. Ezra's all about the rules, you know? And no beer. No drinks. Fucking crazy." He leaned in and whispered thickly, "A lot of us just got drunk before we came. But you got to watch out for Jordan. He'll take your keys, you know."

I got away from Marty as quickly as I could with an "Okay, yeah. Thanks." I ducked my head and continued through the crowd, my phone clamped firmly in one hand. I tried calling Foster again, but I still couldn't get a signal.

As I wandered around searching for both reception and Foster, I took in the surroundings. The porch was strung up with lights, and in the center of the backyard, there was a huge pool. The lights were on underwater, and soft wisps of steam rose from the water's surface. Everywhere you looked, there was a cooler full of soda, a sea of plastic cups. So many brightly colored Homecoming dresses, music that was just loud enough (I was coherent enough to appreciate that), and everywhere the happy, raucous sounds of (mostly) sober partying.

The delicate wisps of steam floating from the pool were upset as someone cut through the air and broke the water's surface, quickly followed by several more people. A cheer rose among the crowd. It was hard to recognize the shapes in the water when they were thrashing around like that, but one figure was undeniable: Ezra.

I was surprised. He was the last person on earth you'd ever fancy jumping into a pool on a whim. I scanned the crowd for Foster once more and tried not to care.

It was only when someone cried out that I looked back at the pool. More people—mostly guys from the team—had jumped in and were all trying to dunk each other. Girls on the sidelines squealed as water splashed their ankles. The boys were all yelling jubilantly, laughing loudly. Someone cried out again.

I blinked. Stanton Perkins, square-headed Stanton Perkins of the defensive line, was gripping Ezra hard and forcing his head under water. I wouldn't have placed the sound if I hadn't seen it escape from Ezra's own lips: a strangled cry caught up in the general chaos.

Stanton pushed Ezra under and wrenched him back up hard by the front of his shirt, only to shove him back down again. Ezra's arms were flailing, but he wasn't fighting back.

All the other guys in the pool were busy messing around. The onlookers were laughing, drinking, dancing, talking loud, taking no notice.

Why weren't they doing anything? Stanton shoved Ezra back under. What was wrong with these people? It wasn't right.

Stanton pulled Ezra up again and I caught sight of Ezra's face. He looked terrified.

All thoughts of Foster left my mind. All thoughts of the crowd were gone. I dropped my phone, kicked off my shoes, and threw myself into the pool.

The water was pleasantly warm, but I took no notice as I kicked over to Stanton. I had never swum in clothes before—a Homecoming dress, no less—and I wasn't ready for how much the fabric would pull me down. Those bridal shop commercials where the bride and groom happily hop into a fountain at their reception are so full of shit. No one would elect to do this.

I had no plan for when I reached Stanton and Ezra, but I knew any attempt to reason with a guy as probably drunk and as definitely stupid as Stanton Perkins was useless. I ducked under the water (a rainbow of ugly dress socks flailed out at me) and closed the distance between us.

I reached them as Stanton was middunk. Stanton looked at me blankly for a second when I surfaced, and I took the opportunity to kick him, hard. I wasn't aiming for any particular place, but I managed to connect with one that was pretty effective.

He let go of Ezra at once, and I seized the front of Ezra's shirt. I don't know what I expected Ezra to do. . . . I guess I figured he'd break away, all offended, and claim that he didn't need my help. Maybe he'd accuse me of crashing his party and have armed security guards escort me from the premises, just for good measure.

But the split-second look he gave me said nothing of the sort. He just wrapped his arms around my neck and held on.

I couldn't support the two of us. My head slipped under, and I pumped my arms and legs furiously to keep us afloat.

"Come on," I choked, kicking frantically. "Come on, swim."

But Ezra didn't swim. He just clutched harder, sinking us both.

Stanton had yelled out in pain, loud enough to call attention to us. A couple of guys swam over and helped guide Ezra and me to the side. A couple of others were keeping Stanton afloat as he cursed loud enough to draw the attention of at least the first tier of on-lookers standing around the pool.

"You fucking bitch!" he yelled as Marty Engelson helped us out of the water and onto the concrete surrounding the pool. Ezra lay on his back, taking big gulping breaths, and I sat there in a puddle of formal wear, unable to stand. I realized I was shaking. "What's your problem?"

I couldn't speak. I had successfully saved Ezra from Stanton, but who would save me?

Before I could think, an object flew through the air and hit Stanton square in the head. It took me a moment to recognize what it was as it bounced off Stanton and landed on the ground nearby: a leather dress shoe.

I looked at the pair of feet standing next to me—one shoe on and one shoe off—and I turned my eyes up to take in Foster's face. There was firm defiance all over it.

"Don't talk about my sister like that."

Stanton pulled himself up and pushed his way through the crowd to our side of the pool. Foster stepped in front of Ezra and me, and in front of Foster stepped Emir Zurivic.

Stanton stopped short.

I hadn't seen Emir all night. His hair was slicked back and he was wearing all black. He stood perfectly at ease, a small smile on his face, his hands in his pockets. "Something wrong?" he asked.

Stanton's lip curled, but he stopped a few feet short of us. Emir wasn't big like Stanton, or aggressive like Stanton, or a bully like Stanton, but Emir was not to be trifled with.

"Yeah. We were just having some fun, and then that bitch went and kicked me for no reason."

"Excuse me?" Emir's smile was dangerous.

Stanton faltered for a moment. "Tell your dumbass friends to leave me the fuck alone," he snarled, and then he shoved off through the crowd, followed by two or three guys who eyed Emir with as much anger as they dared.

Emir turned to Ezra, who was still gulping air, and pulled him easily to his feet.

"There we go," he said, slapping him hard on the back a few times. "No harm done." He turned to the crowd at large, which was looking on in a stunned hush, and gave a simple cry of *"Party time!"* which broke the ice and revived the sounds of conversation.

"Nothing like an evening swim," Emir said, now pulling me up with surprisingly strong arms.

"Thanks. Thank you," I said weakly.

"Don't mention it," he replied, and then, touching two fingers to his forehead in a cool salute, he melted back into the crowd.

I looked over at Ezra, but the spot where he had stood was empty.

31

We found Ezra throwing up on the front lawn. I wasn't sure what to do, but Foster just went up and put a hand on his back, stooping a little with him and saying quietly, "It's okay." Ezra retched a couple more times, spit, and stayed bent over, as if waiting for more to come.

When he finally straightened up and looked at me, the game and the dance and crashing the party all seemed light-years away. "Are you okay?" he asked. He had puke on his shirt, and that black tie was a limp rag.

"Yeah." My voice was strained. "Are you?"

Ezra nodded but didn't speak.

A silence followed that Foster broke only when I gave a particularly violent shiver. "Maybe Dev could have, like, a towel or something."

"Yeah. Shit, yeah, sorry." He turned abruptly and headed up the front steps of the house. After a moment's hesitation, Foster and I followed.

The inside of Ezra's house was just as impressive as the outside, but somehow still managed to feel . . . accessible. Not so chic or expensive-looking that you were afraid to touch anything. Not like walking into a museum.

Ezra had disappeared by the time we got inside, so Foster and I hovered in the entryway; he eyed the rooms branching off the hall past the staircase, and I gathered up the ends of my dress to keep from dripping on the floor. It wasn't really helping.

In a moment Ezra emerged with a big, fluffy towel. He handed it to me and said, "I can grab you some dry clothes if you want."

In Jane's time, that was the sort of thing that propriety called upon you to refuse. The other party would then press you to accept, and then you'd refuse again; and then when they pressed a second time, I guess you'd know they really meant it, or they'd know you'd shown a proper amount of restraint or selflessness or whatever. But people in Jane's time didn't have scratchy department store Homecoming dresses for 45 percent off, and they certainly didn't have them soaking wet.

"Thanks," I said.

Foster stayed in the foyer while I followed Ezra upstairs. I waited in the hall while he went into his room.

There was a whole host of framed photos lining the hallway. A quick survey showed the same cast of characters: a pretty, dark-haired woman and a middle-aged, slightly balding man, posing together on beaches and on the decks of cruise ships. Ezra appeared at varying ages, frowning out of a junior-class portrait, posing on the field in uniform.

I stopped in front of a picture of a middle school–aged Ezra, standing on the banks of a creek and holding up a fish proudly. Behind him, a lanky teenager with a tight smile looked on, a fishing pole resting against his shoulder. What struck me was that I didn't think I had ever seen Ezra look that happy before. Amused, for sure, or pleased, or sheepish, but not like that, not that undiluted, unabashed kind of happy. Was that the kind of thing you lost with age?

"Cute, huh?" someone said. I wheeled around.

I hadn't noticed a door opening, but now light flooded the hallway, and here in its glow stood Marabelle. She was wearing a fuzzy bathrobe and SpongeBob slippers.

"What—what are you doing here?" I asked, even though it was a stupid question. One of her child beauty queen portraits smiled eerily at me from just a few feet away.

"I live here," she said. "Part of the time, anyway. Mostly I stay with my mama, but my daddy got this house so we could all be together, and they have a nice room for me here." She gestured to the picture. "It's cute, isn't it? His daddy used to take them fishing."

"Ezra's dad?"

"Uh-huh."

"I thought he didn't have one."

"They don't talk anymore."

This was news to me. But before I could speak, Marabelle looked over at me, and as if she was seeing me for the first time, said, "Why are your clothes wet?" And in great imitation of Foster, before I could answer, she continued, "Why are you inside? Is Ezra here?" Her eyes grew as wide as saucers. "Did you have sex with Ezra?"

The only thought I could manage to express was, "Why would my dress be soaked?"

"Maybe you were in the shower."

"With my dress on?"

"Who am I to judge a person's tastes?" she said as Ezra's bedroom door opened and he emerged with a bundle of TS warm-up sweats.

"Are you doing okay?" he asked Marabelle.

"Better than Devon," she said. "She's getting water all over the floor."

"Here." Ezra pressed the clothes into my hands. "There's a bathroom at the end of the hall."

"Thanks."

I went into the bathroom and peeled off the dress, letting the ring of fabric slump gracelessly to the floor around my feet. Obviously my bra and underwear were soaked, too, and I silently debated over how to handle that, meanwhile admiring that this bathroom was fully as big as my bedroom.

I resolved to wring out my bra and underwear in the sink and then put them back on, hoping they wouldn't make damp spots through Ezra's clothes. I slipped the T-shirt over my head and pulled on the standard TS warm-up pants, finishing off with a Cavaliers sweatshirt.

The whole house was silent. That is, until I heard footsteps pounding up the stairs, and a small cry.

"There you are!"

Ninety-eight percent of me said I should stay put. But the other stupid, persistent two percent forced my hand to the doorknob and cracked the door a bit so I could stare through.

Lindsay had her arms around Ezra. Why did she have to hug people so much? They were positioned so that I could see her face in the crook of his neck. Her eyes were squeezed shut, and she didn't seem to mind that his hair was still wet as she pressed up against him. Ezra had changed into a getup similar to the one he had lent me—TS sweats and a T-shirt—but Lindsay probably wouldn't even have cared if he was still sporting pool-water formal wear.

"Are you okay? I just heard what happened."

"Yeah, I'm fine." Ezra's voice was soft. "Thanks."

"Where's Devon? Is she all right?"

"I think so."

Why was she standing so close? Why hadn't he let go? I wished I could see his face, but at the same time, I wanted to slam the door shut and never come out again. I could live in this bathroom. It had almost everything I needed. There was even a television on the wall by the bathtub.

But I couldn't tear my eyes away from them, and I couldn't tamp down the dread that welled up inside me at the sight of Lindsay's hand on Ezra's face. For a moment I had no idea why I felt that way, but then all at once the truth rang clear: I wanted it to be my hand. I wanted the license to stand close to him like that, to smooth his hair back from his face.

And suddenly it all made terrible sense. I couldn't account for Ezra, but Lindsay's feelings were crystallizing before my eyes. She had asked me to hint to Cas about Homecoming. But she had never said Cas's name outright. . . . Only that she knew we hung out. And she wanted to *gauge his interest*, but what was there to gauge of Cas? He was clearly into her. Ezra's feelings, however, you needed a fucking Rosetta stone to decipher.

The look she had given me when we were at the mall shopping for dresses, when Maria asked about Ezra and me . . . Her cuddling up to him in the van on the Reeding trip . . .

But she was into Cas, wasn't she? Was I terrible at judging feelings? Or was I only seeing more than what was there between them because I was jealous of her? Because I wanted Cas to trail after me like that?

And all of a sudden my own feelings came into stark contrast as well. The idea of Cas and Lindsay as a couple was annoying, but it could be borne. The idea of Lindsay and Ezra, however . . .

I let the door fall shut.

I don't know how long I stood there, but after a while a knock on the door jerked me out of my thoughts.

"Are you okay, Dev?"

It was Foster. My voice stuck in my throat the first time I tried to speak. I cleared it and tried again. "Yeah. Yeah, I'm fine." I balled up my dress and tucked it under my arm.

Lindsay launched herself at me as soon as I left the bathroom. I hugged her back numbly.

She held me at arm's length. "Devon, you are just so . . ." She looked like she might cry. "You are just the best. You saved Ezra's life tonight, do you realize that? You know he can't swim at all? He never had lessons—you should've had them, Ezra, this is why people need lessons." Yes. This situation right here. They should use it for swim-lesson advertisements at community centers across the country. I could just see the brochure now—Ezra in sweats, me looking bedraggled, and in the forefront, Lindsay Renshaw, glowing and beneficent with a speech bubble above her: *This is why people need lessons.*

She was still holding on to me. "Stanton Perkins is the biggest dumbass—pardon my language—that I've ever met in my entire life, and you're great, Devon. You did a great and brave thing—"

I couldn't deal anymore. It was too much.

"Yeah, no." I broke away and stepped toward Foster, who was holding my phone and my shoes. "It was nothing." I didn't look at Ezra as I said, "Thanks for the clothes, I'll get these back to you. . . ."

Ezra spoke. "Devon."

"We got to get going. Curfew was, like, an hour ago. Come on."
I slipped my shoes on and jostled Foster toward the stairs, but Ezra
followed.

"Dev. Wait."

"We really gotta go," I said, and then I took the stairs two at a
time, burst outside, and powered down the front path, desperate
to put as much space between me and Ezra Lynley as possible.

Foster was quick on my heels. Or at least I thought it was Foster. I neared the end of the front path, but in a few quick strides,
Ezra caught up to me, circled in front, and stopped me dead in my
tracks. If the vast majority of the defenders in the state weren't faster
than Ezra, I don't know why I thought I would be.

"Wait," he said, and he had his hand outstretched toward me,
fingertips just brushing the sleeve of my sweatshirt, gently rooting
me to the spot. I wanted to shrug him off, but at the same time, I
wanted to fall against him and bury my face in his shoulder. I wanted
to commiserate about what had just happened, and make sure he
was okay, and discuss how Stanton really is psychotic. I did none of
the above. I just stood, burning under the light pressure of Ezra's
hand and trying not to cry.

"You're . . ." Ezra searched me out. "You're sure you're okay?"

I concentrated on looking normal. "I'm fine," I said, though
there was a 66 percent chance that the effort it took to keep from
bawling might cause my throat to explode. This was probably not
an accurate statistic, but still. "I'm just tired. I want to go home."

"I'll drive you," he said.

"No." It came out sharper than I intended. "No, it's okay."

"Please."

Over Ezra's shoulder, I could see Lindsay and Foster lingering
on the front steps together. When I looked in their direction,

Foster whirled around to face the house, leaning forward as if something about the storm door was really fascinating. I almost smiled. But then I caught sight of Lindsay, her hands clasped in front of her, biting one lip in a perfect look of friendly concern.

Ezra followed my gaze to the two of them. Lindsay blossomed into a smile at the sight of him, a hopeful sort of smile, like maybe their evening could be salvaged once I left.

I looked away. "It's fine. Really." I stepped to the side, and Ezra's hand just hung there for a moment, reaching for nothing.

He let it fall to his side, and I dared to look at him. Concern played across his face. There was a little crease between his eyebrows that was just begging to be kissed away.

I had to get out of there.

"Well. Yeah," I said, in a loud and flat tone that would've appalled Jane, who had crafted heroines that were much better at exertion than me. "Good party."

It was not a good party. I could think of at least fifteen parties I had been to that were better than this party, and that included one in sixth grade where I was struck with a stomach bug and threw up repeatedly in Ashley Price's bathroom until my parents could come and get me.

On that fucking idiotic statement, I departed.

A pair of footsteps pounded after me, and I braced myself for another encounter with Ezra. But this time it really was Foster.

"I'm sorry," he said. "I'm sorry I didn't come out on time. It's just Gwin kept talking and she had my arm in this death grip, and then she didn't even want to ride with us anymore. She left with Taylor and Jessica and—"

"It's fine," I said, as we motored down the sidewalk.

"It's not. I'm sorry."

I wrenched my car door open.

"Are you mad at me?" Foster said.

"No." Once we were inside the car, the sense of urgency in me began to subside. "No, I'm not mad at you."

I had lost Cas and Ezra in the same night. I stood up to Stanton Perkins, I feared for my life, I ruined my party dress. All at once, I was too tired to cry. So I just rested my forehead against the steering wheel and squeezed my eyes shut.

Foster touched his head to my shoulder, a strange sort of hug. And I was comforted, somewhat.

32

A night like that warranted nothing but sleep—a heavy, all-consuming sleep that would wash away the immediacy of it all. But it wasn't as refreshing as I had hoped, and when I saw Foster's face the next morning, it read as if his sleep had been as restless as mine.

We sat on the couch for most of the day, playing video games and watching crappy TV. I looked over at Foster at one point and wondered who I would've spent a day like this with before he was here. Cas, maybe. But not even Cas could be pinned down for this long. Foster was content to hang out with me for any amount of time. It was kind of funny—the thing that had annoyed me so much about him in the beginning was what I dearly appreciated now.

Gaming and marathoning reruns were a pretty decent distraction, but I couldn't keep last night out forever, and eventually it began to slip in. Cas came first. Fresh indignation welled up in me at the thought of his expression as we stood outside the gym, but there was also embarrassment, and some kind of hurt. There's no way to break up if you never dated someone in the first place, but that's a little how it felt. Maybe not necessarily as final as a breakup, but something had changed between us, intrinsically. I didn't want to think about it too much, didn't want to pick it apart, because it made me sad.

But pushing Cas to the back of my mind just drew Ezra into the forefront. Ezra, with that inexplicable look of concern. Ezra, who was patient with Foster, who didn't question it when we needed him. Yet I wrote him off immediately when he probably needed us.

What did he say on the bleachers that day? *You're easy to talk to.* It was an offshoot of what Rachel had told me: *You're good at talking to people.* I mean, that was a patent untruth right there. If I were so good at talking to people, I would've just talked to Ezra about the Lake Falls game. I would've talked to Lindsay about Homecoming.

Lindsay, golden last night in that gorgeous dress. I realized that she had extended the offer that day at the mall, the offer for us to room together, even knowing that I was planning to go out with the guy she liked. She had treated me better than I had ever treated her, never holding her feelings against me, never begrudging me her regard.

Each revelation made me want to sink deeper into the cushions of the couch. Eventually I would soak right into the fiberfill, a puddle of regret.

It could have been avoided. This couch misery spiral, this . . . loss . . . I could've avoided the bulk of it simply by doing more. I could've given a shit, like Rachel said. Put the effort in.

But what was there to do about it? What could I do now but play *Super Mario Kart* with Foster?

I was quite possibly the worst.

Foster and I stirred from our spots on the couch only for dinner, and that's when my mom and dad broke the news to us—over a meal of Foster's favorite foods.

They were going to California to "finish the process"—finalizing the adoption. It had to be done in the state of Foster's original residence, my mom said. Legal stuff.

"We'll leave Thursday morning and be back late Friday. Do you think you'll be okay, or should we ask Mrs. Patterson to stay over?"

"No!" Mrs. Patterson was our elderly neighbor, and my childhood babysitter. Not that I didn't like spending the occasional evening with her back in the day, but I was way too old to be "minded," as Mrs. Patterson always put it.

"We're going to be fine," I said, taking the volume down a little. "We can look after ourselves for one night." I looked emphatically at Foster. "Right?"

His eyes were on his plate. "Sure."

It was quiet for a moment. "Foster, I know this is all happening really fast," my mom said. "We haven't talked to Elizabeth personally about this, but we thought maybe you'd like to come with us and see her?"

Foster didn't skip a beat. Not a moment's hesitation. "I don't want to miss the game."

"But—"

"He doesn't want to miss the game, Kath." My dad twirled some pasta around his fork and then looked at Foster. "It's a big one, right, bud?"

Foster nodded. "Districts."

"Districts," my dad repeated, and then gave my mom the same kind of emphatic look that I had just given Foster.

We went back to the couch after dinner, only this time Foster set up the Monopoly board on the coffee table. I watched as he arranged the brightly colored bills. He was always banker.

"How come you don't want to see your mom?" I couldn't think of a good preamble, so I just went for it.

"She doesn't want to see me," Foster answered simply.

"You don't know that."

"Don't I?" His face never changed, but he tamped down the Community Chest cards with a little more force than was necessary.

"Maybe it'd be good for . . . closure. Or something."

Foster just shook his head, and when he looked up, his eyes had this odd shine to them. "It's kind of like an inside joke, Dev. You can't really get it because you weren't there. You can't really understand."

There was a pause. I cleared my throat. "Well . . . I wish I could."

"No, you don't."

"You know what I mean."

He looked at me for a moment, and then nodded. "Yeah. Thanks."

33

I wasn't looking forward to school on Monday, but it came and went with little fanfare. I half expected Stanton Perkins to attempt an attack on either Foster or me, but I never even saw him.

I didn't see Cas, either, or Lindsay or Ezra. After such a whirlwind of a weekend, school was actually a little anticlimactic. But blessedly so. I didn't really want any confrontations. I just wanted to do calculus homework and write an essay on Chinua Achebe. To hide myself away in the study cave. I was for college now, remember? I would get into Reeding and someday when I was studying under those oak trees, all this would seem light-years away.

Miraculously, gym class on Tuesday was canceled, and we got a free period. I worked on my college essay in the library and sent up sincere thanks to whoever gave Mr. Sellers's kid pinkeye.

It wasn't until Wednesday afternoon that I saw Lindsay. She flagged me down in the hall on my way to "office hours." At least, she tried to flag me down.

"Devon!" She waved me over from where she stood at her locker. "Could we talk?"

I slowed a bit as I neared. I wanted to talk. I did. But then . . .
I didn't.

"Ah, sorry," I said. "I gotta get to my tutoring thing."

"Just for a second?"

"Super late!" I said, gesturing to my wrist to indicate a watch
that wasn't there.

And I powered to the English room, making it to the door just
as Alex, my tutoree with the Gatsby essay, broke off from a nearby
group of freshmen and jogged up. Excellent. A distraction from my
sheer and utter cowardice.

"Hey. Got questions?"

"Not today. Look!" She flipped back the cover page of her essay.
A big red 87% was marked at the top of the first page.

I deadpanned. "That's not an A."

"Are you kidding?"

"Yeah. That's great. Congratulations."

"High fives for metaphorical shirts."

I slapped her hand, and then she headed off down the hall to
catch up with her friends.

I watched her go, and even knowing that I wasn't really responsible for her grade, that I hadn't done anything wholly remarkable,
I still felt oddly gratified, like I myself had achieved something.
Was this how teachers felt? Was this why they taught people? I
had never given much thought to what it was like to be a teacher.
If I'd had to summarize it before, I would've guessed that it probably sucked. Maybe your students don't necessarily want to be
there, or listen to you, or do your homework. But I guess you can
teach someone something in spite of that. It must make it harder,
but maybe that makes it feel better, somehow, when you actually
succeed.

I was about to head into the classroom when someone called my name. Jordan appeared, cutting his way through the end-of-day crowd with Ezra in tow.

"Champ," Jordan said. "Been looking for you."

"What's up?"

"I, uh, wanted to see if you had the notes for German today."

"I take Spanish."

"Ah." Jordan bobbed his head and then said, "Well, that's all. See you later." And he walked away, leaving Ezra and me standing there.

I glanced at Ezra. He was glaring at Jordan's retreating back.

"Uh," he said after a moment. "So."

"I sort of need to get to tutoring," I said, but the English room was clearly empty.

"I just wanted to . . . So, about Homecoming—"

"Yeah, no, what a night. Cherished senior-class memories. Will scrapbook accordingly."

"Listen, Dev . . ."

Nothing good ever started with *listen*. It was never "Listen, you just won twenty-five thousand dollars." "Listen, I have a huge crush on you." I think the general theory was that you had to tell the other person to listen because you were about to tell them something they didn't want to hear. And I definitely didn't want to hear the end of Ezra's *listen*, because it was probably something along the lines of "I hope we can still be friends."

Did I still want to be friends? What I really wanted was to kiss Ezra's face off. And punch him in the arm. And then kiss his face off some more. That wasn't quite an ideal friendship, was it? That one-sidedness. I didn't want that. But I didn't want to lose him, either. Maybe I could key in on that arm-punching inclination and eventually the kissing thing would subside. Maybe. But not today.

I cleared my throat. "You better hurry or you'll be late for practice," I said. "Got to set that good example, right? Team morale . . . and . . . whatnot." I tried to smile and then retreated into the English room.

The next day, I found myself in the lunch line, scanning the cafeteria to see if Cas was around. We had managed to avoid each other all week; whether this was intentional or not, I wasn't quite sure. And while I looked, I couldn't tell if I was hoping to see him or hoping not to see him.

When the search turned up fruitless, I let out a sigh. The girl in front of me glanced back and gave me a quizzical look.

"New York deli again," I said, pointing to the cafeteria menu by way of an explanation. "They're hitting the pastrami really hard this month."

"True facts," she said, and then faced forward again. A beat later, she turned back. "We have gym together, you know."

For all the marbled rye in the world, I couldn't have told you that this girl was in my gym class. I tried picturing her in the uniform, maybe with the T-shirt tied up, but I drew a blank.

"Yeah," I said, and tried to pretend that wasn't the case. "Hey. Sorry. How's it going?"

"Good."

To try to make up for not recognizing her, I gestured in the direction of another gym class–goer up ahead in line, the hard-core PT–slash–future valedictorian, Amanda Jeffers. She and another girl in line were taking a selfie. Hashtag lunchtime, hashtag adorbs, I could only imagine.

"It's, uh, like a gym class meetup in here today, huh?" I said.

The girl followed my gaze. "Guess so."

"It's funny," I said, watching as Amanda fiddled with her phone, no doubt choosing the best filter to capture that cafeteria glow. "She's actually really smart."

"I know. I have Biology with her. She always scores highest."

I shook my head. "Crazy, huh?"

"Why?"

"I don't know. Because . . . I mean, look at her."

"Just because you like hair and makeup doesn't mean you're stupid."

She said this like it was the most obvious thing in the world.

And I started to say, "I know that," but then I swallowed it back, because . . . did I?

We slid our trays onto the runner, and I glanced over at the girl. I had a nagging feeling that she was judging me, and I didn't like it, which was probably very hypocritical of me.

"Um . . . what's your name again?" I asked, reaching for some fries.

"Sophie," she said.

"I'm Devon."

"I know. We all know." She didn't say this as if it was a bad thing, but again, a glaringly obvious thing. This seemed to be one of Sophie's special skills.

"Sorry, I didn't . . . sorry." I shook my head. "Sometimes you get in, like, a bubble."

"A senior bubble?"

"Maybe. Or just like . . . a person bubble."

A two-person bubble, maybe. Me and Cas against the world. We had always had each other. And with him, I didn't have to bother to have anyone else. I had never really thought about it before, but it was easier to lump people together that way. Like Amanda Jeffers and the PTs—roll them up, an undifferentiated mass of glitter, and relegate them to the periphery. Stick Sophie and all the other Sophies in my life back there, too, indistinguishable, inconsequential. That's what I was used to doing. But that wasn't even remotely fair, was it?

We neared the end of the line, and I scanned the room one more time. Finally, I saw him—Cas, sitting alone at a corner table with an egregiously large pile of cheese fries. We were the last two seniors in the whole fucking world eating cafeteria food, because it was greasy, and more important, it was cheap. But perhaps most important of all, it was convenient. It didn't get easier than crappy TS cafeteria food for lunch. And Cas and I, we were good at what was easy.

I wanted to go over there. But at the same time . . . I don't know. It's a cliché for sure. But maybe easy wasn't good enough anymore.

I looked at Sophie. "Do you want to eat together?"

She raised her eyebrows. "Popping the bubble?"

"I don't know if we can be friends if you're continually sassing me, Sophie."

She grinned. "Can't make any promises. Sass levels are high."

34

On Friday after school Rachel Woodson approached me in the hallway, positively beaming.

"I've been looking for you all day," she said.

"I'm just about to head home—"

"Don't. Come with me."

Rachel was brusque and kind of intimidating, but at the same
time that made everything she said sound like a good idea. So I went
with her to the writing lab.

"I found it this morning," she said as she stuck a sheaf of paper
under my eyes. "The piles got mixed up, the *Herald* stuff got stuck
under the yearbook stuff, so I didn't see it. I don't know when he
even dropped it off, but—"

"What are you talking about?"

"Read it. Read fast."

I looked at the top of the page, which read:

To the editor of the *Herald*:
This letter is in response to your article in last month's
issue about the politics of high school football. I was

featured in that article, and there are a couple of points concerning myself that I'd like to address. That may sound pretty egotistical, and it probably is, but I heard from someone recently that a few details here and there aren't so terrible. So here are some details.

First of all, thanks for the handsome comment.

Second of all, I wanted to speak to the portion of the article that discussed strategies some high school players use to improve their records outside the realm of practice, hard work, etc. I was used as an example in this discussion; as it was stated, I played the first two years of high school at Shaunessy High School, which is a Class 6 team. It was suggested that I made the move from Shaunessy to Temple Sterling's team my junior year in order to get more field time, and thus more opportunities to improve my overall record.

While it's true that stats are really important in high school football today, I can't admit to such a calculated move myself. The truth is that I came to Temple Sterling because my mom got remarried the summer before my junior year. My stepdad's daughter already lived in Temple Sterling with her mom, and he wanted to be closer to her.

I don't typically spread this information around, because I feel like it's no one else's business. At the same time, it's hard for me sometimes to talk about personal stuff, especially when it comes to my family. But I've realized recently that that can be a hindrance, and that maybe sometimes what I justify as reserve is really just not giving people enough credit.

As long as I've got you here, I'd also like to address

the Lake Falls game. Anyone who was at that game may have seen me exercising some pretty unsportsmanlike behavior. I'm embarrassed by how I acted that night, and I'd like to apologize. What I'm about to say isn't meant as an excuse for it, but as at least a little bit of an explanation.

The truth is that Sam Wells's death resonated with me personally, and not just because I knew him. Anyone who knew Sam feels the loss of someone who was a great player and a loyal teammate. But I felt a personal connection to this loss because it isn't the first time I've lost someone in that way. When I was in seventh grade, my brother was killed in a single-car accident caused by drunk driving. My dad was behind the wheel.

It sounds weird that a victory against Lake Falls would mean so much, but for me it would have been sort of a victory against people who act without thinking. It's selfish to think of a game that way. I won't deny that. I try not to let my feelings get the better of me when I play, but I did at the Lake Falls game. For that, and for the way I acted both on the field and off, I'm truly sorry.

The idea that it doesn't matter what other people think about you gets thrown around a lot in high school, and in many instances it's true. But I do care what certain people think of me. I hope that if my actions caused these certain people to lose faith in me, that I can restore that faith, or at least that they'll let me try.

On that note, keep up the good work, editor. I enjoy the Op-Ed pieces, and also when you print the cafeteria menu.

Ezra Lynley

There was a big old lump in my throat. I swallowed hard.

"Are you going to print this?"

"Fuck yeah," Rachel said. "It's good stuff."

Why didn't he tell me? That was the first clear thought I arrived at. I was mad. I was mad at Ezra, not for being a jerk at the game, not for going to Homecoming with Lindsay. Not for anything in the realm of high school bullshit. I was mad because he didn't tell me this. It was like walking into the team locker room after he got the news about Sam, that thought of not knowing when Ezra's business had become our business. But it had. I should've known. Then I would've understood.

"I researched the crap out of him for that article and I didn't find anything about any of that," Rachel continued. "The stepdad, his brother, any of it. Why do you think he'd talk about it now?" She shook her head. "Maybe how he acted at the game . . . maybe there were scouts there. Maybe he had to try to justify getting pulled out so he wouldn't lose face with other schools. . . ."

It was too much. I had too much to think about to deal with Rachel Woodson and her utter hypocrisy.

"Not everything is about college," I snapped. "Not everyone is thinking about their résumé or their record or how to make themselves look good."

"Well, he was trying to make himself look good to someone. I mean, a public apology? It's a bit much. Varsity players act like jackasses at games regularly, and you don't see them waxing poetic about it."

I didn't speak. When I finally glanced at Rachel, she was looking at me critically. "You and Ezra were supposed to go to Homecoming together," she said.

"Yeah, so?"

"So he wrote it for you."

"What?"

"You guys fought after the Lake Falls game, yes?"

Damn small towns with their small high schools and their small high school populations. "How do you know that?"

"Please. Pick a less public spot to have an argument." Her face did something that on a normal person would be considered a smile. "Ezra wrote this letter for you. To save face with you."

"No, he didn't," I said, but looking at the papers in my hand, I had the same suspicion. *Certain people.* Was I *certain people*?

But what about Lindsay? But then again, maybe I was staring down the barrel of two totally different issues. Just because Ezra wanted to clear the air with me didn't mean he wanted to date me.

"Congratulations," Rachel said, and took the letter from my hands. "Your relationship drama got us a major scoop. Star Player Speaks Out: Turmoil and Tears at the Lake Falls Game."

"You're a really shitty journalist, Rachel," I said, and shouldered my bag. "But you'll rule the world one day."

"Tell me something I don't know," she said as I made my way out of the room.

35

I searched for Ezra after I left the writing lab that afternoon, but I couldn't find him anywhere. And I didn't want to text him, or call him—this was a face-to-face kind of conversation.

When I finally located Foster, he told me that Ezra had taken Marabelle to an appointment and wouldn't be back until that night's game. So I went home and tried to study, tried to focus on homework. But fragments of that letter kept surfacing in my mind, and Rachel's firm assertion—*He wrote it for you*—kept ringing out above it all.

The minute the clock struck six thirty, I took Foster back to the field.

But they were already warming up when we arrived. It was the first district game of the year, against Steeleville High School, and no one was taking it lightly.

I positioned myself on the sidelines, as usual, Mr. Harper's faithful luggage rack. He had begun to crack the occasional smile at some of my comments. I think I was slowly wearing him down. By the end of the postseason, he might just trust me with the lens cap, too.

But I wasn't particularly focused on camera duty tonight. I just wanted to talk to Ezra.

The game was good, at least—Steeleville was giving Temple Sterling a run for its money. By the third quarter, we were down by six. Foster had kicked two field goals, and with the field situation, TS seemed primed to take another one. Coach sent Foster in as expected. The center snapped the ball, but no one set it down for him.

It was the fake-out play. The one he had told me about in the Taco Bell/Pizza Hut parking lot, what felt like ages ago.

I didn't even see the pitchout, it happened so fast. Steeleville was quick to catch on, but not quick enough to catch Ezra. He took off up one side of the field, leaving crushing tackles in his wake as the offensive line wiped out Steeleville's defenses.

He stepped over the white line of the end zone. The touchdown was good. The stadium erupted in cheers.

I looked for Foster, but he wasn't in sight. Everyone was picking themselves back up. But Foster was nowhere to be seen.

And then there was this crowd of guys, our guys, forming at one spot on the field.

A call came from them: "We need help over here."

I knew. Like some sick intuition. I just knew. And I didn't think. I dropped the camera bag and ran.

I beat the coaches out, elbowed through the guys, and burst into the center of the circle, and there was Foster.

I thought maybe he pulled a muscle or something. Broke an arm. But he just lay there, unbroken, as if he had simply fallen asleep in the middle of the field.

He looked just like he was sleeping, Dev.

Mr. McBryde and Mr. Evans emerged through the crowd, and

I was jostled aside. The stands were buzzing now. Ezra appeared, too, pushing his way through, still clutching the ball.

"Get back, give us some room, go on," Mr. Evans said, while Mr. McBryde knelt at Foster's side.

"Son?" He tapped Foster's face lightly and then barked "911" at Mr. Evans.

I was numb. I watched, helpless, as Mr. McBryde gently eased Foster's helmet off and said, "Come on now, son."

Ezra dropped to his knees at Foster's side. "Foster." He put a hand on Foster's chest. "Hey. Foster."

Foster's eyelids fluttered.

"How many fingers?" Mr. McBryde demanded.

"Two," he croaked.

"What day is it, son?"

"Friday."

"And who's winning?"

"I don't know. Did we fumble?"

"That's my boy. No, we didn't. Don't try to sit up. EMTs are on their way."

"I'm fine," Foster said, but he didn't look fine.

Mr. McBryde ignored Foster's weak assurances, standing up and ordering the other team members to clear away. I stayed, and so did Ezra, kneeling at Foster's side.

"It'll be okay. It's going to be okay," Ezra said, and he was saying it to both of us, Foster and me, but he looked at me when he said it, and his voice was so steady and calm that I believed him.

After what felt like forever, the paramedics crossed the field with a stretcher.

They asked Foster a series of questions as they checked him

over, shining a light in his eyes and doing all the usual medical drama stuff.

"Are your parents here tonight, Foster?" one of them asked.

For the first time, I found my voice. "No. But I—I'm his sister."

"You want to ride with him in the ambulance?"

I nodded.

"We're probably looking at a concussion," the EMT closest to me said. "Losing consciousness is never good with a head injury, so we need to take him in, get him checked out. But he should be just fine."

We stood watching as they loaded Foster onto the stretcher. He looked particularly gray.

"Are you coming, Dev?" he asked as they started to wheel him off.

"Of course."

Foster threw up in the ambulance. They took him to get a CAT scan as soon as we reached the county hospital. I called my parents while I waited outside the room. They had just left our airport, and it would be an hour or so before they reached home. You would've thought they were still a thousand miles from home, as panicked as I felt, but I tried to keep my voice from shaking when I told them Foster would be fine.

I didn't want to hang up the phone, and when I did, it was just me and the distant hum of machines, the squeak of shoes on linoleum floors. I wanted to call my mom back. The phone felt like a tin can with the string cut, perfectly useless, marooning me here alone. I squeezed my eyes shut and rested my head against the wall behind me.

When Foster got out of his CAT scan, the consensus was that he would be fine. They told me they wanted to observe him overnight. As a minor, he couldn't be released to anyone but an adult anyway.

They put us in a room that was teeny tiny—barely enough space for the bed, one plastic chair, and all that equipment you usually see on TV. They hooked Foster up to a machine that monitored his vitals. Then we were alone.

"Mom and Dad are coming," I said after the nurse left. "They should be here soon."

Foster nodded, and then it was quiet. When I looked at him again, his face was still gray. But not in that just-concussed way he had looked on the field. Jane would say that Foster looked *drawn*.

"You okay?"

"My dad died in a hospital," he said after a pause.

I wasn't expecting that. I just . . . sat. Stupidly. "Yeah?"

"Yeah. And I had to go to one once, after that. I passed out at school and they took me to a hospital. They tried to call my mom, but no one could get ahold of her, and when they finally did, she never came to get me. That's when I got a social worker."

This was one of those times. Like in the kitchen after Sam Wells's funeral. Foster was working through something.

"I could hear them calling," he continued. "On the field? I heard them saying 'son, son,' but I didn't know who they were talking about, because I'm not anyone's son. Not until Ezra said my name . . . then I realized they were talking about me."

Foster's eyes were glossy, and his voice was small when he spoke next. "She never even came to get me from the hospital."

I nodded.

"I know nobody says it, but she was never going to come for me here, either. I know that was never part of the plan."

I looked at the machine, ticking off Foster's heartbeats.

"I'm sorry," I said after a long time, and I was sorry, but I was also uncomfortable, and unsure of what I could possibly say to make anything better. So I didn't speak again, until Foster said, "You said it would be okay if we hated her."

"It is."

"Well, I do."

A pause.

"I think she loved me, though. I think she wouldn't have sent me away if she didn't love me." He looked at me earnestly. "Right?"

I wished very much that my mom and dad were here. They would know what to say to make him feel better. My mom would hug him, and my dad would say the right stuff. But I just let a few selfish tears slip out, not even capable of comprehending how he must feel, because I knew my parents were coming back.

"Right," I said, and it was the first time I ever truly understood what it meant for him to live with us. I had always assumed that he didn't *really* miss her. That he was happier here, because who wouldn't be? We had good food and new clothes and my parents were nice, regular parents who asked you about your day and told you to do your homework. Wouldn't it be a welcome change from someone who cared very little about your existence, and even less about her own?

But she was his mom, and that was his life. It was all he had known.

I looked at Foster. I had also never realized before that I loved him, but I did. And his pain was my pain, and it hurt, but it also felt good in a strange way, knowing that we could share in it together.

I hugged him, and he cried, and it was a long time before I realized that Ezra was standing in the doorway.

"Hi," Foster said thickly as he pulled back from me.

"You want me to come back later?" Ezra said.

"No," Foster wiped his nose on the back of his hand. "It's okay. You can come in."

Ezra stepped into the room.

"Did we win?" Foster asked.

"I don't know," Ezra said. "I left right after you did. They wouldn't let me back here, though. Had to sneak in." He paused. "Are you okay?"

"No," Foster said. His mouth twisted and his eyes flooded again.

Ezra considered this for a moment and then said, "You know what you should do?"

"What?"

"Close your eyes, real tight, and then count to three hundred. That's all you have to do. You just count to three hundred, and when you open your eyes, five minutes will have passed. And even if it hurts or things are shitty or you don't know what to do, you just made it through five whole minutes. And when it feels like you can't go on, you just close your eyes and do it again. That's all you need. Just five minutes at a time."

Foster's eyes were red. He nodded weakly. "Okay."

"Let's do it." Ezra sat down on the edge of Foster's bed and glanced over at me. "We'll all close our eyes."

I closed my eyes, and we counted, "One . . . two . . . three . . ."

By fifty-four, fifty-five, fifty-six, Foster's breathing became even. By one hundred seventy-eight, one hundred seventy-nine, I could hear him settling back against the pillows. At two hundred fifteen, two hundred sixteen, two hundred seventeen, I reached out across the blankets and found Ezra's hand. I squeezed it hard.

We reached three hundred.

I opened my eyes.

Foster let out a long breath, looked at me, and nodded ever so slightly.

I nodded back. He squeezed his eyes shut.

And started to count again.

36

Ezra stayed with us until my parents arrived. My mom was beside
herself. "I can't believe we weren't here," she just kept saying. She
fluffed Foster's pillows about twelve times in the first ten minutes
she was there.

"I'm fine," Foster just kept replying, which was good, because
my mom seemed to need a lot of reassurances. I swear she was just
shy of making him say the alphabet backward and forward, to make
sure they hadn't knocked a few letters out of his brain.

As my parents tended to Foster, Ezra shifted closer to the door.

"Thanks," I said when I noticed this. "For . . . you know."

"No problem."

Ezra had his phone out, and it struck me for the first time how
late it must be. "I bet you want to get home."

He shook his head. "No, I just . . . don't want to intrude."

"You're not intruding."

He smiled a little. And then he held up his phone: "Jordan's
been texting me, like, nonstop from the waiting room."

"He's here?"

"Yeah. I told him Foster was okay, but I guess I should probably go out there."

My parents were occupied with Foster, and Foster, in turn, was occupied with them. So I went with Ezra to the waiting room.

Lindsay, Cas, and Jordan were all sitting out there. They straightened up when we walked in.

"Champ." Jordan jumped to his feet and closed me in a hug. "How's he doing?"

"He's going to be fine."

"Good. Great." He pulled away. "How are *you* doing?"

"I'm okay."

"You look tired," Lindsay said, and then her eyes grew wide. "Not that you don't look great, I mean, you always look great, it's just that—"

"It's okay," I said. "I am tired."

"I could drive you home if you want to get some rest," Lindsay said.

"No, I'm fine. Thanks. Thought about hitting up the cafeteria, though . . . I'm kind of hungry."

"Oh, we stopped at my house," Lindsay said. "After the game. I brought some sandwiches and stuff. Maybe you guys could find some vending machines? Get drinks?"

"Sure thing," Jordan nodded, and he, Cas, and Ezra headed off down the hall.

"I know what it's like waiting at a hospital," Lindsay said to me. "Sometimes you can forget to eat."

I looked at her for a moment as she began unpacking a big lunch box. I didn't know if we were close enough that I could ask her why she had been waiting at a hospital. I decided that we weren't. But then I looked at the sandwich in her outstretched hand and thought about how she'd always been so kind to me, and I decided that we were.

"Why were you in a hospital?" I asked as I took the sandwich.

"My grandpa. He was real sick last year."

"I'm sorry."

She nodded. "We miss him a lot."

It was quiet. When I glanced back at Lindsay, she had a strange look on her face. Before I could speak, she burst.

"Devon, I'm so sorry. I know you have a lot on your mind right now, and it's been a really crazy time for you—for everybody—but I know I've made it harder on you."

"What are you talking about?"

"I never should've asked Ezra to go to Homecoming with me."

That was not what I was expecting, and it wasn't really an avenue of conversation I wanted to explore. "You don't have to—I mean, you had every right to ask whoever you wanted." My thumbs suddenly became very interesting. All opposable and whatnot.

"No, look, I knew that—I heard that you and he weren't going together anymore, and I just thought . . ." She screwed up her face, near tears. "It's so terrible, it's horrible, I just wanted to make you and Cas jealous. I'm so sorry."

I blinked. "You don't like Ezra?"

"Not like that."

"But Ezra must . . . like you?"

"Why?"

"Because you're you. And . . . he said yes to you, and . . ." And it made sense. He was good and she was good; they just made sense.

"No, he didn't even want to go. I really had to twist his arm." Lindsay's eyes were wide. "And it was terrible, Devon. Literally, we got into the gym, we stayed for, like, twenty minutes, and then we spent the rest of the time at his house setting up for the party. I strung the lights and he just . . . stared sullenly at the ice cube trays."

I smiled a little.

"I was so mad about Cas showing up with that . . . that *fetus* Gracie Holtzer."

It was the most contemptuous thing I had ever heard her say. I couldn't help but grin. "Gracie's pretty fierce, actually. She had a guy punched for me in gym. It was like witnessing a mob hit."

Lindsay was still upset. "I'm sure she's great. I just . . . I felt terrible, and all the worse because I knew that I had wronged you, too."

"You didn't—" I shook my head.

"I should've talked to you. Roommates have to communicate, right?" she said, with a hopeful little smile.

"Right," I said. And then I paused. "Lindsay, I think—I know—that Cas really likes you. He just does stupid stuff sometimes."

"Like Ezra saying yes to me even though he's clearly in love with you?"

I choked, and coughed, and sputtered, and then said, "Sort of. Maybe. If that's the case."

"Devon, that's the case."

I made some incoherent noise of dissent and fumbled with the plastic wrap on the sandwich. For a second I considered further pressing her to consider Cas, but ultimately I didn't say anything. At this point, I didn't know if he even deserved her. I resolved to leave the rest up to fate.

37

Lindsay, Cas, and Jordan stayed as long as Lindsay's curfew allowed. We all walked out to the parking lot together when it was time for them to leave.

Inevitably, Lindsay closed me in a hug.

"Thanks," I said. "Thanks for coming."

She pulled back. "You're the best, Devon."

Another patent untruth. But Lindsay was generous enough to believe it.

"So what we were talking about before . . ." Lindsay looked over to where Ezra stood, talking with Jordan. She then looked back at me, and back at Ezra, and in case I didn't get it yet, raised her eyebrows emphatically.

"What about it?"

"I really think you should, you know, give that, uh . . . soup . . . a chance."

"Soup?"

"You know. That soup we were talking about. I think you should give it a shot. It's a really . . . good recipe. Highly dependable. And obviously delicious." Her eyes widened. "Not that I would know. Not that I've tasted the soup."

"This is not a flawless metaphor."

She grinned. "I'm just saying, the soup obviously likes you; and if you like the soup, too, you should just . . ."

"Don't say 'eat the soup.'"

"That's not . . . you're right. I suck at metaphors. But you know what I mean. You deserve good soup."

"You do, too." I glanced over at Ezra and Jordan, and beyond them, to where Cas was lingering. "But, you know, it's not all about soup. There's also . . ." I waved a hand, encompassing her and me. "Grilled cheese and stuff."

"Yeah." She bobbed her head. "Yes." A pause. "We're the grilled cheese?"

"The grilled cheese is our friendship."

She smiled. "Good."

I hugged her again. Maybe she was wearing off on me a little. "Good night, Lindsay."

"Night, Devon."

Lindsay moved to say good-bye to Jordan and Ezra, and then, with just a glance at Cas, headed off toward her car. Cas watched her for a second and then turned to me.

"You're good, right? Everything's . . . okay?"

I wasn't sure if he was asking with respect to what had happened this evening or if there was some broader question there. "Sure. I guess."

"Cool." He paused. "Maybe you'll call me tomorrow?"

Maybe I would. It wouldn't be like it was, though. Curled up under the covers, wanting him to be the last person I spoke to before I fell asleep. Waiting for the final-act reversal. It wasn't coming, and I knew that now.

"Yeah, maybe," I said.

He nodded and looked to Jordan. "See you at school, man." And then he jogged off in Lindsay's direction.

I could've watched them in the distance. Like watching them in the van on the way to Reeding, I could've drawn up that sting of the unrequited, that hurt that you're willing to bear because at least it connects you to the other person in some way. But I didn't. I didn't want to anymore.

After Cas's departure, Jordan slapped Ezra's hand, kissed me on the cheek, and headed away.

And then Ezra and I were alone.

"Back inside?" he said after a moment.

"Don't you want to get home?"

He shrugged. "I'm good here."

I looked up at Ezra Lynley, who was, according to Rachel Woodson's crap article, one of the best high school running backs in the country. He was also best friend to Foster. He led the charts in generosity and loyalty and honor. At least in my book.

I swallowed and was about to speak, but then I noticed something. Or rather someone, hanging around the big concrete ashtray that stuck unceremoniously out of the ground a couple of parking lot lights down.

"You go inside," I said to Ezra. "I'll meet you in a sec." He raised an eyebrow in question. "I just need a minute to myself."

Ezra nodded and then headed in.

"Emir?"

The orange tip of his cigarette flared as I stepped into his ring of lamplight. He exhaled, blowing the smoke behind him.

"What are you doing here?" I asked.

"I was at the game. I followed the caravan over."

"Did you put money down on Foster making it?"

"If I had, would I be happy?"

"Yeah, you'd be happy."

"Good to hear."

He took another draw on the cigarette. I watched and then took a step closer. There was something I had been meaning to say to him.

"At the party, with Stanton, you looked out for us. Thank you for that."

He shrugged. "Yeah, well. I like you."

I opened my mouth to speak and nothing came out.

"Not like that. Don't worry. I know you'd rather have the strong, silent type."

"How do you know that?"

"Everyone knows it."

That was the same thing Cas had said at Homecoming. I guess I was no sphinx.

"Your family took in your cousin," Emir said after a moment. "And I always see you with him." A pause. "Our family here took in my mom and my sisters and me when we first came. It's nice when people do the hard thing."

"It's not hard."

"It's not easy, either."

"Why did you leave home?" I asked.

"It's complicated."

I nodded. I didn't think he was going to go on, but after a long pause, he threw his head back and looked at the sky and then said, "We had this big old tree outside our house. The kind with a rope swing. Older than the house. Older than my parents."

When he didn't continue, I prompted, "Yeah?"

"Yeah. They burned it down."

He took another draw and exhaled. "And we knew it wasn't safe anymore to be there. It was like . . . a turning point or some shit. We had to go." He smiled a little, up at the stars. "It's funny, it was kind of pretty in a fucked-up way, burning like that."

He met my gaze for a moment and I saw it. Just for an instant, it was the look I had searched his face for before—the indication of past tragedy. I recognized it now, and in that instant, I was grateful to be boring Devon Tennyson, extraordinary in how unextraordinary my life had been.

We stood in silence while Emir finished his cigarette. He crushed the butt in the concrete ashtray, gave me a nod, and walked off into the darkness.

38

After Jordan and Cas and Lindsay left, after the conversation with Emir, after my parents told me for the fifth time to go home and get some sleep, Ezra and I went downstairs, ostensibly so he could give me a ride home.

But I didn't want to go, and Ezra knew it, so we just hovered by his car. He fumbled with his keys, and I said something mindless about the weather, to which he very kindly replied with something equally mindless.

Only after a few more similar back-and-forths did he look at me and say, "I'm glad Foster's okay."

"Me, too."

"I . . . I'm sorry," he said. "I told you I would look out for him and I should've . . . that shouldn't have happened. He shouldn't have gotten hurt."

"Ezra, what would you have done to stop it? Acted as Foster's human shield?"

"I told you I would look out for him."

Like a brother would. "So . . . about that letter—"

"Did you—so you read it?"

"Yeah. You didn't have to do that."

"I did."

"But not like that. Now you're going to have Rachel Woodson trying to buy your life rights so she can write a Lifetime movie."

"'He's Kind of a Dickhead: The Ezra Lynley Story'?"

"You're not," I said. "But you could've just told me. I would've . . ." I shrugged. "You could've told me."

"I know. I was scared."

"Why?"

"Because . . ." A pause. "Because I'm ashamed."

"Of what?"

He didn't answer at first. Just passed his keys from one hand to the other for a moment and then, finally, said, "It's like Foster's mom. He doesn't go around talking about her and it's kind of for the same reason, I think. They're part of who we are. We're like a reflection of them. So what they did is like . . . some extension of us."

"It's not . . . it's not like your dad did it on purpose, right?"

Ezra shook his head. "He didn't have to get in the car. If he hadn't, Nick would still be alive."

Tragic deaths aren't avoidable. That's what Ezra said outside Sam's wake, and even though—to use Foster's phrasing—I didn't know anything about anything, I felt in this moment that Ezra was wrong. What often makes something tragic is that it *can* be avoided.

"I saw a picture," I said, "in the hall, at your house. You guys fishing. He looked . . . he looked like a good brother." I had no rational proof for that assessment. I could barely recall what Ezra's brother looked like in that picture; he was eclipsed in my mind by young Ezra's grinning face. But it felt like something that needed to be said, some affirmation, some . . . recognition, of what was lost.

"He was," Ezra said, nodding. "He was." It was quiet for a moment and then, "It's weird. Sometimes it feels like we're still the ones in the pictures, and everything that happened after happened to other people. And then sometimes we're the other people, and the strangers are in the frames."

I nodded, even though I didn't really understand. It was like Foster said: I could never really get it. I could never really understand. But I could strive for empathy. I could at least do that.

"So with Foster . . . was that the secret? He said you guys had a secret. Is it that you both . . . get it?"

"No." Suddenly Ezra made a face, and when he spoke next, it came out rushed. "Dev, I was really, really stupid to go to Homecoming with Lindsay. I mean, that was just . . . dumb."

I wasn't expecting such an abrupt turn. Suddenly I couldn't meet his gaze. I was too embarrassed. "I don't know. If she had asked me, I probably would've said yes."

He huffed a laugh, but when he spoke again, his tone was serious. "I kind of panicked. I thought you'd be there with Cas. From everything Lindsay said, I thought you and he were . . ." He trailed off.

"Yeah," I said again, forcing more life into my voice. "I, uh . . . I was kind of convinced that you and she were, like, totally in love or something."

"No. No way. I mean, we're friends, and she's really cool, but she's not . . ."

His type? I flashed on Foster saying that in gym class, what his type was. Whose type was less like Lindsay Renshaw?

"What, you like 'em flawed?" I couldn't help but say. "Wooden teeth and backward hands and stuff?"

259

"Backward hands?"

My face was red. "You know, when, like, the backs are where the palms are supposed to be, and . . . vice versa . . ."

"Yeah, I know loads of girls with backward hands. Those are the ones you gotta watch out for."

"Shut up."

He smiled, and some circuit closed inside me, some charge beginning to flow.

"Dev, you have to know by now . . . you were the secret."

"What?"

"You want to know why I partnered with Foster, that first time in gym class? Because I knew he was your cousin. And partnering with you had been kind of disastrous, so I thought the next best thing would be to show you that I could at least be decent to him. Obviously afterward I realized how cool Foster is, and that we had stuff in common, but initially it was just . . . I just wanted you to like me."

It was said in such a guileless manner, like one of those first-grade notes, DO YOU LIKE ME, CHECK YES OR NO. All I could do was stare at Ezra.

"You liked me since that first gym class?"

He nodded. "Since I said 'get a ball' and you said 'get it yourself.'"

"That's when the liking started?"

"The initial liking, yes."

"You had a weird way of showing it."

"Yeah, well, I tend to make a pretty shitty first impression. And second and third and fourth and fifth impression." There was a pause. Ezra shifted back and forth for a moment. "So . . . did I ruin it?"

"Ruin what?"

He shrugged. "Any chance for . . . an attachment."

My hand struck out and hit him on the shoulder before I could think. "That's Jane Austen. You read Jane Austen!"

He nodded. "I went and bought that book you had after I found it at the field."

"*Sense and Sensibility*? Why?"

"So I'd have something to talk to you about. I don't know if you've noticed, but conversation isn't exactly one of my strengths."

"How were you going to work it in?"

"I don't know. Maybe if we were hanging out, and there was a conversational lull, I could be, like, 'Man, that Willoughby's a dick, right?'"

"He's not, really. He is but he isn't. Mr. Wickham's the real douche bag of Jane's work."

"Yeah, Wickham. I fucking hate that guy."

"You read *Pride and Prejudice*, too?"

"I thought it was, like, a sequel or something."

No one had ever read a book for me before, let alone two. Eighth-grade boyfriend Kyle Morris asked me out via text message.

"I don't know how to talk like they do," Ezra continued after a moment. "But . . . I feel about you the way they feel in those books. The way those guys feel about those girls that they don't always deserve."

I met his gaze for a second. That was all I could manage, torn between embarrassment and elation. "Some of them are really deserving," I said. "Some of them are great. And not at all douchey."

He grinned, crooked bottom teeth and all. "Not at all douchey. That's awesome. I should put that on my résumé."

I laughed, a short breath of laughter. And then it was quiet.

And for a moment more there was space between us and I was acutely aware of it, and then suddenly there was significantly less space. Ezra moved, or I moved, I don't know—it doesn't matter, because there was Ezra Lynley, eyes turned down as he slipped his hands around my waist. I rested my hands on his shoulders as if we were going to dance a middle school dance, but there was no room for the Holy Ghost, or being nervous, or awkward; it just felt right. Intensely right, intensely excellent, and then he looked at me and it was that most golden moment of Jane's books sprung to life. It was the getting-together part.

The remaining space between us disappeared. Ezra and I kissed.

A vague thought skirted through my mind of *so this is what kissing feels like*, but then all I could really focus on was Ezra, his mouth, his hair, those arms circling around me and holding tight.

A thousand electric cars could run on how you feel when you know that the person you like likes you back. It feels incredible. Like it shouldn't be possible. Of all the happy coincidences to ever exist, it's one of the happiest.

And yet, when Ezra and I kissed, there weren't fireworks igniting the night sky, or an orchestra swelling, or any of the other hackneyed clichés that feature prominently in tweenhood imaginings of first kisses. We didn't proceed to ride off on horseback to his sprawling estate and ten thousand pounds a year. We just kissed, and it was . . . thoroughly awesome . . . and then I leaned against him and we stood that way for a while, arms around each other. Ezra didn't count to three hundred this time. His breathing was even and steady, and there was just this pure, unadulterated, highly concentrated happy. Baking chocolate for the soul.

After a while, we kissed again and said good night, and then kissed some more, and then, finally—just another long kiss, three short kisses, and a scattering of little ones—Ezra got into his truck and drove away. I watched his taillights disappear in the distance, and then I headed back in, my insides feeling like warm honey, my lips red with fun new sensations.

"You look weird," Foster said when I finally entered his room again. My parents glanced up, but if they noticed anything amiss, they were kind enough not to say.

"Your face looks weird," I replied.

"*Devon*," my mom said, but she was smiling.

39

They released Foster early in the morning. He was ordered to rest and take a hiatus from games for the rest of the season. Foster balked at this, but my dad pointed out that going back in too soon might preempt the three more years of games that Foster had to look forward to. After that, Foster seemed pacified.

My parents drove us to the field so I could pick up my car. To my surprise, Foster wanted to ride the rest of the way home with me. And to my even greater surprise, my parents actually agreed. I didn't think they'd let Foster out of their sight so soon, but as we left the parking lot, I could see in my rearview mirror that they were tailing us closely.

It was quiet in the car, but there certainly was a lot to reflect on. The evening at the hospital had been eventful, to say the least, and I don't think I had ever felt more fortunate. I had friends who came, and waited, and brought sandwiches, and *cared*. I had Ezra, and Ezra's smile, and I had kissed that smile, and it was freaking awesome. I had Foster, and he was okay.

There was so much to appreciate, but at the same time, it pained me to know that in some ways, Foster *wasn't* okay, that he hurt, that he mourned the life he knew before.

I glanced over at him when we reached a stop sign.

"How's your head?"

"A little sore."

"You need some rest." I paused. "You're all right, though?"

He shrugged. And then,

"Marabelle broke up with me."

Foster didn't look upset. At least not by what I could see out of the corner of my eye.

"I'm sorry," I said. "When?" It seemed pretty cold to dump someone while they were actively in the hospital. But Marabelle hadn't even been there last night.

"The other day. After practice."

"Why didn't you tell me?"

"It's not like we were even together, really. But she just said . . . she said she can't be my girlfriend or anything."

"She's got a lot of stuff to focus on right now."

He nodded, and after a pause, said, "I wish . . ." He shook his head. "Sometimes I wish that things were different. Is that terrible?"

"No," I said. "No, I don't think so."

It was quiet.

"Did you and Ezra talk?"

"We did."

And he had texted me, early: *Good morning.*

It is, I replied. *Did you sleep well?*

He had answered with three messages, in short succession:

No.
But in a good way.
I was too happy.

I had stared at the words on the screen, straight from Ezra's fingertips to the palm of my hand. It didn't seem like there was such a thing as too happy, but I knew what he meant, and I felt it, too— that kind of happy that radiates from your core, feels too big to possibly contain.

"So you guys are together now?" Foster asked.

"We're something," I said.

"Well, you were always something."

I smiled. That was Foster. Zip Lip Foster. Early-morning smoothies and the like, the great big giant pain in my ass, the brother I never knew I wanted. A page in the story of my life that I never could've anticipated.

I started thinking about those pages. Reeding, and Cas, and car rides with Foster, and loving Ezra were all their own pages. And suddenly I was filled with this feeling—like the resolve that filled me when we visited Reeding, that insane desire to try harder, to *be better*—I was filled with this feeling that there was nothing we couldn't get through three hundred seconds at a time, three hundred words a page.

I pulled into the driveway and looked over at Foster, and I couldn't help but think of what Ezra had said, how sometimes it felt as if everything that had happened to his family had happened to other people. How would Foster feel, seeing old pictures of himself? Was it all something that happened to another person, or was he the stranger now? Maybe a little bit of both. He and I were different people, before we had each other. But I wouldn't trade places with that other person now.

"Well . . ." I said, finally. "We're home."

He looked up at the house—our house. And after a moment, "Thanks for the ride, Dev."

"No problem."

Foster nodded and then got out of the car. I opened my door and followed.

ACKNOWLEDGMENTS

Thank you to everyone involved in the creation of *First & Then*, with particular thanks to Kate Farrell, editor extraordinaire, and Bridget Smith, champion agent. Thanks to all the lovely and talented people at Henry Holt Books for Young Readers and Macmillan, who have made this such an incredible experience.

Additional thanks to:

Mama and Papa, for everything. Hannah and Cappy, for all the lurv. Becky, Sara, Wintaye, the greatest friends and my earliest readers. Mike and Sarah, for all the awesomeness. Josh, for the enthusiastic support! Rochelle, for the beta. Danting, Sreeparna, Adam, for help in title selection. John, who read half of this book in 2010 and said, "I think there's something there." (It meant a lot to me.)

Thank you to the members of the Elmify and How to Adult communities. Your support and kindness have meant more to me than I could ever express. Consider with these words the sincerest of slow-motion high fives.

first & then

then

Bonus Materials

GOFISH

EMMA MILLS

What book is on your nightstand now?
I like to keep a pile of books on my nightstand! At the moment, from top to bottom is: *One More Thing* (B. J. Novak), *The Real Jane Austen* (Paula Byrne), *Murder at the Breakers* (Alyssa Maxwell), *The Wind-Up Bird Chronicle* (Haruki Murakami), *Persuasion* (Jane Austen), and several copies of *First & Then* (I must admit, I like having it close at hand!).

What was your favorite book when you were a kid? Do you have a favorite book now?
Many, many favorites, both as a kid and as an adult! Of particular meaning to me are the favorites from childhood that have remained favorites over the years—I'd cite *From the Mixed-Up Files of Mrs. Basil E. Frankweiler* by E. L. Konigsburg and *The Twinkie Squad* by Gordon Korman as prime examples! And of course, a cherished favorite of mine will always be *Pride and Prejudice* by Jane Austen.

What did you want to be when you grew up?
A writer!

Did you play sports as a kid?
Not even a little bit.

Where do you write your books?
The couch at home is my standard writing spot. But weather permitting, I love to write outside my favorite coffee shop. There's a chair out front that I consider "my chair." I feel rather territorial about it!

If you could live in any fictional world, what would it be?
Harry Potter's world for sure, but preferably at a more peaceful time in wizarding history.

***First & Then* captures the dynamics of high school so perfectly. What were you like back in high school? Do you see yourself in any of your characters?**
I do see a little of my high school self in Devon—particularly in her ambivalence about the future and her desire for everything to stay the same. But I think I was also a bit of a Rachel Woodson back then! Perhaps not quite so directed as Rachel, but I was fairly focused on grades and extracurriculars and the notion of all-caps ACHIEVEMENT.

The relationship between Devon and Foster is one of the most poignant in the novel, and its progress from resentment to affection hits all the right notes. Can you describe how you went about developing this relationship?
I knew where I wanted Devon and Foster to start and where I wanted them to end up—a journey from being almost-strangers to really coming to love and care for each other. Over the course of the writing process, their relationship developed very organically for me. Foster is so instrumental to Devon's growth, and Devon really becomes an anchor for Foster. Their relationship is one of my favorite aspects of the book and was such a pleasure to write.

Devon's narration is individual, honest, and oftentimes hilarious. What was your process (if any) for writing and staying true to her voice? How did you come up with it?

I think—for me at least—some characters need time and effort to really pin down, while others spring into your mind pretty much fully formed. Devon was definitely more of the latter. In telling this story through Devon's eyes, I just tried to stay true to who I felt she was—someone who may be a little apathetic, a little judgmental, but at her core, has a good heart and such a capacity for growth.

Some of the plot of *First & Then* is informed by *Pride and Prejudice*, and Devon herself makes a few references to Jane Austen and her works. Can you tell us a little about the inspiration behind this?

I read my first Jane Austen novel (*Pride and Prejudice*) when I was sixteen. It had such a profound effect on me, I immediately went out and got *Sense and Sensibility*, *Mansfield Park*, and *Emma*, and read them all in quick succession! So Devon's love of Jane Austen is a little reflective of my love of Jane Austen. Austen's sense of the world she lived in and the way she expressed herself is just so beautiful and witty and creative. I hope to capture even a fraction of that in my writing.

Sloane isn't expecting to fall in love with a group of friends when she moves from New York to Florida. Yet that's exactly what happens. Wrapped up in their world of private tragedies, secret codes, and intense affections, Sloane is in for a life-changing adventure.

Read on for an excerpt!

one

My immediate priority is air.

Bree has dragged me to a house party, and the place is too warm. Everything is a little too close.

I don't like being in a stranger's house at the best of times. Seeing the pictures on someone else's fridge, the knickknacks on their mantel, whether or not their toilet-paper roll goes over or under . . . that stuff is personal. To be so outside of it, and yet still privy to it, feels like some kind of a violation.

I can't say this to Bree. So I just listen in on one more conversation about whether Jen and Asher from calculus are finally "official" ("Do they need to be notarized?" I ask, and no one laughs), and then I make my way to the kitchen to escape out the back door.

Unfortunately, escape is barred.

"It's not a big deal," this kid is saying, pitching his voice over the thrum of the room. Clearly it is a big deal, because a ring of onlookers has formed around him. It's that sort of Shakespearean chorus that pops up at parties like this, to observe and cast judgment and report back to the masses later.

I'm only three weeks in at Grove County High School, but I recognize the speaker from my AP biology class. His name is Mason, and he sits at the lab bench in front of mine.

I also recognize him from the pages of my father's novels. In a few short years, Mason could be the sheriff's son who backhands the preacher's daughter, or the ex–high school quarterback hell-bent on avenging some romantic slight. Guys like him were a dime a dozen in Everett Finch's world, and they usually died in a fire.

"She doesn't want to talk to you," the guy standing directly across from Mason says.

"And how the hell do you know that? Twin magic? When she's hit on, you feel it, too?"

The guy doesn't reply, but there is this look in his eyes, a quiet rage that I wouldn't have messed with had I been Mason.

"Really, you should be thanking me," Mason continues. "I don't think she's a lost cause. I could help her turn shit around."

Mason steps into the other guy's space, eliciting a quiet but firm "Don't."

"Or what?"

The guy doesn't respond.

"Or what?" Mason repeats, and steps even closer. In different circumstances, they'd look for all the world like they were about to kiss. Mason's lips curve upward into a smile. "Is this getting to you? Are you wired wrong, too?"

"Don't" is all he says again.

"Come on, it's not like you're going to hit me. You want to know how I know?" When the guy doesn't answer, Mason reaches out and puts his hands on either side of the guy's head, forcing it up and down in a nod. "Yes, Mason, I want to know." And then he moves one hand to the guy's face, smushing his cheeks between his thumb and forefinger. "'Cause you're a *nice fucking guy, Fuller.*" He squeezes with each word.

The guy still doesn't move, and maybe Mason is right—maybe he won't hit him. Maybe he's too solid to respond.

But I'm not.

"Sorry," I say, angling through the people in front of me. "I'm sorry. So sorry. Don't mean to interrupt. It's just . . . are you for fucking serious?"

Mason looks at me, his hand still grasping the guy's face. Surprise cuts through his smirk. *A girl is volunteering to talk to him*, I think, and in that moment, I know which tack to use.

So I tamp down the outrage and manage something like a smile as I reach out and close my fingers loosely around Mason's wrist. A soft touch. He lets me guide his hand away without protest.

"I mean . . . these hands aren't really meant for that kind of thing, are they?"

His eyes track me as I lace my fingers together with his.

"These hands are for . . . for caressing," I continue. "For stroking, even."

"Oh yeah?" Mason says with a dumb little smile. His target just stands there, altogether forgotten.

"Yeah," I say. "Yourself. In front of the TV. Alone. Every night."

Mason doesn't get it right away, but there's a hoot from the crowd and a few barely suppressed guffaws.

"If nothing else, you can at least use them to grasp for intelligence, or like, some semblance of human decency."

The crowd reaction amps up, like a sitcom soundtrack. Mason wrenches his hand out of mine.

"What's your problem?" he says.

"Your face," I reply, because that's what my sister, Laney, would say.

"Fuck you," he says, but he's lost control of the room. The chorus is already buzzing. "Fuck this." He smiles with too much teeth. "Got yourself a guard dog, huh, Fuller? Emphasis on *dog*." Like this will somehow hurt my feelings. But that's assuming I have them in the first place.

When I don't react, Mason shakes his head and retreats, the chorus folding in around us. I look back to where the guy had been standing, but he's already headed out the back door.

Bree appears at my elbow, clutching a plastic cup. Her cheeks are red, and she is grinning. "Geez. That was—was that a New York thing? Do they teach you that kind of stuff there?"

Yes. Here is your MetroCard, and this is how you publicly dismantle insufferable dicks.

"It was a person thing. That guy was an ass."

She shakes her head, still grinning. "Geez."

"What?"

"Gabe Fuller." She gestures in the direction of the guy's retreat. "You stepped in for freaking Gabe Fuller."

"Yeah," I say, because I don't how to respond to that.

A kid I vaguely recognize from my lit class comes up then, holding his hand up for a high five.

"That was hilarious," he says.

I slap his palm, but suddenly it's too close in there again, too much, so I excuse myself and make my way to the door.

It's quieter outside. There's just the low hum of crickets and the soft smack of a couple making out on the porch swing. The chains attaching the swing to the ceiling rattle as she adjusts, he adjusts. One of them sighs, a soft little sound.

I ignore them, bracing my hands against the railing. The night air hangs thick with late-summer humidity, but a few deep breaths still put me right.

Some scraggly trees populate the backyard, and there's an attempt at a garden—a trellis hung with vines, a couple of thorny-looking bushes. The ground is a study in that patchy North Florida grass, which is mostly just sand and a thick coating of live oak leaves. The leaves shine in the light from the motion-sensor bulb on the garage. That same light throws two figures at the end of the yard into stark relief.

I can't hear them from where I stand. Rationally, I know it's none of my business. But I step off the porch anyway and move across the yard toward them.

"I told you we shouldn't have gone to a non-Frank-sanctioned party," the girl is saying as I near. I'm shielded a bit by the shadow of the trellis.

"Why were you even talking to him?"

"He talked to me first. I'm not just going to ignore another human being. We can't all stare through people, Gabe."

"Yeah, well, try. Look at them, and instead of seeing them, see whatever's behind them. And then ignore that, too."

"Yeah, that's a super healthy approach. Super great social skills."

"Mason Pierce doesn't deserve your social skills. He doesn't deserve the hair in your shower drain."

"Who does deserve the hair in my shower drain? Should I start mailing it to Tash? Do you want me to save you some?"

"I swear to God—"

The end of that oath never comes, because it's then they realize I'm there.

Somehow at the sight of me, the guy—Gabe—looks angrier than before. It's not that quiet-rage burn, but more of an outward hostility.

The girl, on the other hand, smiles wide. It lights up her face. "Hey. It's you."

It's such a strange thing to say—like somehow I was expected—that all I can do is nod. "It's me."

"I didn't need you to do that," Gabe says.

"Thank you," the girl amends, "is what he's trying to say."

"I didn't need you to do that," he repeats, and for some reason, his irritation irks me. I did a thing. Stepped in. Dismantled a bully. I could've gone on and done nothing, like the rest of fucking Solo Cup nation in there. "I didn't need anyone's help. Everything was under control."

"So the part where he plied your face like Play-Doh was a critical step in your plan?"

The girl snorts, and Gabe shoots her a glare.

"I was fine," he says tightly. "Next time, don't help."

I nod. "Okay. Sure." But I am incapable of leaving it at that. "'Cause if this world needs anything, it's more passive witnesses to injustice, right? The U.N. should adopt that model. Amnesty International. Forget the barbed-wire candle—their symbol should just be like a guy leaning against a wall with his arms folded and a speech bubble that says 'Want to help? Next time, don't.' Someone should really get the number for the Gates Foundation and let them know."

"That's not what I'm—" Gabe begins, but once I start, it's kind of hard to stop.

"Hey, I know scientists are super busy trying to find cures for diseases and stuff, but maybe at this point in time they should just try *not* doing that—"

"I didn't say—"

"Humanitarian aid workers," I call out, like the yard is full of them. "Lay down your instruments of change, because 'Don't help' is the societal model we're going with now—"

"Okay," he says loudly. "Okay, fine, yes, I'm sorry. Thank you. For helping. Thanks. Please just stop."

The girl bursts out laughing. Gabe glares at her.

"Sorry," she says. "Just . . . your face. God. So good." She points at me. "You're great. You're staying. We're keeping you."

Gabe looks at her and then at me, and for a second I think he might laugh, too. His lips twitch, at least, and the corners of his eyes crinkle up a little as he looks away. It's almost as if something has been defused inside him. Like the right wire has been cut.

"Who are you again?" he says.

"Sloane," I reply. "Who are you?"

"Gabe. Fuller. This is Vera." He waves a hand at the girl. Framed in the light from the garage, I can see they favor each other—similar in the line of the nose and the curve of the lips. *Twin magic*, Mason had said. Two pairs of dark eyes look out from under thick lashes, framed by the kind of eyebrows that are equal parts impressive and intimidating.

"Nice to meet you," Vera says, and nudges Gabe. "Isn't it?"

"Yeah," he says. And then to Vera: "I'm going to go. Are you going to ride with Aubrey, or . . ."

"No, I'll go with you. Do you want a ride, Sloane?"

"That's okay, I drove somebody."

"Okay. Well." Vera looks to Gabe, who is now staring in the direction of the garage. "Thanks again."

"No problem. I'm here all week."

"You're vacationing?" She looks mildly alarmed.

"No. No, it's just . . . one of those things comedians say? 'I'm here all week' . . . 'Tip your waitress.'"

Vera grins. "I get it. You're funny." She glances at Gabe again, but he doesn't give confirmation. His jaw is firmly set once more. "See you at school, I guess?"

"Sure. I'll be the one who looks like me."

She laughs, and it's weirdly gratifying. I haven't had such a receptive audience in a long time. Laney's only nine, but she knows all my dumb jokes by now.

Casting one last smile at me, Vera grabs Gabe's arm and leads him toward the house, and I am alone once more.

Except for the couple making out on the porch swing, I think, until I look back and see that they, too, have left. Maybe they fled during my humanitarian-aid-workers speech.

I return to the porch and settle down on the vacated swing. It creaks as I rock back and forth. The chains look like they probably won't withstand many more vigorous make-out sessions.

I check my phone. Nine thirty-four. I think my mom will be satisfied if I stay until ten.

You should go! she had said, when I mentioned tonight's party. *Get to know some new people! Do something fun!*

Just different shades of the same things she would say to me back home. So I gave my standard response: *These things are always boring.*

You won't know unless you try, she replied. *Maybe it'll be different here.*

She had a point. Maybe it would. That's sort of what I'm counting on, after all.